THE MY...

JAD EL HAGE

Dec. 2006 - Jan. 2007

First published in the UK by Banipal Books,
London 2007

Copyright © 2006 Jad El Hage

The moral right of Jad El Hage to be identified as the author of this work has been asserted in accordance with the Copyright, Designs and Patents Act, 1988. All rights reserved. No part of this book may be reproduced in any form or by any means without the prior written permission of the publisher

British Library Cataloguing-in-Publication Data:
a catalogue record for this book is available in the British Library
ISBN 978-0-9549666-4-5

Banipal Books
P O Box 22300, LONDON W13 8ZQ, UK
www.banipal.co.uk

Set in Bembo
Printed and bound in Lebanon by
Amioun Printing Press
E-mail: impa@lynx.net.lb

by the same author

The Last Migration
(*Panache* 2002)

For Liz

It had come so softly towards us over the waters; this war; gradually, as clouds which quietly fill in a horizon from end to end. But as yet it had not broken. Only the rumour of it gripped the heart with conflicting hopes and fears. At first it had seemed to portend the end of the so-called civilised world, but this hope soon proved vain. No, it was to be as always simply the end of kindness and safety and moderate ways; the end of the artist's hopes, of nonchalance, of joy. Apart from this everything else about the human condition would be confirmed and emphasised; perhaps even a certain truthfulness had already begun to emerge from behind appearances, for death heightens every tension and permits us fewer of the half-truths by which we normally live.

Laurence Durrell, *Clea*

Instead of the thorn shall come up the fir tree, and instead of the brier shall come the myrtle tree: and it shall be to the LORD for a name, for an everlasting sign *that* shall not be cut off.

Isaiah 55: 13

One

I was on my knees in the olive grove gathering the new olives, called *jerjar*, when the sudden squawk of a blackbird startled me. I looked up. It was young Zahi. His slender body skittered down the rough trail between the terraces, breaking through the dappled sunlight. He landed near me with a thud and crouched, panting, "Adam, your uncle wants you right away. There's an officer with him."

The word 'officer' was reverent in his mouth. His eyes were shining, not with the excitement that sparkles off him when he leads his pack during football games, but with the darker dazzle of the civil war. He was the younger son of our next door neighbour and village shopkeeper, Abu Faour. I'd known and liked him since he was born. But today his demeanour was disquieting. As if his soul had been stolen from him when he wasn't looking.

"I'll be there soon. Stop at Sitti's, tell her I'll be late."

Zahi nodded and was gone in a flash, taking with him my peace of mind.

I looked over my half-full basket and scowled. I'd been waiting for this day all summer, hoping to collect two loads of jerjar: one to share with my grandmother, and the other for my mother in Beirut - a treat from the heartland. Now I had to shelve it and join my uncle. Normally I wouldn't mind, but I hate interruptions when I am working in the orchard. Something snaps inside me when that happens. Still, he wouldn't have sent for me if it wasn't urgent. Reluctantly, I picked up my basket, extracted my pail and stick from the leafy shade of the myrtle tree, and trudged uphill. Yes, I'm still using your stick and pail, Father. The carving you did on the stick is a little more worn every year, but its oak remains as steely as ever and its knob as lethal. And your copper pail is a little more battered than when you were alive, but it still holds my lunch well enough – two boiled eggs, a boiled potato, a tomato, a few olives and a hunk of bread. Your Winchester I no longer use, not since I gave up hunting, but it's displayed on my wall: the third of my treasured possessions, constant reminders of you.

I walked faster than I should, stabbing the nooks and crevices with my boots, forgetting to breathe. "Rest before you get tired, and continue before you become idle." I remembered one of my father's field tips and took the time to regain my wits under a young oak overlooking the valley.

Except for the crickets, an eerie curtain of hush misted the orchards. It was late September, the brief period of respite after the relentless heat of summer and before the furious rush of harvest. The village should have been warming up with songs of *Mijana* exalting fertility and the joys of a plentiful crop. Instead, for the last few days people had been gathering in the square to gossip and speculate, troubled by confusing reports about the spread of the civil war which had started in Beirut six months ago. They disputed armament versus carrying on as normal. Some said, "What's the point of being armed if our granaries are empty? Do we feed our children bullets and hand grenades?" Others said, "But everyone around us is arming. We can't let ourselves be sitting ducks." The arguments buzzed in and out of the houses like a beehive gone awry. Meanwhile the early olives waited to be picked.

With the sun approaching its zenith, I reached the large fig tree in my uncle's front yard. Beneath it was the straw hut he assembled every summer for his wife to cook in. For once the aroma of her cooking didn't make me salivate. I put my basket down under the tree. Amti Wardieh stepped out from the hut, swept her apron across her sweaty face, handed me a towel and followed me silently to the basin. I crouched to wash. Handling a bar of homemade soap had always given me a sense of well-being. Its slippery edges, its resistance to easy foaming, and its organic, earthy smell brought the essence of belonging into my spirit. I thought to myself, this bar of soap can wash out anything: Sitti's long plaited hair, my uncle's blood-soaked dentistry towels, my field clothes, Amti's copper pans. May it wash away our visitor, so I can go back to my orchard in peace.

I lifted the pitcher and let the cool water splash down my face. To the north, on the edge of Wahdeh, the Peacock Castle loomed. This citadel of stone, guarded by oak and pine trees, usually mellowed in the shadows into the soft shape of a breast. Now it seemed forbidding. With the visiting officer, the rumours about turning it into barracks were sounding like reality.

I towelled myself dry, feeling refreshed and ready to listen, for Amti had unspoken words crawling all over her face.

"I had to kill Samson," she said. "The pretty one. I couldn't do it myself. I called the butcher." Her voice was slow, as if she were reading at dusk.

Double shame. Losing her best rooster and asking the butcher for help. A black and green beauty, Samson had been Amti's pride. When in a good mood she'd imitate his bouncer walk and his comical domination over the hens.

"Your uncle and his hospitality," she sighed.

"Did our guest come alone?" I asked.

She nodded and pointed at a jeep parked outside the house. "He was surprised to see your uncle in his jellabia. 'Oh, you're still in your bedclothes, Hakim,'" she mimicked. "Raji would meet the President in his jellabia, never mind a runaway officer."

"Do we know who sent for him?"

"Nimer and his beach bums, who else?"

'Nimer and his beach bums' was my aunt's label for the restless young men who lived away from Wahdeh most of the year, mainly in Beirut, and came only to spend the summer here with their families. For them Wahdeh was a holiday resort. Separate from our own local lads, they drove in and out like tourists. They never had to work the land or live out the winter with us. Now they were eager for action, any action. So they grouped behind Nimer, the Mukhtar's son, cheering him and egging him on. To me, as to most people in Wahdeh, Nimer was a lost cause. Beaten excessively by his father as a child, he'd frittered his youth away roaming the neighbouring villages, making bad use of his family's good name. He was the only son among six well-educated, well-behaved and happily married sisters, but far from the heir the Mukhtar had hoped for to bequeath his stamps and legislative power to. Nimer had truanted from school and been considered a wimp, sucking at a dummy until he was four. Then he fleshed out during puberty and became a bully instead. The Mukhtar had tried everything to keep him out of trouble. But the boy was out to compensate for his miserable childhood. First he'd scarpered off from his uncle's blacksmith shop, then he'd let down his family – and the whole village – by refusing to keep the mill house going. Nothing so menial for him. Nimer the hot shot 'abaday'. The bully from Wahdeh, a unique phenomenon in our largely peaceful village.

By now the sun was directly overhead. Only a few puffs of cloud disturbed the blue sky, but it could turn nasty if the northerly died out. Across the road young Zahi and a couple of his friends were inspecting the jeep, awed by the big roaring toy they'd seen so often on television this summer – the television that had changed their games, taught them about Kalashnikovs, mortars, anti-aircraft missiles, kidnappers and snipers. Seeing me they ducked behind the jeep, feigning invisibility, and then charged off noisily. I wondered if Zahi had delivered my message to Sitti, my grandmother. My wife and daughter were at her cottage, preparing the winter provisions. I was supposed to meet them for a late lunch. But I dismissed the idea of Zahi breaking a promise: his reliability as a messenger was his forte among the grown-ups and his source of power over his peers. Now he would be telling everyone at the square that we were about to have lunch with the officer.

I pegged the towel up to dry, pondering how to tackle a situation utterly beyond my experience. I walked towards the entrance repeating to myself: whatever it is, we'll fix it, we'll fix it.

"Adam," Amti called, "don't let your uncle drink too much."

I nodded and climbed the stairs.

The door to my uncle's dentistry practice was open just a crack. I hesitated. Only on the coldest days of winter was this door shut, keeping the southwesterly at bay. Otherwise its old cedar planks were flung invitingly open. Uncle Raji was not just the village dentist, he was also our doctor and vet, on hand round the clock, freely available to all creatures great and small.

More to the point, he was the unofficial leader of Wahdeh, possessing an uncanny gift for solving any problem.

I looked through the gap, saw a crossed trouser leg with a sharp crease ending in a long black ranger boot, heard a biting voice:

"I'm not enjoying this either, Hakim. I'm a trained, educated officer. I had a great career ahead of me. Now that the army is breaking into factions, I'm just a wanderer going from village to village, taking lads away, disrupting their lives to give you all a shield against the coming storm. That's not easy. But I'm a soldier. I'm made to fight. And this war is spreading, Hakim. Spreading fast. Take it from me. I could leave at any time, have a good life abroad. No problem. My father is rich. He wants me out of the country. But then nobody would be left to fight. Some people criticise us for forming our own militias. They're calling us warlords. Rubbish! We're facing an international conspiracy. We must take control of our country."

I walked in.

My sudden appearance brought the two men to their feet. "Murshed effendi, this is Adam, my nephew." The officer gave me a crisp handshake. I matched it with a firm grip: Beware, soldier of misfortune, this hand means business. Then we sat down around a coffee table arranged with a few pre-mezze dishes: olives, nuts, pickles, balls of labneh conserved in olive oil, and a small carafe of arak.

To indulge his guest my uncle had changed hastily into a grey shirt and navy trousers. One button of his fly was undone. His worry beads drooped in his left hand like a dead vine. His face was heavy with anxiety. "Excuse my nephew's attire, Murshed effendi; he's come straight from the fields." The Hakim was mildly apologetic. "You see, sir, the land is Wahdeh's lifeline. Always has been, always will be. We still use the old methods, each bartering his surplus crop with others. It's a perfect system," the Hakim continued, ignoring Murshed's hawkish eyes and tightened lips. "It's kept us going for hundreds of years. There'll be a catastrophe if just one of the cogs breaks down."

Our guest was clearly unimpressed. Bartering in this day and age? I thought my uncle was trying too hard. As if by awakening his nostalgia for a lifestyle free from price tags this army alligator would shed a soft tear and leave us alone.

"Our village economy, Murshed effendi," I said, trying to bring the Hakim's argument down to earth, "depends on mutual contributions. If our young men have to leave before the harvest, the crops will rot and so will the sharing that has bound us together for centuries. There'll be severe shortages. Some families will have nothing . . ."

Murshed cut me short with a wave of his hand. "No need to worry about provisions. We have more than enough flour, rice, grain, canned meat, dried milk . . ."

"Dried milk," the Hakim muttered, shaking his head. His chest wheezed. He pulled out a cigarette and lit it, frowning. I hoped he would notice the mutinous button. Instead he changed the subject. I prayed for a new tactic, but he was still determined to preach the merits of our idyllic isolation. "Murshed effendi, this area has never known violence. We don't have vendettas and bloody feuds like in the North, no history of arms and bloodshed. If there's an international conspiracy, as you say, if our homeland is dragged into it, as you say, surely we must try to save small villages like ours rather than throw them into the fire."

Murshed spoke with a world-weary sigh, "Hakim, open your eyes. Most villages are already armed. Your neighbours across the valley have amassed medium range machine guns and heavy artillery. They've been training for months. Not only are you closer to the fighting than you think, you are dangerously unprepared."

The Hakim fiddled with his worry beads. He stared balefully at his half-consumed drink – a saviour who was letting him down. He turned to me. "What do you think, Adam? You're a university graduate and the same generation as Murshed effendi. Give us your thoughts."

I suspected that my uncle was manoeuvring for time in which to formulate a compromise.

I spoke to the officer as if to persuade an old friend. "Murshed effendi, this is the most crucial time of the year for us. The bad news about the war has already disrupted our normal life. The olives are heavy, about to drop. You should see them; they are like pregnant women in labour. We have fourteen wheat fields. God knows how many orchards. Grapes. Figs. All needing to be harvested. And that's only the beginning. Then there's taking the olives for pressing, making the burghul, distilling the arak, drying the figs and the grapes, making the preserves and the kishk and the kawarma . . ."

The Hakim took up the theme. "And if we don't harvest, the crops will rot, the village will be infested with rats and foxes, the terraces will crumble. Generations of hard work will be washed away in a season. This land is dear to us, sir. Our fathers had to grind the rocks to make it fertile. What you see around you wasn't made in days but in centuries, and not with modern technology, but with sweat and tears. You can't ask us to throw it all away now, for surely you too are a patriot. Give us a month.

We'll meet again to talk about your plan in a month, how does that sound?"

Murshed's slow ironic smile conveyed pity that we poor peasants were failing to appreciate his efforts to save us.

Amti Wardieh came in with fresh glasses for the next round of arak. The officer lifted his first but the Hakim won the toast. "Peace!"

"Let's pray for it," the officer said dubiously. Then he thanked Amti as she was leaving, and resumed his officious manner. "Time is short, Hakim. Much shorter than you think. A month will be too late. Harvests and land are nothing compared to the danger at hand. You're not alone in making sacrifices. Other villages have done it, have turned themselves into fortresses." His voice took on a sharp edge. "You have to understand, this is an emergency. Otherwise I wouldn't be here."

My uncle was unmoved. "But we heard on the radio that a compromise . . ."

"Radio talk. It's their business to sedate. It's ours to protect."

"Couldn't we try to reach an agreement with the neighbouring villages?" I asked.

The officer shook his head. "If it were that simple, I wouldn't have bothered to come. The neighbouring villages are already fortified. You'd be negotiating from a position of weakness. If you want a treaty, get armed, train, fortify. Then you can talk."

The Hakim shifted uneasily in his chair. "We could call a gathering of the elders from all the villages and talk amongst ourselves. We could sit down as friends. Hundreds of years of common living and common survival must count for something."

"It's too late. You've lost that opportunity."

At last the Hakim aimed his spear straight at the officer's heart. "Murshed effendi, is there any way to spare us this war?"

The officer registered the emotion in the Hakim's words. But though he spoke kindly, nothing could soften the harshness of what he had to say. "Your isolation is suicidal. We can't let you wait any longer."

My uncle gathered his worry beads into his fist and threw them on the table.

The outline of young Zahi suddenly blocked the sunlight. His eyes were drinking in the scene in large, thirsty gulps. "Excuse me," he mumbled, standing sideways at the door.

The Hakim scanned the boy's face. Then he nodded for him to enter. Zahi came forward and whispered something in the Hakim's ear. Their expressions gave nothing away. A few seconds later the boy was gone. The Hakim stood up, noticed the missed button and quickly did it up.

"Murshed effendi," he said, "There's an emergency in the village I must deal with. I'm sure you understand. I won't be long. Needless to say, this is your home. Excuse me."

It was normal to send for him any time of the day or night. But why the secrecy? Usually the messenger would barge in screaming, "Our cow is rolling her eyes in labour, *yalla ya Hakim!*" And uncle Raji would grab his leather case and rush over to help. Whoever had asked Zahi to fetch him today must have stressed the need to whisper. Such secrecy meant serious trouble.

Two

The abruptness of the Hakim's exit left me in an uneasy vacuum. What was I to do with Murshed effendi? My father used to say, "Listen to strangers, keep listening until they're strangers no more." But the more I listened to Murshed the wider the gap between us opened. What I saw beneath his strategy of 'defence' was burning the green and the dry, firing cannons at fleeing olive trees. Shall I take him on a tour of the old olive press, Father? Pretend to be showing him a small piece of recent history and then casually, very casually, tell him about you, about your devotion to Ghandi and your conviction – which became my conviction – that non-violence can defeat a whole empire?

I tried to keep the conversation light, trivial, as shallow as possible. But the officer wasn't going to humour me. Soon he became more personal. "Surely you can't make a living just from the land, can you?"

"I work at the bank in Delbeh," I said, naming our nearest sizable town. "I'm a chartered accountant."

"Ah. And what's the work like these days?"

"Dead, since the start of this war."

He didn't seem to understand. He obviously assumed all banks were doing well. In reality, only the city banks and those in coastal towns were flourishing. The militias had money. So did the looters, the money launderers, the drug and arms dealers. So after our stock market collapsed, the coastal banks installed satellite connections to the international market, operating under heavy shelling, wheeling and dealing as if they were next door to Wall Street. No such luck for us in the heartland. Business at our small agricultural branch had taken a sharp fall. With roads sometimes too dangerous to move the crops, many farmers had already left their farms, withdrawn the bulk of their savings. Some had started new businesses closer to home – the kind that would allow them to leave at the first sign of peril. Others had emigrated.

"Are you saying your bank is closed?"

I explained that although we had no transactions to speak of, the door had to stay open; a few clients still had money wired to them or wished to wire money abroad. The commission from these and other small services helped to keep us going until such time as head office would decide our fate. Meanwhile, our bank was in effect a coffee shop where we met with friends and relatives, read newspapers and listened to the news.

"Pretty boring," I admitted.

"Then come with us," he urged, and offered to recruit me to an office position with his faction, though he stressed that I'd be obliged to do initial training like everyone else and that would involve "a bit of the rough stuff".

"I'd be useless," I said. "I don't have the killer instinct. I've even given up hunting."

"I understand," the officer said. "That's why we give our fighters a cat or a rabbit to tear apart with their bare hands."

My stomach churned.

"Because you see," he went on, "all humans have the killer instinct, but sometimes it lies dormant – it's never called upon. But believe me, it's there," he said, poking a finger at my chest. "And it's our job to bring it out. That's what our training is all about: awakening it, preparing you to use it, teaching you not to fear it. Because fear is your worst enemy. Kill or be killed, that's what war is all about. And if you're afraid, you die. Simple as that."

"It's not a question of fear. I just don't want to kill."

He narrowed his eyes. "Are you saying you're a pacifist?"

"I'm not into labels, Murshed effendi; I just can't see the point of a war about beliefs or ethnic groups."

The officer inched his body towards me, his eyes floating in pale mercury. He carved out his words. "Adam, I have just come from the battlefield. I can tell you from experience that the time is coming when each of us, *each one of us*, will face the moment of truth: if I don't pull the trigger, the enemy will. No third choice. You get my drift?"

I was unimpressed by his words and had no intention of being caught by his hook. As far as I was concerned, people were accountable for what they did, not for who they were. You don't choose your place of birth or the sect you're born into. You choose your deeds. Moreover, I had a lovely wife and a gorgeous daughter, and fertile land and a dream to revive the olive press left to me by my father. I wasn't going to crumble. "There's always a third choice," I said.

"Such as?"

"Stopping the escalation."

"You think we haven't tried? Don't you follow the news? How many ceasefires have there been in the last few months?"

"I'm not counting ceasefires. I'm counting the days before my daughter can start school, my wife can stop worrying about her job, my bank can reopen properly. And some days I find myself counting how many people have been killed in the name of this and that."

"Sometimes you *have* to die for your country. For your ideals. For your honour. For your way of life. What's more, you are proud to become a martyr."

"The only martyr in this war is our country."

"Right! Unless we decide to die for it."

"Only under one condition might I consider taking up arms: if my country were attacked by an invader. And then I would want to be a normal soldier. I won't accept favours."

"War is a science, Adam. Every element is evaluated according to its potential. A nuclear scientist will be protected by a hundred foot soldiers, not sent to the trenches to die. Likewise every capable brain. The simple man will be taught simple things. And yes, we can afford to lose many of those, whereas the skilled are rare and precious."

"I'm not versed in the science of war, Murshed effendi. To me every life is precious. So if I had to defend my country, I'd want to be in the front line. Not because I'm a good shot, but because I won't tolerate others dying to save my skin. Matter of principle."

Our encounter was moving beyond casual chat. Murshed's throaty drawl was beginning to hit a nerve. He spoke about war like a coach about a game of football. He had the blueprints of coming battles all grafted into his brain. I dreaded pushing it any further for fear of ruining the Hakim's efforts. A trickle of sweat seeped under my arms as I began:

"Let me tell you, Murshed effendi, how I quit hunting. It may give you an idea how far apart we are on the issue of killing. Last winter we had two heavy snowfalls. On the morning after the second, I took my rifle and walked down to the valley. The sun was so bright off the fresh snow that you couldn't raise your eyes without sunglasses. A stunning day, one of those when your heart sings to be alive. I'm stressing this weather report because it affected my mood so much. Anyway, when I saw the shadow of a bird gliding over the white slopes, I turned and in a split second brought it down. It was a blackbird who'd found a morsel of food. It fell with a cry and hit a flat slab of rock, still alive, still holding the food in its beak, panting, bleeding dark red dots onto the snow. I'll never forget its bewildered little eyes, Murshed effendi. Those eyes were saying: you wouldn't starve if you didn't kill me. So why? That day I decided to stop hunting for good. Because through the death of that blackbird I was given a rare insight into the tragedy of another creature. And now you expect me to tear apart some animal to resurrect a killing instinct I've consciously chosen to bury?"

The officer stood up, flushed. He paced the practice room, scanning the recliner, the workshop table with all its broken and mended dentures, the stove, the medicine cabinet. He seemed at a loss for words. He went to the window and stared at my uncle's back yard before turning back to me. "I had no idea people like you still existed, Adam Awad. I mean no offence, but yes, there's a huge gap between us. As wide as that between reality and dreamland. I envy you this bliss. At the same time it shocks me, because it is, frankly, the bliss of ignorance."

"Don't worry about offending me, Murshed effendi. But there's nothing about this war that makes me want to kill. I know I can't stop it, just don't ask me to be part of it."

"If you don't leave the country fast you're going to be part of it whether you like it or not. I know this for a fact. If you don't want to bear arms, fine, but you could help us organise the logistics. We need someone like you."

"What exactly are you up to?"

"We're going to use the Peacock Castle as a training camp. We'll do all we can to keep the area out of immediate fighting, but nothing is guaranteed."

"Opening the Castle is a bad omen for the people of Wahdeh. Many will see it as the end of life as they knew it for generations. Besides, the Castle has been left to disintegrate for more than thirty-five years. It would take you some time to fix it. Why not squat an empty building in Delbeh instead?"

"The Castle is a strategic marker on the map of the army. Though legally it belongs to the government, I have the authority to break the lock and take it. But I prefer to do things peacefully. Unlike you, I believe your uncle understands where I'm coming from."

I felt the urge to sneer, Oh *please, spare us the farce of your 'peacefully'*. Luckily, the Hakim chose that moment to walk in, calm as a fallen tree.

"Sorry to have kept you waiting, Murshed effendi. There was an urgent meeting of the elders. They came together in the square and asked me to carry their greetings. Come to the table now. Lunch is ready."

Murshed was visibly taken aback by the feast Amti Wardieh had prepared. "You shouldn't have gone to so much trouble," he said.

Amti dutifully recited the standard formula: "When you are in our home we are your guests, Murshed effendi."

He bowed, palm on chest. Whether he read between the lines, I couldn't tell. But Amti had made a slap across the face look like a red carpet. Her display of every dish of mezze, presented as if for a royal banquet, was really saying: There you go, you nobody from nowhere. If you think you've come to a piffling village to deal with muddy peasants, think again. This house has seen nobleness and ranks far above your petty self. Now eat and tell!

The Hakim seated the officer to face the wall of memories where dozens of pictures and trinkets chronicled Wahdeh's history: the fish fossils found on the slopes by the cliff, old pistols from French and English officers, muskets from the Ottoman times, the Deer Manifesto stamped with the *turra* of Sultan Suleiman, the sepia photographs of major events – many of them featuring the Hakim himself shaking hands with dignitaries. In pride of place, the key to the Castle gate. Under these symbols of acquired authority we sat, washing down our meal with homemade arak.

Our conversation was light and carefree. The officer tasted every dish with affable appreciation. But Amti would only nod, nibbling slowly, as if she had no teeth. She was done with small talk, concentrating on keeping an eye on her husband's drinking.

Meanwhile the Hakim was playing detective, winkling out information about Murshed's life. Not that it took much effort. Murshed was expansive now, lolling importantly in his chair.

"Yes, my father is a judge. He wanted me and my brothers to follow him into the law. Very disappointed when I joined the army, but after a brace of medals and a judge's daughter for a fiancée he came round."

"A fiancée! Congratulations!" The Hakim raised his glass.

"We plan to get married after the war."

"Well, here's to a large and prosperous family," the Hakim toasted, adding, "Adam here has a four-year-old daughter. We're hoping he'll add a boy next time."

We drank to this too.

"Is that you there, Hakim?" the officer asked, pointing at the old photograph where my uncle, young and elegant in a white suit, leaned forward to shake hands with General Gouraud.

"Yes, just imagine: the same hands that delve into open mouths and open wombs once met with those of a great general."

"Bless them." The officer was sincerely impressed.

"The mouths or the wombs?" the Hakim joked.

The officer laughed.

Amti left the table, blushing. When her husband starts making dirty jokes, he loses his gravitas, and this was not a binge with the locals, where he could let his hair down with no fear of consequences. After all, she'd sacrificed her best rooster and produced an impressive lunch to help him out. The least he could do was control himself.

A minute later, she brought in the slaughtered Samson on a silver platter, roasted brown, fragrant with cumin and thyme and the seven spices. But the circumstances dimmed my appetite. I was playing the worst role ever given to me by my uncle, participating in a game where the rules had not been disclosed to me. Amti leaned towards me, urging me to eat. I shook my head. Then she gave me a pleading look, *dilute his arak.* I poured a slug of water into my uncle's drink. Surprisingly, he didn't object. He even murmured, "Thank you," and spread his palm on top of his glass, a sign he would drink no more. So. He wasn't as light-hearted as he pretended.

A little later, glassy-eyed from the arak, the officer was again staring at the wall. He pointed at the inscribed deerskin. "Is that Turkish?"

The Hakim cleared his throat and relaxed back into his chair. "Indeed it is; the Turks used our Arabic script right up to the time of Ataturk. But what did they leave us with after more than four centuries of rule? Hashish, bribing and backgammon. Still, our fathers did the best they could. Believe me, there's a lot to learn from a piece of deerskin hanging on an old geezer's wall."

The officer's antennae were erect. He was breathing heavily from the good food and the powerful alcohol. A good time to attack.

The Hakim made his move. "Would you like to hear the story, Murshed effendi?"

"By all means." At last the officer was trapped.

"During the Ottoman rule," the Hakim began, "our ancestors were forced to pay the *miri* taxation once a year. All males over sixteen had to queue in the village square, heads bowed, to be slapped on the neck by a Turkish tax collector as they paid their dues. It was an unbearable humiliation that pushed many to join the maquis. Now in those days, Murshed effendi, there lived in Wahdeh a wise man called Saleh el Saleh. A gifted hakim, God bless his soul. His curing hands were famed throughout the region, and his door" – the Hakim pointed at his own – "was never shut to the needy and the sick. One day, Murshed effendi, a messenger from the Supreme Porte in Istanbul shows up in Wahdeh looking for Saleh el Saleh. The Sultan's daughter, he says, has tuberculosis. She's been pronounced incurable by the palace doctors. 'With God's help we will cure her,' answered our hakim. 'Bring her over here. I'm too old to take to the sea.' The princess was duly carried from the port on a sedan bed. It took three days and three nights before she was brought to the old hakim. In the highest pine a tree house was built for her. Two tents were erected under it for the women who served her. Special food was cooked for her at the hakim's house. Poets and musicians were invited to serenade her. By the end of that summer, Murshed effendi, the young princess who arrived in Wahdeh hardly breathing had rosy cheeks and was completely cured. She was so happy she decided to stay for the harvest. An olive orchard was named after her. When she returned to her father's palace, the Sultan was ecstatic. He sent the ship back with a bag of gold for Saleh el Saleh. Well, our hakim had no need for gold, nor did Wahdeh, my dear sir. All we wanted was to be exempt from the *miri* humiliation. So the old hakim sent back the money with that very request. It was a dangerous thing to do. You don't refuse a gift from the Sultan, let alone make demands. We waited and waited. The whole of Wahdeh was terrified. Any day now the Turkish soldiers might storm it and set it ablaze. But the princess pleaded with her father on our behalf. And instead of a raging army we received a high-ranking *Umbashi* who carried this deerskin. Yes, sir, that's the decree that exempted Wahdeh from paying the *miri* throughout the rest of the Ottoman rule."

"That's one hell of a story, Hakim."

The Hakim nodded slowly. "Now tell me, Murshed effendi, what lesson do we learn from this story?"

The room held its breath as the Hakim moved in on his prey.

But the officer wasn't cornered yet. "Self-denial?" he ventured.

The Hakim nodded again. "Self-denial, to be sure. But first and foremost, patience. Patience gains the best prize, Murshed effendi. For haste is the work of the devil, don't you agree?"

The officer took a deep breath. He hadn't missed the point of this rural diplomacy. He looked straight at the Hakim. "How long do you need to get your act together, Hakim?"

The Hakim sat back. He shifted his worry beads into his right hand and ground them rhythmically. Then he said in a blank voice, "Three weeks. That's what the elders agreed just now. Three weeks to get organised."

I couldn't believe my ears. But I sensed my uncle's urge for my complicity. If he was playing a dangerous card I had to be his partner. I kept quiet.

The officer relaxed. "Excellent." The two men shook hands.

Amti stood up. Her face was so red I feared she'd burst into tears. She carried away the leftovers of Samson together with my disappointed hopes.

Three

The old rooster let out a wheezy crow. Amti Wardieh waved it away. "Ah, you can crow now, now that the young king is dead," she said, shoving Samson's bones into the bin. Then, turning to me: "Go and check on your uncle, will you, Adam?"

I found him leaning against the almond tree in the back yard, smoking a cigarette. Instead of trying to find out what was eating him, my bottled-up anger spoke. "What have you done, Uncle? Three weeks? What can we do in three weeks?"

The Hakim wasn't listening. I waited. From afar the bells of the returning herds were carried by the wind. The rain was coming.

"Bloody fools. They could have spoiled the whole thing."

"Who, Uncle?"

"At the very moment I'm trying to save the village, they're disgracing it." He continued to stare at the ground. Then he let go of his cigarette, crushed the butt with the tip of his shoe and sighed. "Nimer got it into his head to join our lunch, because it was he who contacted Murshed and asked his help to get Wahdeh armed. As if treason gives him a place in negotiations! He argued with his father and . . ."

"Slow down, Uncle, for God's sake. Are you telling me there was no meeting of the elders at the square? Just a tiff between the Mukhtar and his son?"

"That's how it started. Abu Faour sent Zahi to fetch me before things got out of hand. I rushed over, but it was too late.

They were already at each other's throats. Can you imagine? Nimer and his beach bums attacking our Mukhtar?"

"Nimer wanted to invite himself to our lunch, and his father wouldn't let him? Is that all?"

"It got worse. The Mukhtar tried to reason with Nimer. So did Abu Faour and others at the square. They told him to let me deal with Murshed, and then we could get together later and discuss the matter among ourselves. But Nimer was on fire, he couldn't wait. He jumped up and slapped his father across the jaw. The Mukhtar lost his tarboosh and would have fallen in the stream if he hadn't hung on to a branch of the poplar tree. Then Nimer took off towards the mill house, followed by his cronies. I helped the Mukhtar home. First he was cursing the day Nimer was born, then he was sobbing like a child, asking me to go easy on his boy. I sat him down. I took his pulse. He was fine. I asked his wife to mix sugar and rose-water for him and make him rest."

The Hakim's troubled eyes seemed to be framing the event into the wider picture of Wahdeh's history: Not only to hit your own father but to compound the outrage by doing so in public! An episode that would be remembered for generations, told with shaking finger to fledgling Nimers. He put his arm around my shoulder and walked me towards the house. "Me too, I need to rest. It's been a hell of a day."

We strolled down the pebbled stone path that had been one of his little prides; he'd ordered its material all the way from the coast and bartered the fees for dental services with the truck driver. Now such minor triumphs seemed as old and dry as the weeds that sprouted across the path.

"Uncle, I've never seen you like this before."

He nodded and tightened his grip on my shoulder. His arm was stiff, vibrant with fatigue. I put mine around his waist, wanting to transfer my strength to him, wanting to restore his old fighting spirit. For without him on form, we were in deep trouble. He was the pillar of Wahdeh, the one and only. And to me, the closest and the dearest man alive. Amti and he had looked after me after the death of my father and my mother's departure to Beirut. Not having children of his own he adopted not only me but every life in need of care in Wahdeh. His caring was reciprocated; I'd been beside him in every major crisis since, and I was determined to keep it that way.

He left me at the foot of the stairs. I watched him go up, stooping with Wahdeh's weight on his back. Just before reaching the door, he turned.

"Come early tomorrow morning. I want you with me when I talk to the village."

"Did you call for a gathering, Uncle?"

"I asked Abu Faour to inform everybody."

With the change in the weather there was no point in going back to the olive grove. In any case, my heart was too heavy to restart a broken day. The westerly was rising, shaking the almond tree. I decided to pick the nuts before the wind scattered them. I got a basket from the straw hut and a ladder from the back yard.

From the tree top I could see Wahdeh closing its windows against the coming storm, but the shutters of the Mukhtar's living room were rattling freely. I imagined him after the brawl taking his anger out on his wife. And her wailing, "*Ya dilli, ya shehhary*. My shame, my misery. He's my only son. If it wasn't for him I would be called *Um al-Banat*, mother of girls. It's that damn fever. All night I stayed at his bedside carrying him around like a gypsy. He never fully recovered from it. And now he wants to take up arms!" And the Mukhtar shouting back from his corner under the window: "The fever, the fever – he just takes after your side. You're all crazy. I tried to make a man of him. I handed him the mill house and he turned it into a hideout for his cronies. I killed myself to teach him my trade but whatever I say to him goes in one ear and out the other. He can't even write properly. Now he hits his own father!"

The sun was moving away further westward. The pair of hawks I'd seen this morning, basking in the blue dome as if patrolling the eastern hills against intruders, were leaving. When I was a child, one of their forbears had saved my life. I was eight or nine, and the cliff had seemed to me the visible half of an immense jaw that opened each morning to release the sunrise. It had intrigued me: how, after it sank behind the opposite horizon, did the sun come back to us? I wanted to see for myself the house of the sun. So early one summer morning I sneaked away, climbed over stone walls and through the deserted square, trying not to be spotted. I'd pushed on through the woods until I reached the high rocky foothills under the cliff. There I paused to catch my breath and looked back. From there I could see the winding lanes of Wahdeh snaking between the leafy yards. Looking at it from above made clearer than ever its appealing geography: a wide plateau, forming the seat of an immense throne, with a curved back rising to the north and east, and the foot sloping down to the south and west. Protected yet fertile. "It's called Wahdeh," my father had told me, "because it's on a hill sheltered by higher hills. Neither a towering peak nor a valley bottom, which is what Wahdeh means." Why had I never asked him about the sun? He would have told me and spared me the trouble ahead.

That unforgettable morning, the cool fresh air had given me a second wind and a push out of the scrub onto the rocks. It soon became harder underfoot. My sandals wobbled. The climb was getting steeper by the step. I had to use my hands to help myself along. Crawling on all fours, I didn't notice how close I was to the cliff face until it was a nose away. The stone was warm, rough like a grater. I was terrified by the sudden height looming over my small self. My resolve started to shake. Although my feet were still on firm ground I felt I was about to fall back into nothingness. I walked along until the sheer wall leaned a little. Heart thudding, I began climbing. Below me the drop to the valley floor seemed an abyss. I held back my fear and kept close to the wall: belly and chest and jaw. One move at a time, looking neither up nor down, searching carefully for crannies to hook onto. My sandals slipped off and fell one after the other. My limbs were trembling, it was becoming harder to clutch and push. Each pull up was draining my strength.

Then I was stuck. Both my hands were on the same level. My feet were glued to the rock. I tried in vain to lift myself but couldn't see what was ahead. If I leaned back one inch the weight of my head would topple me. My spine ached as if stabbed. The desire for exploration had vanished. I'll be here forever. I'll die. They'll think I'm lost in the forest, or drowned in the river. They'll be looking everywhere but here. I wanted to fall into my mother's lap. I wanted to see my dad. Sitti. My uncle. My sister. I wanted to fly back home. But my voice was bolted to my throat. Centimetre by centimetre I started to move my neck and look up. A hawk. Still as a picture, less than a handshake away, the huge bird of prey was looking at me. A sudden heat washed away the chill in my ribs. I was growing wings. With one thrust I pulled myself up and fell flat on my face in a wide field of golden wheat. When I looked up again the blue sky was empty.

Today the sky was darkening. Far off thunder was announcing the coming of rain. I climbed down the tree with my basket full of almonds. My aunt had left the piece of homemade soap by the basin. I washed the stickiness off my hands. Two familiar sounds chorused through the closed shutters: the puffing whistles of Amti, who slept half seated with her head sunk on three feather pillows, and the static gurgle of my uncle's apnoea. The rhythm of their siesta brought the wings back to my spirit. I left the basket in the straw hut and set off for Sitti's cottage.

Four

Sitti Khatoum, my grandmother, was nearly ninety-five. She lived on her own in an old stone one-room cottage on the northern edge of the village. The ceiling was supported by oak beams blackened with soot. A large pillar stood in the middle, reinforcing the hard-packed dirt roof. In the left-hand corner, near the narrow corridor leading to her tiny kitchen, a hanging larder stored her food: "Better than your fridge," she boasted. On the straw mat covering the floor, flat bolsters and cushions lined the remaining walls, forming a living space centred on the wood stove, her only 'modern' item – she'd installed it three years earlier when her lungs could no longer bear the fumes of the traditional hearth. The whitewashed walls displayed her sole decorative items – two photographs: one of my father in his jellabia (short thick curly black hair, black moustache trimmed closely above his pronounced lips, serene face and solemn eyes), and one of me at my graduation (my father's hair but longer, my father's moustache but thicker, wide brown eyes from my mother looking earnestly out from behind my glasses).

A respected clairvoyant, my grandmother relied on nature for help. Animals were her favoured medium. She started her day long before dawn: praying, watering her plants while talking to them as if they were friends, eating her breakfast of milk and bread, rolling the leftover bread into balls, and then walking to the fountain where the village mongrels would surround her eagerly. She would throw the balls high in the air and watch with glee as the dogs caught them. Then she would feed the old blind dog by hand. Some years ago, on hearing the dogs yelping like wolves and the hens crowing like demented roosters, she'd gone to the square shaking her stick and shouting, " Get out of your houses, everybody! Let the animals out too! – they'll come back when it's over." She was simply so awesome that everyone trusted her, which had saved Wahdeh the devastation of an earthquake that killed many in other villages. She routinely treated the ill effects of an evil eye, using olive oil, water and prayers. And she had herbal medicines for every malady, including stubborn ones like infertility, asthma, arthritis, and acute stomach disorders. Pregnant women came to her in their third month to find out the sex of their embryo. She was right most of the time; if not, "It must be something that woman has eaten . . . must be!" Even sceptics like my wife Yousra and me couldn't deny that Sitti had a gift beyond our comprehension.

Sitti and her son the Hakim hadn't spoken to each other for as long as I could remember. I loved them both dearly, and I knew they both loved me and my family. But I failed to mediate a truce between them. I remember them standing far apart, heads bowed and tears rolling down their faces at my father's funeral. I was eleven. Their rift hurt me even more than the loss of my dad. They always made me feel caught between a hammer and an anvil.

Sitti disowned the Hakim for many reasons, all of them moral. It had begun when he eloped on a drunken spree and brought young Wardieh from the North without the consent of her folks. It was degrading for someone of his stature. "Not only does he snatch a poor innocent minor from the bosom of her family, he celebrates his marriage for seven days and seven nights as if he were a prince, while a distraught family is looking for their daughter. Doesn't even let them know where she is. Too drunk to remember!" To Sitti, recklessness was an unforgivable sin, and she claimed this sin had been apparent in Raji from his earliest years:

"Your uncle was about five, playing in the back yard as usual. I was keeping an eye on him but also on something I was cooking indoors. Suddenly I smelled burning. I rushed to my kitchen to check and Raji, the little devil, climbed onto the rim of the well and knocked over one of the pots. He was startled and let out a yell and I heard the splash of the water at the same moment. I screamed and ran to the well. No Raji. He'd run off and hidden. I flew to the square and came back with men and ropes. And what did we see? The little scamp playing in the back yard as if nothing had happened."

Her son disliked this story. For him the past was a well of wisdom, not a storehouse of anecdotes. Still Sitti told it, repeatedly, for the moral at the end: "If I'd given him a good spanking that day instead of hugging him to bits with relief, he might have learned the price of recklessness."

And then there was the Hakim's refusal to take up the mayorship of Wahdeh, which appalled her and furthered the rift between them. Sitti thought her son's attitude shameful. "If you are given strength or wisdom from God you should honour the gift and put it at the service of others."

True, had he wanted, he could have become the first and only mayor of Wahdeh. But the Hakim maintained that winning was just the other side of losing; you never knew when the coin would flip to the wrong side. He preferred power without title, leaving us with the current Mukhtar, who'd held his official legislative and council position for over two decades. Wahdeh's people needed the Mukhtar to stamp the formalities of sales and for registrations of births and deaths. For everything else they came to the Hakim. He'd never been challenged as the village leader, the last word in all communal matters. But Sitti maintained he should have 'the word and the sword' in his hand.

No shoes were allowed inside her cottage. I took mine off on the porch and pushed the door open.

"Ah, here is Adam," Sitti cried, as I filled my lungs with the comforting smell of childhood: dried lavender, sage, mint, oregano, thyme.

Mariam jumped gleefully on me. I lifted her up on my shoulders. She dug her fingers into my curls. "Your poor hair!" laughed Yousra. "Her fingers are sticky."

I peeled Mariam off with mock horror and plonked her on the mat. Then I kissed the three generations – Sitti's hand, Yousra's lips, Mariam's ticklish neck – and joined them on the floor around a big white sheet. On it were newly-rolled balls of cracked wheat thickened with yoghurt, ready to dry in the sun for later use in my favourite soup. Yousra, in her usual jeans and her green jersey, had tied up her amber hair with a scarf from Sitti's black-only wardrobe to keep it away from the messy dough. My city girl, who'd learned – for love and with love – the menial chores of the heartland.

"What did you have for lunch?" I asked.

"*Shish Barak*," Mariam answered.

"We ate Samson."

"What?" they cried in unison.

"With the man in the jeep?" asked Mariam.

"Yes. Did you see him?"

"I saw him driving past. Everyone cheered." Mariam waved her arms and mimicked the victory sign.

"So, Wardieh sacrificed her best bird," Sitti said scornfully. "Something big must have happened at the Serail today."

'The Serail' – Government House – was her sarcastic name for her son's practice.

I didn't want to play piggy in the middle yet again, so I tried to delay my report on 'the Serail' by asking if they'd heard about Nimer hitting his father.

"Nimer! That bum!" cried Sitti. "Why does God allow such creatures to be born, God forgive me. And it's all my fault. If I had lied and told his mother she was expecting another girl, she'd have jumped from the roof to abort."

"So it's all because of you!" I joked.

"What's abort?" Mariam, always wanting to know everything.

Sitti ignored her. "Enough of that. What about the Serail?"

I gave in. "Okay, you win. An officer came to get the key to the Castle. He wants to turn it into barracks and train the lads. But Uncle managed to delay it three weeks."

"Three weeks?" Sitti sneered. Then she shook her head and closed her eyes. "That Castle is haunted. Opening it will bring bad luck."

"Honestly Sitti, Uncle tried his very best. But that officer was hard to crack. By hook or by crook he's going to open the Castle for training."

"Are you going to the Castle, Baba?"

"I don't think so, Mariam."

"Why aren't you going? Are you afraid?"

"Your father is as brave as your granddad was," Sitti snapped.

"Was Jeddo never afraid?"

"Never. He was a lion."

"Are you a lion, Baba?"

"No. Now fetch me the pitcher, I'm thirsty."

"Can't you see I'm busy?" Mariam protested, showing me the crushed ball of kishk in her little palm.

Sitti burst out laughing, grabbed Mariam and hugged her tightly. "Bury me, this generation is so bright."

"God help them," Yousra said. "We want to give them the moon but we're taking even their schools away."

"Don't be so pessimistic," Sitti replied. "There are still schools."

"Not for long." Yousra, a political animal, had been following the news closely. "Wherever they open a training camp the schools close down. They're taking kids as young as twelve."

"The shame of it!" Sitti said. "Even in the Ottoman days we had schools under the oak tree."

"Perhaps we should go back to the tree," Yousra muttered.

"Let's hope the Hakim comes up with some way to keep us out of this war," I said.

"If he stays sober long enough." Sitti curled her lip.

"He's doing his best," I repeated curtly. I didn't want Sitti to think that I was taking sides, but her face darkened at my short answer. So I decided to relate in detail what went on from the minute I shook hands with Murshed until his last sip of coffee on the Hakim's veranda. I stressed the fact that my uncle had controlled his alcohol consumption deliberately and that he'd used the story of the Sultan's daughter to our advantage. I reiterated the Hakim's attempts to reach into the officer's heart, making him feel at home and free to speak about his personal life. Then how Zahi walked in and took the Hakim away to the brawl at the square. "Had he been drinking, you think he could have managed to keep the lid on such a scandal?" Mariam had stopped rolling the kishk and was listening attentively. Yousra and Sitti carried on working. They were both sceptical about the Hakim's methods – Yousra thought they were old-fashioned – but deep down they couldn't deny that Wahdeh had no one else to speak for it except the Hakim.

"If war is coming to our doorstep, we're out of here. I'm not going to waste my time fretting and begging a living in my own country. I'd rather clean toilets somewhere else that still has peace and dignity." Yousra spoke slowly but with carved precision. Like someone reading a will.

I was stunned. Staying in Wahdeh was the challenge we'd long ago chosen. We were a rare species: young, educated professionals who'd opted out of city life. We had sealed our love beneath the vaults of the olive press we'd vowed to revive. But one look at my wife's face told me she was dead serious. It was obvious she'd been fermenting this brew of thoughts to herself for a while. Sure, we both objected to the war, but we had never considered leaving the country.

Mariam had a more immediate concern. She pierced the balloon of silence with her own needle. "Baba, will Amti keep our share of the almonds if we leave? I don't want her to crack them for us; I want to do it myself."

"I'm still thirsty, Mariam. Hand me that pitcher, will you."

As I drank down the cool water from the earthenware pitcher, my father's portrait was telling me: "Scream in the storm, no one will hear you; whisper in silence and everyone will."

Which is just what Yousra had done, choosing the perfect moment to whisper her bombshell.

Sitti must have sensed the tension and decided to defuse it her own way. "We need more salt if we're to finish this lot," she said. "Will you go over to Abu Faour's, Adam, and get some?"

Five

I walked over to the shop aslant the wind. The clouds were ready to burst as soon as the temperature dropped. Only a few of the dozen dogs were by the fountain, among them the blind hound, Sitti's favourite. An empty square is usual before funerals, when Abu Faour and the butcher bolt their doors to join the mourners. It's usual too during siesta on hot summer days, when the noon heat freezes life until the first breeze reaches us through the cooling valley. But today the wind alone had virtually emptied the square.

Except for Rameh, the bailiff. His stick across his shoulders or hooked in the crook of his elbow, he was walking in circles like a Chinese water carrier who'd lost his buckets.

"Hey, son of Awad," he called. "Tell me, are we mice or men? Me, I'm afraid of no one. I'm ready to defend my village. How about you, hey?"

"Are you ready to lead us, Rameh?" I smiled, slapping his broad back.

"Of course! Who else knows Wahdeh like the back of his hand?"

"Any one of the children, or the dogs. Even your goat knows her way around."

Rameh unhooked his stick as if to hit me. I ducked into the shop, laughing. Had he really wanted to hit me he could have felled me like a watermelon. But Rameh's heart was as high as the cliff and deeper than the valley. Though the same couldn't be said about his brain.

Rameh was truly a piece of the wild. From an early age he had followed his tinker father and their mule along the rough mountain roads, carrying goods and provisions to remote villages. On his memory was engraved every nook and cranny of these mountains. He had roughed it in caves, faced wolves and snakes and scorpions. He had learned the old ways of hunting and trapping and listening to the sounds of the night. At fourteen he'd walked into the square clasping a live hyena by its ears, a showcase of his strength and courage. Then his world had collapsed in one day, the day his father died. He was only seventeen then, too young to be trusted by merchants. So he'd sold the mule, taken over an old tree house by a stream, and lived on game and wild vegetables. It was a hot summer. The heat had made Wahdeh's people lethargic. They hardly managed their daily chores, so it was easy to forget about the tinker's son in his eyrie. They couldn't know that Rameh was experiencing the first stirrings of love. In his hideaway, he would wait for Hilweh, the butcher's buxom daughter. In the heat of the day she would come out of the village to cool off in the stream. Unaware that she was being watched, she would undress, and slowly, dreamily, wash her white skin with loofah and soap, humming to herself all the while. Until then, Rameh's sex life had been confined to goats and sheep. No one had told him it was different with humans, so one day when his excitement reached boiling point, Rameh lumbered down to the stream, taking Hilweh by surprise.

Whenever the Hakim told this story he would shake his head and close his eyes in pained memory: "Suddenly, there she was, all naked and bleeding in the middle of the square. A distraught fifteen-year-old screaming and running, arms stretched out like a crucifix."

In a matter of minutes the whole village had known. An angry mob gathered, the commotion grew like thunder and rumbled towards the stream. Rameh heard the stampede approaching. He realised he'd done something wrong and took off, not to be seen again for four years.

The shock had impaired Hilweh's brain. Her brothers swore they'd hunt Rameh down and bring him in like a rabid dog and slay him in the middle of the square for all to see. But their bloody threats didn't help Hilweh. For some she became a poignant curiosity, for others a theatrical distraction. "*Dabkeh!*" a boy would shout, and she'd start jumping up and down mimicking the traditional dance. "Goat! Goat!" And she'd gallop like a goat. But if anyone uttered Rameh's name, she'd run off blindly, howling, bumping into people and animals and trees until the Hakim could be summoned to give her a sedative.

Time had passed with still no sign of Rameh. Some said he'd thrown himself from the cliff. Others came back from travels abroad saying Rameh was married and living in America, in Australia, in Brazil. Once, the unexpected disappearance of the wild boar that caused havoc to the crops ignited another legend: Rameh had gone after the boar, to compensate for his crime, to prove he was worthy of Wahdeh. Like Adonis he fought the boar until they both collapsed and died. At times Rameh's image as a noble savage overshadowed the trauma he'd inflicted on Hilweh. She was even dismissed as a feckless seductress who deserved her fate.

One day Abu Faour had come for a private audience with my uncle. The door had closed behind them. "I saw Rameh," the shopkeeper said. "I saw him with my two eyes, may I lose my sight if I lie. He's living in a cave down by the river. I almost shot him. He looked like an animal. I cornered him. He confronted me. But in the end we sat and talked. Rameh knows what's going on in the village. He comes out like a mole at night and listens. He may look like an animal but he's a grown man now. He says he wants to marry Hilweh if her folks will agree. He wants you to plead for him, Hakim."

The Hakim had a strong weakness for Hilweh, what with all the running after her to inject her with sedatives, and the sobbing breakdowns she spent in his arms. As usual he opted for the middle way: if such a marriage could mend what was broken through a freak incident of innocence and lust, then so be it. He'd taken it upon himself to persuade the butcher's family. He told them that there was nothing to gain by killing Rameh or sending him to prison. And no one else would ever marry Hilweh now. Perhaps she would settle down if she was married off to her aggressor. That way "neither the wolf dies nor the herd perishes," the Hakim suggested. It was a hard task. It took him several days to cool the angry blood of the butcher's family. Finally it was agreed that Hilweh should be carefully prepared, told that the best man for her was the one who had deflowered her. That he was not a bad man but, like her, hadn't known what he was doing. He hadn't meant to hurt her and now he wanted to make her his wife. She'd be fine once married; she'd have children, a home and so forth. She might even regain her mental faculties. The Hakim called Abu Faour and asked him to bring Rameh to the practice secretly. "We spent the whole night lifting him out of the Neanderthal age!" the Hakim had said.

Next morning Hilweh was dressed up, groomed, powdered and manicured. Although it had been four years since the incident, the moment Rameh marched in, Hilweh freaked out. She started haemorrhaging and running through the narrow alleys. She was found a few hours later by the stream, drenched in blood and tears.

After that she became aggressive, hitting the children, throwing stones at passers-by and chasing the dogs. Her family had no option but to lock her up in a barred room overlooking the square. But while they cared for her needs lovingly, she remained at her window, haunting the whole village.

Rameh had gone back to the woods. He guarded the land, watched over herds and crops, made sure shepherds did not cross their designated territory. He trapped jackals and foxes, protecting Wahdeh's livestock, and slept in caves or tree houses. But he kept in touch with the Hakim through trustworthy messengers. Hilweh's family, known by the name of their trade, Lahham, cooled off with time. After extensive negotiations with the Lahham family, the Hakim won a plea for clemency, and Rameh was officially appointed bailiff and permitted to move into a cottage in the eastern woods.

Today, Rameh's face was knotted with belligerence. He walked into the shop after me, took off his hat and threw it on the counter. Faour – replacing his napping father – pulled down a quarter bottle of arak and poured a handful of peanuts onto the rim of the hat. Rameh grabbed the lot, snatched a wooden chair, marched outside and sat himself in front of the poplar by the stream. He jammed the bottle between two stones in the water and started tossing the peanuts in the air, catching them in his mouth. For each one he caught he rewarded himself with a swig. Taking heart at my presence, Faour came to the shop entrance and started nagging Rameh about going to the Castle. "And who'll look after the village?" he said. "Who'll control the irrigation? Who'll keep people from stealing each other's water and diverting the power lines? Who'll stop the gutters from flooding?"

"I'm going to the training when the Castle opens," Rameh repeated.

Faour raised his arms in exasperation: "Leave it to us, you can't do everything. Anyway it's against the law for bailiffs to join the militia."

"The law," Rameh said scornfully. "The law is on the side of the guy with the biggest gun."

"You can't just go off with the boys; your goat will miss you." Faour was getting personal.

"Leave my goat out of this!" Rameh yelled.

"But you love that goat," Faour persisted.

"Ah, you're getting on my nerves!" Rameh tucked the bottle in his pocket and stood up. "You're all rabbits! Run to your holes!" he cried and stormed off towards his cottage.

At her window, Hilweh was nodding and rocking from side to side, her wide green eyes looking into a space of their own.

Faour shook his head, "The curse of his life. Even if she pulled out the bars of her window or howled all day, Rameh would never look up and meet those eyes." Then Faour raised his head and blew Hilweh a kiss.

As I walked back to Sitti's, I contemplated Rameh's current dilemma. Maybe he needed an excuse to leave the village and his haunted past but was too proud to slink away. But if he went to the Castle he could lose his job – his hard-won status as Wahdeh's guardian. And he might have to take orders from Nimer, the Mukhtar's son, whom he despised. On the other hand, if he didn't go he would be branded a coward, unworthy of defending Wahdeh. He was between a rock and a hard place.

Then it occurred to me that perhaps a symbolic gesture would incline him to stay.

Rameh often pestered me, trying to borrow my father's Winchester. "You never hunt. I could bring in some good game with this. Lend it to me, son of Awad, your dad would approve, I swear." His one-barrel Spanish rifle was light, unsteady, always jamming. He loathed it, and given his undoubted hunting skills, he felt he deserved the Winchester. True, I'd stopped using it. But the rifle was heritage. And memory. Hours of cleaning and carrying and holding. Unforgettable moments of pride. My father, down near the myrtle tree, teaching me how to shoot. I'm eleven. He lines up bottles, tins, caps and pegs. He hands me his Winchester loaded with light cartridges. "You don't need speed but precision. Only fire when you're sure." That single precious summer when he began to see me as a man, just before he died.

But now I was thinking like the Hakim: to keep Rameh away from Nimer's lot, get him to stay in the village, we'd have to strengthen his sense of loyalty, remind him, without hurting his dignity, that he wouldn't be where he was if it weren't for the Hakim, and that the Hakim needed him by his side more than ever at this time. The rifle would be a token. If he got it for keeps he wouldn't let us down.

The more I pictured Rameh with my father's rifle, the more I was letting it go. For the first time ever I felt I could relinquish the treasured Winchester. And with this idea came a strong sense of your presence. Perhaps it *was* you, Father, putting the idea in my mind? You want your rifle to be useful – useful for a new purpose, is that it? You never did like waste. What we own is nothing if nothing is done with it.

I delayed delivering the salt and went home. Like the Castle key on the Hakim's wall of memories, the Winchester had pride of place on our living room wall. I lifted it resolutely from its pegs and walked to Rameh's cottage. With every step I felt my spirit lighten.

Rameh's face when he opened the door, dressed only in his grubby underwear, registered the bewilderment of a man awakened from an arak dream. I held out the rifle. "Here. The Hakim wants you to have this. May you have many good seasons of hunting with it."

His face cleared. He took the rifle from me and cradled it as if it were a long-lost child. "You mean it?"

I nodded.

Now his face broke into one of his rare smiles, as big as the man himself. "Son of Awad, I'll never let anyone harm a hair on the head of you and yours."

I went back to Sitti's with the wind behind my back. Once I'd made up my mind it had been easy, like peeling a scab off a healed wound.

Six

Back at our house, supper was marred by noisy rows from the neighbourhood. The closeness of Wahdeh's homes seemed to draw the faraway war nearer, breaking long-guarded truces in almost every household. Murshed's visit had been the stick that poked the hive. All the uncertainties it raised had rekindled dormant – or so far tolerated – differences. Screams answered threats. Children left to howl while their parents brawled heightened the cacophony. Slippers flew from mother to daughter and crockery cracked against walls. Disrespect elbowed the elders aside. But most of the din came from young men defying their parents about joining the training. Prudence of the parents versus imprudence of their young. Classic. But seldom breaking out all at once.

Mariam couldn't sit still, jumping up and running to the windows every time she heard a new fracas. She had to know who was doing what and why. Why should the village explode just because we had a stranger visiting? She was seriously concerned, demanding detailed answers. Unfortunately not everything could be explained to her and you never can be sure if you've hit the right balance with an inquisitive child.

Finally we managed to close the shutters and tuck Mariam in bed. She was still wide awake with excitement, so we sat either side and began reading to her a story from the Arabian Nights. I read about Shatir Hassan sailing the seven seas in quest of Sitt Bdour, the beautiful daughter of the Red King. I raised the waves high and low like a hypnotist. Then Yousra described the golden hair of the fair princess and how she had two attendants combing it softly . . . softly . . . until Mariam's limbs went limp and her eyelids drooped.

Yousra sighed as we sneaked back to the living room, still grieving the loss of the Winchester. "I'd imagined Mariam proudly showing it to her children one day, telling them how their grandfather had stopped hunting. It's a good story."

"You think good stories need material evidence?"

"This one would have worked better with a showcase."

"I had to do something before tomorrow. Rameh is important to the village. He has to stay, for the good of us all."

"Are you sure he got the message?"

"He was pretty tipsy, but he heard just fine."

Explaining that Rameh was too overwhelmed by surprise and alcohol to say anything concrete did not satisfy my wife. She thought I should have made him promise to stay in Wahdeh. After all, he was acquiring a slice of the Awad legacy. No small thing. "You can't expect him to read your mind, Adam. State your requests clearly. Not everyone has the same insight as you, *habibi*."

"I have to trust my hunches sometimes. It came to me like a revelation – give Rameh the rifle. I'm not saying I heard a voice from outer space, just a hunch."

Yousra and I went out to the back yard to close the hen house. She still didn't believe Rameh would be able to stay out of it while others were going to bear arms. I said, "Let's wait and see."

"Rameh feels responsible for our safety, how could he watch the lads getting hold of firearms while he's stuck with a hunting rifle?"

Suddenly the windows next door rattled. It was Abu Faour, storming up into his house and banging the door behind him. Through his veranda windows, we could see him clearly, waving his arms and kicking his legs like a crazed dervish. He was cursing in language neither we nor his children nor his old mother had ever heard from him. Um Faour, his wife, rushed from the kitchen holding up her hands in horror and stared at him. Zahi and his little sister Nour recoiled and retreated to their granny's lap. Abu Faour silenced the TV. His speech was jumbled except for his curses. Obviously his status as father and master of his own home had been shaken. But every time he came near the source of his fury his temper got the better of him and foul language obliterated all meaning.

At last we got the gist of Abu Faour's wrath: Faour, his eldest, had disobeyed him and gone to a meeting at the mill house organised by Nimer. An eldest son going against his father's will was a mortal sin, even the beginning of the end of a distinguished dynasty. Faour would be copied by Zahi, then little Nour could become infected by the same virus of disobedience.

"Let the boy be! He's a man now! Let him find out for himself!" Um Faour screamed.

"He'll never step inside this house again!" Abu Faour roared back.

But Um Faour held out for her son's free will. No doormat, she. She stood her ground and yelled, "You wouldn't let him join his cousins in Venezuela. You wouldn't let him go to Beirut, not even to carry on his studies. At least let him be his own man out here. If you say another word to him I'll take the children and leave you."

That's when Abu Faour lost it. Threatened? By his wife? In front of his children? He snatched his mother's walking stick and raised it high. "Back to the kitchen, you! My grandfather was born in this house, my great-grandfather and my father. Over my dead body will anyone leave this house without my permission! To go anywhere, you hear me?"

The children's eyes were wide with panic. They'd seen him cross before, even angry, but never had he raised his mother's stick to his wife, or to anyone else for that matter.

Next Abu Faour declared that he'd close the shop if the Castle was opened for training. Um Faour screamed again, "You have no right to close the shop!"

"The place will be swarming with thugs and hooligans!" Abu Faour thundered back.

"And where will they buy their tobacco, their booze, their food?"

"In hell!" Abu Faour stamped the floor fiercely.

So far Abu Faour's mother had been keeping her peace. Now she sprang up on her shaky legs, grabbed back her walking stick and snapped: "The shop will never close. Not while I'm alive. It's your livelihood and your children's." Her voice vibrated with emotion. "Your grandfather was master of the market. His word was a contract. One hair of his moustache weighed an ingot of gold. He never closed the shop. And your father never did either. Never."

Abu Faour flung himself onto the sofa. "Don't contradict me, Mother. I am the head of this family. I make the decisions. When the Castle opens I shut the shop. I will not hear another word on the matter."

Old Fatat was white with indignation. Her family had owned the shop in Wahdeh for generations. It was the only store besides the butcher's. It provided everything from food and medicine to fodder and agricultural tools. Abu Faour had expanded the business. He had made it the throbbing heart of Wahdeh. Until now he'd been known for his devotion towards his mother. He took her blessing every morning and bowed to kiss her hand at the end of each day. Now he was pulling her down from her pedestal in front of her grandchildren. His wife hid her face and sobbed. Her mother-in-law was the good spirit of this house. You don't bully a good spirit. Zahi and Nour thrust themselves back towards their granny to shield her. On the sofa Abu Faour was breathing heavily. Fear and anger were pulsating through the thick walls and shut windows of Abu Faour's normally serene home.

"Look," Yousra whispered, staring at the far corner of Abu Faour's house.

Faour was approaching the back door of the downstairs apartment intended for his future use, stealthy as a cat on a high plank. His thin figure swayed unsteadily. He must have been listening to his brawling father just like us and wanted to sneak into the apartment until the storm passed.

Faour had always been a favourite with us. I in particular felt a strong kinship with him, despite the age difference. A bit like a son, a bit like a younger brother. I'd helped him with his maths and we'd also worked the land together, though he spent more time reciting poetry and singing Ataba than digging dirt. I called him over.

"Psst. Over here."

Visibly relieved to see us, Faour crossed the vine pergola, climbed up a step and greeted us.

"Man, what happened to you?" Yousra exclaimed, looking at his torn shirt and crumpled trousers. It was uncharacteristic of him. He was usually such a quiet lad with books all over his lap and his head full of dreams.

"Oh, that's nothing, you should see the other guy," Faour joked feebly.

The wind was gusting. We took him inside to wait until his father cooled off. Our stove was on. A hot bowl of soup, not the rod, was what the lad needed. His face was as battered as his clothes. He held the bowl with both hands, sipping and staring at the lentil broth. I asked whether he'd fallen in a ditch or had a row with someone at the mill house.

Faour didn't stir. His face barely registered my question. He was breathing slowly like a partridge in hiding. Something had deeply disturbed him. That glazed bewilderment reminded me the blackbird I'd shot by mistake and the river of questions that poured from its beady eyes.

Yousra gave me a quit-pushing-the-boy look. He'd been her student for the last couple of years and she had her own insights into him.

Faour carefully placed the bowl back on the little table near the stove, as if the bowl were still full, and made a move to leave. Yousra put her hand on his shoulder. Pedagogy plus love thy neighbour. "Are you going home or sleeping downstairs?"

"I have a mattress on the floor downstairs. I'd rather use it."

"Can I ask you a favour?"

Faour looked at Yousra with a guarded willingness.

"Don't sleep with whatever is bothering you. Put it down on paper, okay? We'd like to read it, Adam and I. Got a pen and paper?"

"Always." I glimpsed a shadow of a smile on his bruised mouth.

The next morning we found this under the entrance door:

Honour thy father, yeah. Does that mean worship him? Blindly? I mean not even dogs obey their masters blindly. There are limits. But my dad sees none. Faour, do this, don't do that, period. He strips me of my own reasoning; my mind belongs to him or else I'm a traitor. Figure that! All I wanted was to keep up with what's going on in the village. I'm no hero, but I'm no snail tucking my head inside a shell and hiding. I need to be able to make up my own mind about things, for God's sake. I don't mind discussing whatever with him, only he turns everything into an argument, ordering me around like I'm a slave. I had to be at the mill house last night. I regret what happened but I'm not sorry I went.

When I arrived Nimer was sitting on top of the old flour bags under the kerosene lamp. He was glaring at the stragglers like a sentinel in a medieval prison, so I sneaked in quietly. 'Close the door,' he ordered, 'and stop smoking. Now listen,' he went on, 'tomorrow at ten sharp I want every one of you in the square. I want you in the front. When the Hakim speaks, talk back to him. Ask him questions. Interrupt him but don't mess it up. Remember, we have to convince him to open the Castle as soon as possible. We need to keep on the right side of the elders. I lost my temper today and hit my father. If Murshed effendi hears about that, he won't trust us. We have to win his trust. So let's not blow it. It won't be long before the village is in our hands.'

At this stage Abu Janjoul - you know, the one with the muscles - shouted, 'To hell with that old fart. Let's just go to his house and grab the key.'

That was too much. Rameh, me and a few others told him to shut up. After all, when you insult the Hakim, all Wahdeh is insulted. But Abu Janjoul kept ranting: 'There isn't time for all that crap. We should get the key and kick the Hakim's arse.' That's when the shit hit the fan. Rameh slapped Abu Janjoul. He started spitting blood and charged at Rameh. They tore at each other. The beach bums rallied behind Abu Janjoul. Us locals, we were trying to push them away, punching and kicking. Then Abu Janjoul fell back onto a pile of flour bags. He flicked open a butterfly knife and looked ready to use it. Nimer roared for them to stop, but he didn't move, so I leapt at Abu Janjoul and grabbed his wrist and whirled around with him, trying to squeeze the blade out of his hand. While we were struggling, the knife slit open a few bags and the flour spilled out, all rotten. It smelled horrible. Then suddenly an avalanche of rats fell down on us and everyone freaked out and ran and Nimer was yelling, 'Come back! Come back you stupid idiots,' jumping up and down like a tap dancer among the rats. The shame of it really got to me. You know me, I'm not into brawls and stuff. Somehow I felt like I'd been molested.

Sorry about last night. I'll go up now, make some coffee and apologise. Abu Faour is not going to change. We have to make do, I guess. And thanks for the broth.

Faour

Seven

A thin rain had fallen that night. When I opened the door, the fresh aroma of a replete earth embraced me. The sky was spotless blue as if newly painted, except where the sun bleached it white above the cliff. There was a vibrant feeling after a thorough bath in the air. The kind of feeling that makes you sing a smiling song.

Even Uncle Raji was in good spirits, ready, shaven, dressed to the nines in his black jellabia and white collarless shirt. Amti Wardieh, however, muttered a good-morning as if she had pebbles in her mouth, piqued at the prospect of him meeting up with hooligans and beach bums. I sipped another coffee with them on their veranda and told the Hakim that I'd given the Winchester to Rameh on his behalf, and why.

"Good move, lad. We need Rameh on our side."

Then I reported the previous night's mill house fight.

"You see?" my aunt argued. "Better to leave them to finish each other off."

"Wish us luck, Wardieh. We should be back before lunch. Let's go, lad."

Finally Amti softened and asked the Almighty to walk with us.

At the square, a group of women gathered by the fountain, pretending to scrub their copper wash pans. In front of the shop, under the poplar, older men fretted and smoked nervously. With them, in his best attire, stood Rameh, leaning against the tree trunk, tapping his newly shined boots to punctuate the conversation. Abu Faour and his battered son stood on opposite sides of the shop entrance, arms crossed, waiting. They seemed to have reached a partial truce. Between them, on a chair at the threshold, sat our Mukhtar, his tarboosh as straight on his head as a cork on a bottle of syrup. Zahi and his gang crouched on the shop's flat roof. Nimer and his crew were gathered in the centre. The white powdery marks on Nimer's back suggested that he had braved the rats and spent the night in the mill house rather than go home. Cuts and bruises on all of them spoke volumes about the debacle. On seeing us, Abu Faour moved swiftly. He snatched up a small wooden chair and banged it down for the Hakim, startling the Mukhtar. It was a message aimed at Nimer et al: Right, you scum, now you're in for it.

After last night's sparring at the mill house I thought that things could get out of hand. I feared for my uncle's safety. I walked half a step behind him, scanning the scene at the square and his reactions. There was a jungle tension, the sort that calls for a machete in your hand. I could feel the Hakim preparing a move, but I was as surprised as anyone when, with a resolute pace, he walked over to Nimer and pulled him out of his flock like a hair from a ball of dough. Nimer's entourage stood stiff, flabbergasted.

This was a far cry from the steamy summer day that June when Nimer had arrived at the square battered and bruised. His fan club had gathered around him excitedly as he narrated his adventure:

"It all happened so fast, I'm lucky to be alive. I was on my way to order a new suit, my wallet bulging, when four robbers attacked me. Four of them!" He'd held up four fingers and ticked off: "One had a dagger, the second a pair of knuckle dusters, the third a big knife, and the fourth a club. I headbutted that one in the stomach grabbed the club and went for the others." Nimer had mimed the whole fight. "I polished them off just like that and left them bleeding in the gutter." A few days later it had transpired that Nimer had been beaten up on the bus when he tried to take someone else's place. No gang of robbers, no loads of money, no new suit. Nonetheless, the charged atmosphere of the summer had provided him with more listening ears than ever. And now the beach bums had convinced him to seek 'military assistance' for Wahdeh. So he'd gone to a militia HQ and put in jeopardy an otherwise safe village which had until now been shielded from the worst fratricide in Lebanon's history.

And yet here was Nimer meek as a lamb while the Hakim took him by the arm and escorted him straight to the shop entrance. I felt the cobble stones under my feet ticking with anticipation. "Nimer," the Hakim whispered, "you know I never had children, and you know how I love you like my own son. Your father and I go back a long way. Believe it or not, at your age we too did foolish things. But we are old men now. Your father has done much for us. We all owe him. He is our Mukhtar, but first and foremost he is your father. I want you to go over to him now and kiss his hand. If you do this I shall let you stand in my place and speak your mind to the village. Are you with me?"

Nimer's confusion was apparent. He hadn't expected this. No doubt he'd lain awake all night with his fantasies of becoming a warlord. Now he was being led for all to see to bow before his father. His head drooped. His eyes tightened. His steps became heavy. His pack looked like a football team locked in an uneasy huddle. The men near the poplar fell silent. The women at the fountain gave up all pretence of work. Hilweh stopped rocking behind her window. But it was the Mukhtar who was the least prepared, bewildered that his errant son was suddenly so submissive.

"Sorry, Father."

The older men murmured approvingly.

Then relief turned to indignation when Nimer jumped onto the wooden chair. No one but the Hakim had ever stood on this chair to speak. What was Nimer up to? Nimer himself wasn't sure. His apology to his father had drained his aggression. Breathing erratically, he began:

"Gentlemen, firstly I thank the Hakim for his support. Secondly I apologise for hitting my father. It won't happen again, ever. Now I wish to ask you all a question. How are we to protect ourselves without weapons and training? Other villages have bought weapons. They didn't worry about losing the olive crop or the vineyards or the sheep. They worried about the lives of their women and children. They worried because they didn't want to see their villages looted and their women raped and their children killed. To stop that from happening here we must move now. If we are shelled we must be able to shell back. If we are shot at we must have the means to retaliate. This is what I think and this is what the youth of Wahdeh are prepared to do. We are ready to defend our village. I hope the elders won't let us down. Once again my thanks and my apologies."

Nimer was sweating like a shearer at midsummer, perspiring from his thick straight hair down his long face and his stubby neck. His whitened back was now blotched. When he stepped down from the wooden chair for a moment he failed to control his nerves but regained his composure when his cronies woke up from their surprise and applauded.

So far the Hakim's tactics were working. He had nipped in the bud the seeds of rebellion. Standing near the bewildered Mukhtar, he was now looking steadily at the young rebels. Then, as if sensing that they were now tame enough to listen, he stepped up onto the chair.

"Nimer is not speaking nonsense," he began. The two groups slowly started converging on the shop entrance. "Yes, there is war in our country. A war that has nothing to do with us here in Wahdeh. Some people say foreign hands have played a foul game to divide our motherland. Others believe it is the plea of the poor so long ignored. Either way, it's become a looting party and a vicious insurrection out of control. The national government and army have all but collapsed. Nimer is right to advise defence. He is right that we must make a crucial decision. Our young men want to train and arm themselves for protection. Fine. But we must keep a low profile, extend the olive branch before the gun, refrain from unnecessary aggression. We have agreed to hand over the key to the Castle in three weeks. Until then, I declare a state of emergency. We must all work at a tremendous pace now. Save what we can from the harvest. Repair the orchards to face the coming winter. Fill our granaries in case we receive the destitute and homeless. We can do it. Your fathers and their fathers kept this land fertile not with guns and swords but with sweat. Remember this before you allow division to creep into your ranks. Standing together is our best defence. I say to the young ones, in three weeks you shall leave your families and learn the art of fighting. But when your training finishes you'll come back here to organise night guards and remain vigilant, ready to defend your land if, God forbid, we come into the line of fire."

"Hear! Hear!" Rameh declared. He extended his hand to Abu Janjoul. They embraced. The others followed suit. Excitement mounted, became a wave that lifted the Hakim up on its crest. Even Nimer joined in the chanting of an old resistance anthem from the Ottoman times.

Hold your head high
Open your eyes
You have earned
Every loaf of bread
Every drop of wine
By the sweat of your brows
Lift your head!
Lift it above the clouds.

The Hakim was hauled up onto Rameh's shoulders, paraded through the streets of Wahdeh, waving his arms to people who'd come out on their verandas and balconies to cheer him. But fewer showed up with their children in their arms, or pushing their elders in wheelchairs. And no one showered him with the traditional confetti of rice or rose petals as in his days of glory.

Eight

The next day Faour caught up with me as I walked to the orchard. Neither of us felt good about yesterday at the square. The Hakim had done his best, but was it enough? Nimer and his cronies were back at the mill house getting all stirred up, and the Hakim was resting on his laurels believing he had averted disaster. Something more had to be done. I looked south across the valley towards the slopes on the other side, at the distant red roofs of Nahrieh.

"I've been thinking. Perhaps I should go there, pay a visit to Sayed Bey," I said, "just in case he has any ideas. He and my father swore blood brotherhood years ago. I'm sure he'll remember me. Yousra and I talked about it last night – she thinks it's a good idea too."

"It's worth a try. I'll go with you," said Faour.

We found Rameh grazing his goat by the myrtle tree. He couldn't see any objection to our plan, but neither could he guarantee our safe passage. "Things change every day. A while back they said all the mountain paths would be kept clear for emergencies. Next thing, boom. A young shepherd from Delbeh lost his legs. Take the normal road. At the checkpoints tell them you're on a mission to Sayed Bey. He still has clout."

"I don't trust the militias," Faour said.

Rameh scratched his head. Then, reluctantly, "I suppose you could take the cave tunnels..."

"Cave tunnels?"

"Only tinkers and shepherds know about them. Some are wide enough to shelter a herd of goats if a goatherd's stupid enough to get stuck in the snow."

"Stupid?" Faour frowned.

"Have you ever seen a billy goat before a snow storm? Your smart goatherd notices how his billy starts eating frantically as soon as the westerly blows. That won't be just rain on the horizon but snow, which means no food for a while ahead. Even a donkey grazing away from home lowers his ears and heads back before snowfall. Animals read the weather; we only predict it."

"Will you show us the way to Nahrieh through the caves?" I said.

"I'll go with you to the other side of the river. After that you're on your own."

"Let's go then," Faour urged. I could see the traffic of expectation bumper to bumper in his eyes.

Not more than ten metres wide and two or three metres deep, our winter stream was called 'river' just because 'stream' was too condescending for its roaring flow during the winter months. But now that the snow was long gone from the peaks which fed it, the translucent trickle was only knee-high at its deepest. We rolled up our trousers, took off our shoes, hooked them to our belts and, balancing precariously on the stony river bed, stumbled along behind Rameh, the man who knew these lands and waters better than he knew himself.

We reached the other side, where Rameh uncovered a cave mouth hidden in the rock behind a thick bush.

"Gentlemen, your path to peace. Keep moving forward and up. Don't veer downward or you may get stuck. When the light starts to brighten, that's your exit. Climb out, you'll see the Bey's house on your left."

"Rameh!" Faour was scowling at the black hole. "We have no torches!"

Rameh dug his hand in his pocket and fished out his old silver lighter. "First, get used to the darkness: close your eyes and walk with your hands touching the top. Push on like that until you can't feel the top anymore. *Then* open your eyes. You won't need the lighter, but use it if Faour starts crying." Rameh laughed as he pushed us into the black void.

We shut our eyes as instructed and lifted our hands and felt the dented roof. It was steadying but didn't make me feel safe. Even when playing blind man's bluff, I'd always failed to grasp the fun of putting oneself in total darkness.

A strong smell of decay and mould seeped into us as we moved forward. After a while Faour spoke. "I'm kind of enjoying this. I'm all inside me and I'm nowhere at all. Imagine what might come into one's mind in a lifetime like this. I wonder if there's ever been a sect where people stayed blindfolded their whole lives." I felt his humid breath brushing my neck. His murmuring voice reminded me of whispering under the eiderdown with my sister when sharing a childhood secret. It lit a smile in my own darkness.

A few minutes later, my hands ceased to feel the rock above and my next step fell away into nothing, like being on a branch that had suddenly snapped. I yelled and reached out to hold onto something. Faour bumped into me and both of us landed on new footing, our eyes blinking open at last. The faintest illusion of light showed that the space around us was the size of a tent shaped like a two-spout funnel. Unlike the tunnel we had just left, with its moist sandy floor, the ground here was hard packed with rough dirt and crushed manure. I pictured the 'stupid' goatherd huddled by the fire, weathering the storm and wondering what had gone wrong.

We moved on, crouched over, until we faced the two black holes in the rock. Then we stopped, staring at each other as if held up at gunpoint. Faour's scowl made him look more apprehensive than he really was. I could read him like an open book. His imagination was the main source of his reactions. I wouldn't say he purposely exaggerated, but he had a tendency to dramatise the unknown.

"You take the right, I take the left. We walk and count, say to a hundred, and then we come back here. We'll choose the one that's going up. Remember? Up," I said.

"Up. And the lighter please, or I'll start crying."

We entered our respective spouts. I held my hands before me and began counting. After ten, a nauseating stench of decay hit me and I plunged into muck. I could feel the slide, but I had to make sure before turning back. I continued counting, twenty-one... twenty-five, twenty-six... Now the darkness was absolute. I was drenched in cold, sticky sweat in this tube of sludge and rock, and going down with every new step. I gasped for air. My whole weight seemed dumped into my chest. I crouched and crawled back.

Faour was squatting between the two gaps, breathing heavily from his mouth, trying to ignite Rameh's lighter.

"A hive of bats," he reported. "I need to get this bbbloody – ..."

The lighter responded, with a precious blue flame which snapped Faour out of snarling irritation into full blown enthusiasm. He stood up, brandishing his tiny torch, and led the procession.

The right-hand passage was long and veered gradually upwards to a wider cave, where we heard an eerie fluttering and smelled something like a mixture of pus and decay. Then the bats attacked. We slipped our shirts over our heads to keep them out of our hair and held our noses. Faour waved the lighter in a futile attempt to scare them off, and cursed them loudly. The bats continued to piss on us, their strident screams piercing our ears.

Finally we reached the next tunnel. Although it was darker in there, the bats were behind us and the path was still climbing.

Every branching had to be checked out, before a decision was made, but deep down, I was starting to feel confident about the journey. Our path was now gaining in steepness and the soil was getting drier.

"Adam?" I knew that tone of voice: slow, almost liquid, as if pouring diluted words into a narrow tube. Throughout his childhood, in the middle of his ordeals to comprehend maths, he'd interrupt me to ask an out-of-context question in that voice. Today it was, "Do you ever stop to ask yourself why on earth you are here, doing this, at this particular moment?"

"Once in a while. I'm sure everybody does. Why?"

"I do it all the time."

"You ought to study philosophy. *The Old Man and the Sea* won't help you in this."

"I like stories more than philosophy."

"Then you'll carry on being bugged by unanswered questions."

"You really think philosophy has the answers?"

"Look! Light!"

We quickened our steps toward the stabs of sunshine at the end of the wider grotto. Faour clapped shut the lighter. Relief came like a splash of cold water after a drunken binge. And warmth; I suddenly realised how cold I'd been inside the caves.

Outside, I was in familiar surroundings, though the landscape was more overgrown than I remembered.

Sayed Bey had given his land incomparable masonry; no one else built terraced groves with hand-chiselled stones. His forefathers, like ours, had created the terraces by piling up rough stones found in the ploughed soil or brought over from nearby quarries. And they, like we, spent considerable time and effort every year restoring the fallen sections. Then one year, when I was about seven, a bruising winter caused havoc across our region, crumbling all thirty-six terraces that climbed the hill from the Bey's house to the main road.

"Enough is enough, my friend," he had said to my dad. "I'll rebuild the terraces better than the Pyramids. Nothing will ever again shake the soil that holds our roots." The words of that impressive man had left a warm imprint on my memory. *Nothing will ever again shake the soil that holds our roots.* I had no idea then that I was drinking in the love of the land and sealing it into my bone marrow forever. At the time, I was just a boy who liked visiting and listening.

The sky was a serene dome but the silence incited doubts and fears. After all, we were broaching another's territory. I felt a flinch of dread, the dismay of walking on a neighbour's grass like a trespasser.

The citrus trees had not been tended; they were tangled with weeds and thorns. Neither the vines nor the olive trees had been pruned for at least two years. The large vine pergola which crowned the entrance of the Bey's house had been renowned for its formidable black grapes and the breeze it stirred on hot summer afternoons. The vine was still there but its straggling shoots drooped like the branches of a weeping willow and grapes hung untouched, to be eaten by wasps and bees. A neglected home in a small village suggests despair behind it. I thought of the melancholy Fairuz song:

> *Ma fi hada, la tindahi, ma fi hada*
> *Babun msakkar wal-ishib ghatta e' deraj*
> *Shou awlkoun sarou sada . . .*

> No one is here, do not call, there's no one
> Their door is shut, and the weeds cover the stairwell

Could they, may they, have become mere memory . . .

We approached with vigilance. I longed to raise my voice in the high, assured tone of my father: "Brother Sayed Bey, we are home." Not *here*, but *home*. And the answer would reach us like a resonating bell: "Indeed you are!" Instead, Faour and I tiptoed like thieves towards the pergola.

Then the smell of Sitt Kattura's cooking broke through my painful alienation and I glimpsed her black dress behind the branches of vine at the far end of the pergola. She was cooking over an outdoor hearth made of rough stones. A steady fire glowed inside it, neither smoking nor sparking. Not using the kitchen gas stove whenever the sun shone was the ancient way. It meant perseverance. Identity. Hope. I took heart.

Sitt Kattura looked up, startled, the wooden spoon a stilled pendulum in her hand. Her round, refined features squinted as if looking into a flashlight. Then she dropped the spoon in the pot and parted her arms, stepping towards us. I ran to her. She held my sweaty head in both hands, kissing me repeatedly on the brow. It was some time before I could introduce her to Faour.

"I knew your father and your grandmother," she said to him. "A fine woman."

Sitt Kattura matched her husband the Bey in size, though she was not as broad around the waist and was firmly busty. Despite her seventy-plus years, she held her head like a Canaanite queen. Her almond eyes were deep brown; their quizzical gaze used to have me wondering if she could read my thoughts. Her hair was braided down to her thigh in one long silver rope. Her mouth, that once held the secret pleasure of a judge about to set you free, was now carved into lines of exhaustion.

"Sayed is bedridden, my son. Since the beginning of the troubles he's approached his maker several times but was never accepted."

"God forbid."

"And so He did. But Sayed is feeling like an outsider. You can imagine: a deputy, a minister, an honorary councillor and the chief of this village, now humiliated by hooligans, disrespected and ignored. Death will be a mercy to him, my son."

Sitt Kattura's manner was level-headed. There was sadness in her voice, yes, but she was making sure that I would grasp the situation.

"I must see him, Sitt Kattura. We came here through the cave passages so we could have a word with him. And even if he's unwell, we can't just leave without taking his blessing. Would you let him know that we're here to see him, please?"

Sitt Kattura's expression admonished and forgave me at the same time. "You are your father's son, Adam," she said. "Walking with you, young Faour will learn to be a good man. God bless you and keep you both. Follow me."

She used her dress to grasp the handles of the pot and carry it ahead of us through the front door. We followed a sharp smell of medicine towards the main bedroom. I felt my pulse pounding and heard myself say the old familiar words of greeting: "We are home, Sayed Bey!"

"Holy Eternity! Is that the son of Sámi Awad? You have your dad's timbre. Come, boy, come."

His voice was scratchy. I felt a surge of emotion. I grabbed Faour's wrist and rushed past Sitt Kattura just as she was turning kitchenward. "*Shway, shway,*" she said, warning us not to tire him.

The colossus of Nahrieh had grown a white beard down to the middle of his chest. He was pale against the white bed linen, but his sunrise blue eyes were glowing.

"You have come like messengers from time immemorial. Telepathy still works. If you look hard enough you'll see it laughing above the telephone lines!"

His own attempt to laugh ended in coughing. He gestured me to lift his shoulders. Faour hastened to the opposite side and helped by pushing the pillows up.

"Where did you find this fine boy?" The Bey's hand brushed Faour's face.

"This is Faour, my neighbour and part-time student. I try to teach him maths. He hates it, but he's passionate about reading."

"As long as you have a purpose to your passion. A passion without purpose is a ticket to eccentricity. But Faour will not become a mere collector of books. Mountain boys inherit a sense of purpose. It's in their blood."

The picture above the Bey's bed posed a striking contrast to his present state. Standing proud in long cavalry boots, an English carbine strapped to his shoulder, an Arabian keffiyah crowning his head, his twirled moustaches about to take off like eagle's wings: this was the man who had thundered at the French Mandate officials: "Good friends don't overstay their welcome; they leave on time from the front door, unlike thieves and intruders. Are you friends or thieves?" He knew full well that Paris had invested too heavily in Lebanon to be kicked out by force. He also knew better than to risk losing the support of a great power. Ironically, I thought, the Bey had helped remove the French but had failed to keep his own clan in order.

There was a protocol to visits, as I well knew. You showed patience and tact. You didn't state your wishes up front, and never before the preliminaries of traditional hospitality. But while I was composing the formalities in my mind, Faour jumped in with: "Is Nahrieh and the villages around it going to war against us? We heard rumours of armaments and militias and land mines. People are scared. We don't want this war. We don't want our homes destroyed and our lives . . ."

The Bey was taken by surprise. He stopped Faour in mid-sentence and grasped his arm. "Son! I can hear the pounding of your young heart. Bless you. I wish all the fools brandishing arms were like you. But believe me, civil war is an incurable disease. Like the one eating my lungs. The good people of this land have never managed to stop it from recurring. Don't you read the history books?"

"I'm reading about the French Revolution," Faour tried.

The Bey shook his head impatiently. "All fine and good, but ours is a tribal society. Even the word society doesn't apply. We are a ragbag of refugees: escapees from ancient genocides and banned religions. Everyone fleeing persecution in the Near East ended up hiding in these mountains. So how can you make a silk purse from a sow's ear? I don't mean to upset you, lad, I can hear the thunder in your mind. I wish I had the lightning to bring the refreshing rain."

He paused for breath, then said, "And it's been the same right back to the Phoenicians. Even then, each city fought its wars alone, and lost. We have too many hearts for one body, lad." According to him, despite the proliferation of different factions and militias, there were just two sides in the current war: those fighting to change the power structure and those hanging onto their power. The winners, if anyone ever won, would crush their enemies to the point of humiliation.

"And who in their right mind wants to live next door to a vanquished neighbour? How long before the buried hatchets are dug up again?"

Perhaps it was the dismay on Faour's face that softened the Bey's voice: "But I don't think history repeats itself forever. In my religion we believe in the eternal continuity of life, and in purification through trial and error. A time may come when people will refrain from soiling their hands with the blood of their brothers. This is the dream of my soul. And looking at the pair of you today, I can almost believe it will come true."

Throughout, he had kept his hand clamped around Faour's arm, his weary gaze moving slowly between the two of us. Sitt Kattura had been standing inconspicuously a few steps inside the room. She'd brought *charab* for us, and her husband's soup, but had placed the tray on a side table, waiting for him to finish speaking. Now she served us. While we sipped the sweet charab, she sat on the edge of the bed watching her man unsteadily eating his soup. From time to time she handed him a small towel to wipe his mouth.

When Sitt Kattura left again with her tray of empties, the Bey glanced at me sideways, pursing his lips. He was hesitant, yet what he had to say was going to come sooner or later. "How's the Hakim coping with all this?" he asked finally.

The Hakim had no clue I was here. I had to choose my words with care. I gave Faour a *be quiet* look: *Wahdeh's reputation and my uncle's credibility are at stake. Your honesty can wait.*

"My uncle sends his regards, Sayed Bey. I'm sorry for not relating his greetings before. He values your opinion dearly and is looking forward to hearing from you. In his own judgement Wahdeh should keep a low profile. He tells us: In times of turmoil stay as calm as when a snake is passing between your legs – if you don't move, it won't feel your presence. We'd been doing fine like that, but lately we've had a visitor. A militia officer who wants to reopen the Peacock Castle and start training the lads. The Hakim is trying to delay that plan until after the harvest, but he can't stop it altogether. Some young men are keen, especially those with no land to work or crops to harvest. They're feeding on the panic and the news from elsewhere. Therefore we need to establish an understanding with someone in control over here, in Nahrieh, or wherever you can direct us. A sort of non-aggression agreement. Prevention before facing a difficult cure."

The Bey was silent, his eyes half closed. He had lain down again after his soup. His breath stopped fluttering the white sheets. I feared he was falling asleep. Faour looked alarmed and he cleared his throat loudly. A shadow of a smile rose from the corners of the Bey's mouth, relaxing the ripples of his brow. It said, I am here, be patient.

"The Hakim, God bless his good spirit, is right of course," the Bey said at last. "He bases his attitude on the old tradition of invisibility. He aims at handling things with care, as if tackling a sick baby. That's fine. Because he's keeping his flock together. It may not seem a great achievement to you, and it's a big gamble. But the Hakim has no other cards in his hand. As for your noble mission, I fervently wish I could help. But you can see I am no longer in control over here, and no one knows the number of factions roaming this side of the mountain now. Add to those some vengeful individuals and others crazed with drugs. I advise you to back the Hakim. Stay behind him even if you don't like his methods. And please, Adam, do not tell him that you found me. If he knows that I'm sick and the way things are around here, he may become disheartened. Tell him I wasn't here, which isn't far from the truth anyway." The Bey's eyes grew heavy. "My siesta time," he sighed. "Please excuse me . . ."

Moments later the Bey's breathing filled the room with broken whistles and light snoring. A crushing wave of defeat rolled over me. However 'noble' our mission, it had failed.

Nine

Every morning, at the rooster's second crow, Mariam sneaked into our bed whispering, "In the middle," a ritual that usually took place while Yousra and I were drifting out of sleep.

It was three days before we were due to hand over the key to the Castle. We'd worked hard yesterday and stayed up a bit later than usual talking. But neither the rooster nor our daughter sympathised. Mariam was flipping around in my arms like a fish. Yousra moaned and migrated to the edge, dying for an extra wink of sleep. I tightened my grip on Mariam, whispering, "Let Mama sleep."

"Why?" Mariam whispered back.

"'Cos we were up late."

"Why?"

"We were talking."

Mariam paused a second or two. Then another, rather dubious, "Why?"

Suddenly Yousra turned and took her from my arms. They locked together like magnets.

I jumped out of bed and stepped outside the back door. The cliff was a huge uncut jewel. The pines were a fresher green. The rain must have come late in the night. I hoped the soil wasn't too muddy. The proverb that promises another summer from October till the end of November had been confounded by restless weather over the last three weeks. This period used to be the softest spell of the calendar, a reprieve permitting us to prepare land and cattle for the winter. Not so this year. The blue northerly was lasting only a few hours before giving way to the wicked southwesterly that crowded the sky with dark clouds. Soon thunder clouds were beheading the mountains.

Yousra gave me a hug from behind and rushed Mariam to the kitchen. I felt good. Given that she wasn't a morning person, I didn't expect her to resume last night's discussion. Her students had been visiting lately – a couple from Wahdeh, the others travelling from neighbouring villages. They arrived hitching a lift with anyone, even the militia. Sometimes their parents drove them over, together with gifts from their fields. Disheartened by the threatened closure of their school, they were desperate for advice. She couldn't help them but neither could she stop worrying. What if the boys were infected by war, taking up arms and dropping their education? And what would the girls be doing all winter? Her concern was genuine and she did her best to help, but this counselling service run from home had to stop. Not only because we had to tend to our land but because the students had to help their parents with similar chores. Their visits had been emotionally draining for all of us, but Yousra still preferred to stay in contact with them.

For me, the decline of my job at the bank and the increase of farm work was a blessing in disguise. I loathed the culture of speculation and gossip and conspiracy theory that had turned an otherwise congenial little bank into an ersatz combat zone, where each soldier was a self-decorated general, expert in war and international politics. I'd drop by casually, sort out any paperwork, and breeze away as quick as I could. We had a lot of land work to finish in a short time. Our olive trees were the main asset in building up the olive oil industry we'd been hoping to start this year. I wasn't going to let the trees down. But Yousra couldn't put her heart in the land under the present circumstances.

"I look at my students and I see a lost generation," she had said last night, "It hurts. Can you imagine waking up one day and finding all your olive trees reduced to ashes? What would you do?"

"I'd shoot myself."

"Well, I've been teaching those boys and girls since I came to Wahdeh. Over the years I've seen them struggle, fail, succeed, hope, plan, dream, believe they were building a future. And now what? Where will they go from here?"

"How would I know? We're in the same boat, remember? The difference is, I don't ask impossible questions. I just want to do what's at hand and hope that this war will stop. What else can I do?"

"No. You believe you're King Canute holding back the tide of war. You and your Don Quixote of an uncle."

"Leave him out of this. He's doing what he can."

"Whatever. I just don't see how we're going to survive if the fighting escalates."

"We'll manage."

"How? You spend no time at all at the bank. Have you finished your work?"

"It's all OK. Yousra, don't worry about my job, please."

"If I lose my job and you lose yours, just tell me in figures how are we going to survive?"

"We're better off than many because . . ."

". . . *we still have the land*. I know, I know. But can we live off the land alone? We need at least five years to start making money from the olive press *if* we can get it started at all. What about Mariam getting a proper education? And our next child?"

It had been seven years since our wedding. Yes, time to have another child. And time to restore the *ma'sara*. A couple of years after the death of my father, I'd voiced my desire to revive it, but no one had shared my dream. My uncle had said, "Forget it, that was your dad's passion. Find your own." Sitti abhorred the idea. "Raze it to the ground, it killed your dad." My mother blamed the hard work at the press for taking her husband. She had stayed only one year after his funeral. Then she'd turned her back on the whole business of olives and oil and, taking Hawwa with her, had gone to live near her brothers in Beirut. No one believed I could manage the hard work involved. In their eyes I was still the skinny child. The olive press needed a robust man. You were that man, Father, and I am your son, and ready now to take up where you left off. I can hear you urging me on. I can feel the strength of your arms in mine, the power of your chest is warming my lungs. You're walking with me, and your dream is now my dream, only updated.

After all accountancy was only a means to an end, a way to earn the start-up capital I needed. I had done much else during my student years, travelling north to Kura, the largest area of olive groves in the country. I had visited every new or refurbished olive press, storing up ideas. I would produce only the first cold pressed olive oil, a delicacy of low acidity and rich aroma. I would bottle it in dark glass so that light and oxygen wouldn't damage the golden elixir. It would be more expensive than the fraudulent products mixed with hazelnut oil and processed to prolong their shelf life while parading as 'virgin' and 'extra virgin' oil. I was learning about the health benefits, about antioxidants and fats and how to prevent the loss of nutrients. I was ready. I would keep the grinding stone and the old fibre discs made of hemp, but I would get a stainless steel decanter and upgrade our old hydraulic press. I was still considering whether or not to use the exhausted paste to make aromatic soaps or just sell it to commercial producers. But that was a minor detail. It was time to begin.

When I met Yousra at university I met my soul mate, though not straight away. She was too involved in the politics of change.

Although I saw little point in playing hide and seek with policemen, I joined her in demonstrations, sit-ins and riots. I was in love and love made me do things against my nature. But none of it changed my gut revulsion towards the superficiality and falseness of Beirut. What many later came to believe was the golden age of a Mediterranean metropolis was to me a façade of cool and hype. It was a lie on every level, and the civil war was now revealing its sham. Where were all those revolutionary secularists who had filled the streets with slogans and paraded their support for radical change? Back in their sectarian enclaves. Where were all the café pundits of Hamra street, the holier-than-thou intellectuals who knew, as the saying went, which egg belonged to which hen? In hiding, or putting themselves at the disposal of warlords. My fellow-students had regarded villagers as backward, but I was neither proud nor ashamed. My people don't care for political illusions. They ask straightforward questions: Are you going to asphalt this road for us or just talk about it, like the previous deputy? You're promising heaters for the school, yes? But for every classroom or only for the principal's office? Same with me. I wanted to know if all the demos were going to result in some genuine improvements to our university, or whether demos were just the trendy thing for students to do, copying Paris and Chicago.

The answer came on a normal day during term, when I saw this tiny student standing at the main university gate holding a big banner, inciting car horns and the amazement of passers-by. That day the new Minister of Education was coming to visit the campus, so this olive-skinned girl with the tight pony tail and high cheek bones decided to welcome him with "a basic demand". The banner read: "DECENT TOILETS, YOUR EXCELLENCY!"

I was on the other side of the road when a police jeep arrived. I felt compelled to stand next to the lone protester. By the time I reached her she was saying," You see, officer," disregarding the mocking smile on his face, "our problem as students is that we protest for every cause under the sun, yet our basic facilities are in a despicable state. Ask him," she said, pointing at me. I nodded. The officer shrugged and left. When the minister arrived, there were at least two hundred students standing with us. Yousra and I were holding hands and talking like old friends.

Yousra wanted to stay in Beirut after graduation and continue the struggle. So whenever I talked about olive oil she humoured me kindly, like someone who has never seen the sea indulging a sailor's tale. Then one day she came to watch our spring festival, when the whole of Wahdeh gathers around the Castle walls and the Hakim sits royally on a flat rock overlooking the party in his white suit and his brown and white shoes. The women prepare tabbouleh in big copper basins. The men barbecue young calves and lambs. The children buzz around. And Rameh, wearing his father's silk *gumbaz*, spellbinds everybody with his tricks and the *dabkeh* beats the solid earth.

Yousra had been smitten and found herself swept away to belly dance along with everyone else. Never had she looked more beautiful, with her long amber hair and wide dark eyes and her lithe little body revelling in the dance. All the women had taken to her, clapping her on. At the end of the festival she said she wanted to check out the house of my dreams. We walked back to the village, stopping at significant spots, those overlooking the olive terraces then carpeted with white camomile flowers. "They seem happy," she said of the trees, "like grannies leaning over generations of babies."

"That's the wind, sculpting them. The south-westerly does half the pruning, we do the rest."

"Do they need a lot of pruning?"

"Each tree is an individual, and that's how we treat them. Generally, the younger trees get more pruning. The more you care for them, the more – and better – olives you get. But you can neglect them for years and they'll still keep flowering and fruiting. And if you prune a hundred-year old olive tree right down to its base, it'll sprout again. They can live many hundreds of years – more, even. There's one in the hills above Byblos that's said to be thousands of years old, the oldest olive tree in the world." I carried on, outlining the history of the olive trees, from it's beginning here in what used to be called the Land of Canaan, through its spread by the Romans who took the olive seeds to Cyprus, Greece, Italy and Spain, right down to the present.

"Historically, olive oil was sacred, it was used in rituals of worship. It's also been used for medicinal purposes from the start."

"My mother used to rub my skin with olive oil when I was a baby," Yousra said.

"Me too."

We laughed. I opened the squeaky door of the olive press. The old-vaults and arcades, the bare stone walls, the huge millstone, the baskets, the wooden handel, the fibre discs, the demijohns, the deep window like the mouth of a spring with light flooding through it – all of it entranced Yousra. "It looks like a deserted temple," she breathed, "thirsty for celebration."

"Would you like to be the priestess of this temple?"

Yousra beamed a sweet smile and raised her arms towards me. It wasn't just a kiss but the start of a lifelong commitment. And that commitment had been fuelling our life with energy and excitement; saving, planning, and filling the future with hope.

When I joined her in the kitchen there was a frown between her eyes. The radio was on: A car loaded with explosives, said the news reader, had detonated in the fish market. Seven killed. Eighty injured. Four more schools had been commandeered as training camps. Two others turned into refugee centres. Yousra snapped the news off. She sighed, crossed her arms and stood near the window watching our daughter emerge from the hen house.

Mariam walked into the kitchen showing three eggs in her curved palms.

"Now clap!" I said.

"They're still warm," Mariam murmured, as if the eggs would wake up if she spoke any louder.

After a quick breakfast we assembled the tools and strolled down to the grove; we could put in a good four hours of work before the clouds would gather again to bring more rain. The morning was fresh and fizzy. Wahdeh was at work in earnest. Roofs and yards and verandas were full of women, their hair wrapped in colourful scarves, cleaning, preparing burghul and kishk and pickles and jam. The men were harvesting, clearing irrigation channels, reinforcing terraces and piling up wood and twigs. We planned to pick as many olives as possible, fortify the terraces and tend to the vines.

Mariam skipped ahead of us with the lighter basket. I carried a bundle of supporting sticks and a thin pole to shake the branches. Yousra carried a large basket on each arm packed with sheets to catch the falling olives. We spread the sheets under the trees. I took the pole and started working. Mariam, on all fours, gathered and filled the baskets. Yousra went to the upper terraces to prop up the vines. All over the fields, families worked shoulder to shoulder without a break, each trying silently to outdo the others. Unlike the previous harvests, no one sang or walked over to the next orchard carrying a pot of coffee, a present of freshly picked fruits. The elderly and the babies were absent, too cumbersome to bring over for just a few hours. All we heard were the sounds of tools and adults slave-driving their children. Mariam needed no scolding to get the job done. On the contrary, I had to engineer little breaks, like, "Get me the pitcher from the myrtle tree." Or, "Go to the end of the terrace and check that little tree, is it worth the trouble?"

By the time the wind started to hum in the nearby woods, Yousra had managed to lift our vines off the ground and tie them as best she could. She even had a smile on her face when she came back to the olive grove. "Two full baskets!" she cried, looking proudly at her daughter. "It'll break our backs, carrying them up the hill."

"No problem," came Rameh's voice from behind the trees. Then Rameh himself appeared, with my Winchester and three fat grouse. Mariam ran up to examine the game. "They're so big! Are you going to eat them all?"

"Sure will," said Rameh, fluffing her fringe.

"I see you've been busy," Yousra said to Rameh.

"Oh yes, she's a jewel, never misses a shot." He tapped the gun boastfully, then bent down to pick up the baskets.

Rameh's heavy load slowed him enough to match Mariam's small steps. They walked together chatting about the Castle. Besides the Hakim and a few old men, Rameh was the only person to know the Castle inside out. And Mariam was firing him with enough questions about it to mark the entire way to Jerusalem. In seconds a caravan of rolling clouds obscured the cliff. Rain was beginning to spit. We speeded up. Although we were prepared, our raincoats wouldn't shield our faces when the rain started in earnest. We urged Rameh and Mariam to hurry, but Rameh could sleep in the middle of a storm, and Mariam, wholly protected in her yellow sou'wester, was equally indifferent.

Yousra and I agreed without words not to worry about Mariam. We started to run. The minute we took off, it poured down. Why a minor coincidence like this made us laugh is beyond me. We ran flat out all the way to Sitti's, laughing like fools.

When we arrived, we had to walk around a basin on the floor. This was the first year I hadn't had time to stone-roll Sitti's roof. Now it was leaking, dripping tick, tick, tack into the copper basin. "My ceiling is like a sponge, son. We'd be better off under an oak tree." Sitti didn't mean to make me feel guilty, but Yousra nonetheless came to my rescue. "Why don't you have it cemented? It's the only dirt roof left in Wahdeh."

"Do what you want with my roof when I die. Until then it will remain dirt. I'm only worried about Mariam catching a cold if it gets too damp here. Where is she?"

"Behind us."

As soon as we joined Sitti by the fire, Mariam arrived, panting with excitement. She took off her coat and her shoes and rushed over to throw her arms around Sitti.

All through lunch Mariam rabbitted on about the Castle. She was still bursting with questions. Rameh had told her that sometimes he heard strange sounds coming from it. Was it really haunted? Could the sleeping spirits wake up, strangle the officer, and make all our troubles disappear? What did Sitti think?

The west wind picked up another gear and whined through the gaps of Sitti's cottage. The fire crackled in the stove. As always, Sitti answered with a story:

"A long time ago, even before I was born," she began, "there lived a man nicknamed Ringman. He started out as an honest person living a normal life. He hadn't a clue that his brother was a scoundrel who led a gang of robbers, ambushing travellers and Ottoman soldiers and taking away their belongings. Sometimes they even had to kill somebody. One day they cut off the finger of an Ottoman general in order to steal his diamond ring. But they couldn't sell the ring because the authorities had set eyes and ears everywhere looking for it. Finally the robber chief gave it as a wedding present to his brother, who wasn't called Ringman at the time. He wore it proudly, not knowing its origin, until a spy for the Ottomans spotted it on his finger and snitched on him. The next day Ringman was arrested and taken to the prison in Peacock Castle. The police asked him where he'd got the ring from. He said it was his, not wanting to get his brother into trouble. They tortured him for days but he still didn't tell. It was only much later in prison that he learned from the other criminals about his brother's secret life; one even knew where the gang's cave was. Ringman became very angry. Some say he bribed his jailers. Others that he managed to saw through the bars. In any case Ringman escaped. He surprised his brother in the cave. There was a terrible fight between them. It ended with the brother's death."

"Yes!" Mariam cheered.

"Yes indeed," Sitti echoed. "But then Ringman was stuck. On the one hand the Ottomans were after him. On the other, the robbers would kill him if he left, to make sure he couldn't give them away. So he stayed and became the new leader of the gang. In time, Ringman rose to fame for robbing the rich and giving to the poor. The villagers harboured and protected him from the police because they liked him, even though there was a large reward on his head. But one day his luck ran out and one of his own men betrayed him. He was taken back to the Castle. This time he was chained to the wall and a few days later they hanged him."

"Oh, no!" Mariam was appalled.

"Oh, yes. Terrible things have happened in that Castle and more still may happen. There's a curse on that place, you know. It should never be opened again."

Ten

The Hakim's windows were shuttered and the front door closed: an unfamiliar sight except on those rare occasions when he was profoundly disturbed about some matter. Then he'd drink himself silly; his liver would reach the end of its tether, and his immune system would collapse, driving him to bed with fever, to cough and shake and eat nothing but soup and baked garlic. His visitors would be banned until the smell of garlic and farting was gone and the first cigarette sat in the ashtray next to the first glass of arak. My heart lurched at the possibility that he might be ill. I hadn't seen much of him lately, what with the rush of work during the last three weeks, but I wouldn't expect him to crumble so soon; we need him to maintain Wahdeh safe. We needed him to keep a close eye on Nimer and his cronies when the boys came back from training. A bed-ridden Hakim would be a disaster.

I knocked. While waiting, I noticed that the cooking hut had been reduced to a pile of kindling under the fig tree. Looking at the empty space where the hut had stood for six months, I thought: "Now comes a winter unlike any other."

The door creaked open. The Hakim stooped, stepping on the hem of his pyjamas. He retreated to let me in. He was unshaven. His voice was hoarse. "Come in, lad." He looked like he hadn't slept for days.

"What's wrong, Uncle?"

"Nothing. Everything."

"Where is Amti?"

"Resting. She's worn out. She dismantled the hut on her own."

In a far corner of the kitchen I noticed the large enema syringe. Perhaps Amti Wardieh was worse than just tired. The enema wouldn't be used to treat mere fatigue. Perhaps the Hakim had used it on himself. Perhaps his worries were too stubborn to numb with arak and his bowels had rebelled accordingly. "Root out the rot and you'll be fine," he always said. I didn't feel it appropriate to mention the enema, so I asked if Amti was asleep.

"She is, lad, I gave her a couple of aspirins. You want coffee?"

"I should be going; we can't keep Murshed waiting, can we?"

I tried to be light-hearted, but the atmosphere was crushing. The Hakim stood staring at his crowded wall, his gaze meandering among the pictures and relics and souvenirs. His breath whistled. He looked hard and deep at the castle key as if intending to melt it down with his stare. So many people had tried to take that huge key off his wall in the last thirty years. Bailiffs had pleaded with him to let them use the castle as a watchtower and shelter. Travelling merchants, tinkers, shepherds. He'd held his ground. Even smugglers, and they had offered big money. But the Hakim could not be bought. Most recently, commercial developers had wanted to turn Peacock Castle into a tourist attraction. No way. Like Sitti and many others in Wahdeh, he believed that opening the door of the Castle would bring bad luck. Now he was cornered. He was suffering, and it showed. Then suddenly he flinched, his shoulders narrowed. He snatched the key from its hook and handed it to me. Its shape left a mark on the wall.

The key was heavy and cold. Heavier still was my uncle's hand that clamped round my wrist. His face was tight. His little eyes flickered ominously. "Son, after this I want you to be ready to leave. I don't want you here if it gets ugly."

"Uncle!" I cried. But the Hakim turned away abruptly and shuffled off to his practice, closing the door.

His despair engulfed me as I drove to the Castle. *I don't want you here if it gets ugly.* His words hammered into my skull. It distressed me to think that my uncle, of all people, could think for one moment that I could leave.

The square was unusually full, the crowd hovering around the shop as if about to loot it. Faces frowned and heads shook at my speed but I didn't slow down. I was miles away. "When the watchdog goes under, it's banquet time for the wolves." My father again. But also my uncle. Brothers reciting the wisdom of old, as different from one another as the waves and the rocky shores, yet just as close. Where on earth would he expect me to go? And why was he feeling such terrible humiliation?

I turned off the road and drove across the old stone bridge, up the leafy hill, under the ancient pine trees that guarded the entrance. At the forecourt, an army truck was being unloaded by Nimer, his beach bums and – surprisingly – Faour. They greeted me, I nodded. Faour avoided eye contact. But I knew – peer pressure plus his father's rigidity. Murshed effendi jumped out from the front seat.

"Ahlan wa sahlan, welcome." He came towards me with open arms. The sharp creases were gone, his fatigues dishevelled. "You're early," he added.

I said nothing. Something about him made me want to stop breathing.

"So you haven't changed your mind?"

I handed him the key.

"What's wrong? How is the Hakim?"

"He's not a happy man today." I wished I hadn't opened my mouth. I just wanted to give him the damn key and leave.

"Is there anything we can do?"

"Anything?"

"Sure."

"Give me back the key and take your war away from here."

I walked to my car feeling angry with myself for airing my anger.

But the officer was unperturbed. He followed me, putting a light hand on my shoulder. "I am truly sorry, Adam, but I need your help out here. Just an hour or so every day. I need someone to handle logistics. Just some book-keeping, at least for this round of training. Besides, Wahdeh's boys look up to you."

"What do you want me to do? Count how many bullets are fired each day?"

The officer laughed, "A bit more than that. All the book-keeping. We'll provide you with bills and receipts. A simple inventory will do."

I was about to refuse, when the look on Faour's face, his sad eyes as he watched from the back of the truck, made me think twice.

"On one condition," I said stiffly.

"Yes"

"Promise to go easy on Faour, but don't tell him I asked."

"I'll do my best. But I can't guarantee anything with Bou-Youn. He goes by the book."

"Bou-Youn?"

"The best trainer this army has ever had."

"I don't care if he's the best in the world. Give me *your* word."

The officer tendered his hand, smiling.

Reluctantly, I took it.

When I reached the square there were even more people gathered around the poplar, and my uncle – still in his pyjamas – was arguing with Abu Faour. They were talking at the same time in a high, angry pitch, obviously not listening to each other. Either the Hakim was not convincing enough to shut Abu Faour up, or the shopkeeper was being even more stubborn than usual. Everyone was agitated, moving in circles and stamping the ground. They were shouting so loudly I had to strain to disentangle the words: "What's come over him? This is unbelievable! He's lost his head! What will I do for clothes? For fuel? For medicine? Where will we weigh our crops?" So. It was for real. Abu Faour was truly shutting up shop

I left the car and pushed through the crowd, but before I could reach the Hakim, a thin breathy scream chilled us all into silence.

At the centre of the square, hobbling on her bowed legs with her stick, Abu Faour's mother was coming straight towards us, shaky as a scarecrow in the wind. But enough resolve emanated from her weak body that a sudden silence fell. Abu Faour rushed to meet her.

"Don't you come near me!" she shouted. She pulled a piece of brown paper from the top of her dress and waved it in his face. "These are the title deeds of the shop!"

"Mother! Mother!" Abu Faour pleaded.

The old woman lifted her stick and whacked him.

"I am selling the shop. Do I have a buyer? Do I have a buyer? Five piastres. On one condition: keep the shop open no matter what."

"Please, Mother, don't shame me any more."

She hit him again, missing his bald head by a whisker.

Trembling with fatigue and emotion, the Hakim approached the old woman. He shielded her in his arms. "Give it to me, I'm buying," he said, as if to a distraught child. He took the piece of paper from her and growled at Abu Faour. "Let's take your mother home. The square isn't the place to sort this out." Abu Faour walked over, covering his face with both hands. I opened the car door and pulled forward the front seat. Helped by the Hakim, mother and son tumbled onto the back seat. She stopped hitting him but continued cursing him to hell and damnation. The stunned crowd parted to let us through. The Hakim sat beside me.

As we took off I saw Zahi crying with shame, pulling the shop's rolling door down.

Against all the odds, the Hakim's rural diplomacy worked. The next morning Abu Faour was back in his shop as usual.

Eleven

The Peacock Castle was built by Severus, the first Roman emperor born in the Near East. He'd already built the Great Law School in Beirut and the magnificent temple to Bacchus in Baalbek. The Peacock Castle was constructed as a leisure centre for the elite of his army. The Hakim maintained that, to this day, the sounds of Roman debauchery echo through its rooms during nights of the full moon. When the Roman Empire fell, the Castle too fell into disuse until Suleiman the Magnificent, the Ottoman Sultan, decided to build a Serail in Wahdeh. By then our village was a prosperous centre of learning. A Serail in it would mean the coming of politics. Regional feuds. Soldiers. Officials. Bribes. Executions. In short, the end of Wahdeh as a quiet campus of culture. The elders were worried. They got together and came up with a middle way. They suggested positioning the Serail over the ruins of the Roman castle. That way it would be kept out of village life, while remaining just within the parish boundaries, for it stood some distance away, near the junction with the main road. To make the offer even more appealing Wahdeh's people donated their labour. The Sultan agreed.

After the First World War German Archaeologists excavated the grounds, wrote reports and put the Castle on the map.

The English shipped a mosaic as significant as the Elgin Marbles to one of their museums.

The French turned it into barracks. And at the end of their mandate General Gouraud handed over its key to my uncle.

Now the civil war was about to write another chapter in its history.

Over the next seven days Wahdeh's men and women put their hands together and their bickering aside to turn a cold, damp ruin into proper barracks. The focus was on providing our lads with a decent place to train. The spirit of *aouneh*, togetherness, made a surprising comeback. What had seemed forgotten during the harsh summer and the hurried harvest re-emerged in the most unlikely place. Perhaps it was common curiosity about the Castle that had been for half a century the source of so much speculation, rumour, and fictitious stories. Perhaps also the general concern for the lads; basic instincts can work wonders.

The weather was terrible throughout, more like midwinter than late autumn. The heavy rain caused havoc all over Wahdeh, unleashing rivulets down the slopes. Debris from fallen terraces and flooded stables was carried along in waves. Whips of wind filled the surrounding forest with sounds that evoked the Hakim's tales of ghosts and the bygone debaucheries of the Roman aristocracy. But we toiled on, installing running water, electricity and telephone, all stolen from the mains. We brought materials from home, from nails and screws to doors and windows and even curtains. Nothing matched, of course, but the deserted heap of grey stone, with its two stories and dungeon, soon became a dwelling fit for human habitation. The only two people who never showed up at the Castle were the Hakim and Abu Faour.

The work finished, the training began. Several of the women, including Yousra and Amti Wardieh and Um Faour, took shifts to manage the catering. Yousra was the shrewdest observer on site, reporting on our lads and on Murshed and the "best instructor this army has ever had" - a scrawny little man, nicknamed Bou-Youn because of his bulging eyes. Yet, Yousra said, he was feared and obeyed as if he were a titan. She mimicked him: "I'm here to lick you lot into shape. Your mothers gave birth to you once. I'm going to give you a second birth!" (Sitti cursed the womb that spat him out. "Such creatures come not from the rib of Eve but from the arse of Satan!")

"Murshed effendi is a little more informative," Yousra continued her report. "You are here to undergo a highly concentrated training. In three weeks you'll learn what's usually covered in a three-month programme. Essential discipline. Attack. Retrenching. Ambush. Barricades. Communication. Interrogation. First aid. Explosives."

Yousra abhorred the tense atmosphere at the Castle, the rigours of the gruelling timetable and the problems caused by throwing together a castleful of men of different ages and widely varied experience. Some came from nearby villages. Others from more distant areas where they'd already witnessed battles and atrocities and destitution. Some were shell-shocked survivors who'd lost loved ones and parents. Fifteen-year-olds mucked in with middle-aged men, and the guileless with the vengeful. Yousra described one man losing his rag during dinner. "Suddenly he jumped up and stood on the table kicking at everybody's food and beating the air with his hands like someone deranged. 'Let me loose on the battlefield *now!* I want the blood of my family to drown the bastards!' "

Murshed had stepped in to restrain the man, but a younger recruit stood up for him, also fuming. "He's not crazy, sir. Lots of us here feel the same. We've had enough shit. We've been made destitute. Our homes have been burned, our trees bulldozed, our children slaughtered, our women raped . . ."

"Enough!" Murshed barked. "Soldiers, we understand your anger, we feel your pain. We're all in the same boat. But we don't want to lose you through high spirits. If you don't learn to fight properly you'll never avenge your dead. You'll be killed by the first bullet. There's a time for training and a time for fighting. For now, *focus*. Don't lose the north. Focus. Okay? Now finish your meal and get some rest. We have a long day tomorrow."

Every minute of the day was packed with furious activity. At six, a bell sounded through the thick walls. In ten minutes sharp the recruits had to be dressed and lined up in the courtyard to do their Swedish exercises, then run uphill for an hour. After that a quick breakfast followed by a run through the muddy fields, chanting songs of war. Their echo travelled the freezing winds to the anxious ears of their parents. The rest of the training took place in the woods, where they were taught to dig trenches, fill sand bags for fortifications, ambush the enemy, climb ropes and cliffs.

As for my "job", I soon discovered it was a cover-up for a scam. Truckloads of food, arms, ammunition, clothes and medicine were scheduled twice a week. I entered their contents as per the dockets handed to me by the drivers. Then the recruits hauled the supplies down to the dungeon. The next day or the day after, the same quantities arrived again. The dungeon was big, but not *that* big. I asked Murshed. He said that the Castle was used as general storage for the whole area. "Not all training camps have this kind of space." I wasn't convinced. Then one day Rameh told me that by night civilian trucks came to take the gear away for sale on the black market. That same afternoon, I caught hold of Murshed. "Find someone else to cook your books. I am out of here at the end of this round of training." I spoke firmly, looking straight into his eyes. He nodded, unable to say a word, and walked away.

Of all the recruits, Rameh was the only one enjoying himself. Nothing was too difficult for the bailiff who'd grown up in the wild. What's more, he slept like a log while everyone else ached and moaned and tossed in their sleep. On one occasion three locals were given command of a night-time exercise: Faour, Nimer and Rameh, each assigned to lead a platoon. They had to capture an enemy post – an abandoned stable at the foot of the cliff. Murshed, Bou-Youn, and a few chosen recruits went ahead to guard the stable. The aim, as explained by Bou-Youn, was to surprise the guards and take over the post. But as soon as one of the attackers was spotted, his whole platoon would have to surrender.

"The advantage of defence on your own turf is knowledge of territory. No matter how professional, an invader can never match the locals if they're well-trained. Let's see who gets there first," said Murshed effendi.

Rameh was in his element. He led his men along obscure paths known only to snakes and rabbits. He was so sure of his success, he even started humming a mocking song. Faour planned a clamp approach in the shape of a comb. It was working until one of his crew slipped and was spotted midway. His platoon was captured, ridiculed and ousted. As for Nimer, he designed a crab-like attack which would have worked perfectly if Rameh hadn't been borne from the rocks with eagle wings. Nimer burst into the stable growling "Hands up!" only to find that his first military manoeuvre had failed. There were the guards already held at gunpoint by Rameh and his men.

"Hey Nimer," Rameh laughed, "Even my goat would have beaten you."

Surprisingly, Nimer kept his cool. With a bland smile he replied: "Let's see who has the last laugh."

Rameh was unsettled by Nimer's reaction. Such calm behaviour made him fret. He began to watch out for Nimer. "He's up to something," he said to Faour as the wind howled outside, smashing hail and rain against the makeshift windows.

Faour was wrapped in his sleeping bag, trying to read. "He's always been up to something. He was born that way. Let me read myself to sleep, I'm knackered."

In the middle of that night the bell rang. The lights went on and off several times. Murshed and Bou-Youn ran into the dorm roaring: "An attack! We're surrounded!"

Murshed had warned the recruits about this exercise at the start. "You never know when the enemy will strike. You have to be ready at all times. When the bell rings I want you all out fully dressed and armed in five minutes."

For Rameh this too was a doddle. He slept fully dressed anyway. In two minutes flat he'd sprung out of bed, splashed his face with water, grabbed his rifle and rolled downstairs while the others thrashed around like a herd of bulls in a china shop, their chilled fatigues crackling like crusty bread in their freezing fingers.

But when Rameh arrived in the courtyard he was dumbfounded. There was Nimer, cool as a cucumber. Rameh longed to wipe the smirk off his face with the butt of his rifle. How the hell . . .? He fumed in silence.

Murshed and Bou-Youn were scathing. "You morons!" Murshed bellowed as the shambling recruits tried to line up. "Look at you!" He pointed to their feet. "Wearing your boots the wrong way round." Everyone looked down fearfully, but their boots were on as normal. Then, getting the joke, they forced an uneasy chuckle.

Murshed continued briskly, "If you were regulars I would have shaved your heads and kept you out here all night to freeze. But you are volunteers. You have chosen of your own free will to defend the motherland. Unfortunately, you cannot be regarded as soldiers yet, nor can we count on you in the battlefield. But don't lose heart. We have a plan for you. We will send you all over the country to the rear lines to work with more experienced fighters until each of you is evaluated. Then we will post you according to your abilities. We're not in the business of churning out martyrs. We'll leave it to others to fill their walls with memento photos of ill-trained young men. Not us. Your life is valued. Your life is cherished. You'll receive more detailed information at the end of your training. Meanwhile, you must regard this new plan as your first military secret. Guard it well."

Back at the dorm there was bedlam. The implications of what Murshed had said freaked everybody in different ways. The more embittered recruits from afar wanted action straight away, not to be stuck on the rear lines. The beach bums also fumed with indignation. They were planning to stay together. Kill together. Die together. And the local lads were dismayed, Faour crying: "We joined to learn how to defend our village. Now they're sending us God knows where."

"They should have told us right from the start!" roared Rameh.

Out of the chaos Nimer suddenly emerged. "Quiet, please, quiet! Comrades, this is not easy for any of us. But there are proper armies out there fighting against us. If we're to join the fight we must climb the ladder one step at a time. If everyone does what they want it'll end in a massacre. We must learn to obey our superiors. 'Obey first, then object,' that's the rule. War is a science, not a fist fight. Your officers know best. Let's keep our cool and take things one at a time."

Although Nimer had convinced no one, he managed to restore order. Because at last everyone, even brick-brained Rameh, saw where Nimer was coming from: the inside. Nimer was an informer. Already he was currying favour with Murshed in exchange for insider information. Working his way up in the militia.

Twelve

Faour escaped the Castle a week before the end of training, leaving the village altogether in the dead of night. The whole village was stunned, no one more than me. But at least he'd managed to write me a message inside the inventory book: "I'm not going to let them play Russian roulette with my life. I'm sorry I kept this plan from you but we never had a chance to talk. I'm going as far away as the seas and the skies can take me." Where on earth did he go?

The weather turned the day the training finished and our lads were coming home. Relieved in every way, Wahdeh's people sat out on porches and verandas with coffee and hubble-bubbles, chatting. Flags flapped in a brilliant blue sky. Our doors and windows were open again. The ashes from our stoves had been spread in the gardens to feed and warm the soil.

Although I dreaded the irony of such a glorious day, I took Mariam up to Sitti's roof to watch the imminent parade. I didn't want her to be among the crowd, so I convinced her that she wouldn't be able to see everything from the square. Sitti's cottage was on a slight rise. Besides, this morning I had rolled the roof; wouldn't she like to try it out?

Sitti and Yousra were even less interested in the parade than I was. They busied themselves with waxing the tops of preserve jars to keep the contents from going mouldy, totally absorbed in their chore.

The Hakim, in his black abaya embroidered with gold, was looking his old self again, jovial and cordial, greeting everybody, confident that the village would be back to normal.

I lifted Mariam up onto my shoulders for a better view. She commented on the dogs gathered around the fountain, sniffing each other nervously. Normally Sitti's best friends would be scattered, each in his own territory. Now, Mariam said, they looked like children waiting for the school bus.

"Will there be shooting?" she asked.

"No – there's no reason to shoot today."

"Then why did they train?"

"To protect us."

"Who from?"

"Anyone who dares hurt us."

"Can't we ask them to shoot?"

"No, Mariam, this is serious."

"What will they do then?"

"Parade through the square. Listen to speeches – here they come."

"I can hear them!"

To a song of victory, an open jeep emerged from among the pines, a flag fluttering on its bonnet. Murshed was driving; behind him stood Bou-Youn, gripping a fixed machine gun. Then Nimer appeared, carrying a rifle before him and jogging ahead of the regiment, then Rameh and Abu Janjoul, each heading a platoon. As they approached, everyone stood up and cheered. The women threw rice and raisins into the air. The boys in the trees sang and whistled. Someone had given Hilweh a little paper flag. She waved it awkwardly from her iron window. From time to time it snagged on the bars, tearing off a piece that fluttered down like a dying butterfly. Even Abu Faour was in festive mode, having spread an old carpet at the doorstep of his shop. There he stood, with the Hakim and the Mukhtar, a mocking, defiant smile on his face. For once he was proud of his son's mutiny. "I prefer they call him a coward than say God bless his departed soul," he'd told me earlier that morning, but he wouldn't reveal where Faour had gone. "In good time," was all he would say.

The recruits lined up in four columns facing the shop. They did their utmost to look decent in spite of the oversized second-hand fatigues given to them the night before. The smaller lads were struggling to keep their hands and feet free of the baggy folds of material. Even big Nimer looked swamped. Murshed stepped onto the bonnet of the jeep. Bou-Youn barked the order for attention.

"People of Wahdeh," Murshed intoned, "today you have every right to hold your heads high. Your boys have done their best. We gave them a hard time but they took it in their stride. Look at them, hardened and disciplined. This is the first step. And we are on course to achieve even more, all the way to victory, with God's help. I thank you for your support. I salute the leadership of your brave community." He extended his arm towards the Mukhtar and the Hakim and continued: "Ladies and gentlemen, here is your prize."

The villagers cheered and clapped. The mothers' eyes glistened with pride.

The officer went on: "These are men whose devotion will never waver. They will not hesitate to do their duty, they will never fear death."

The Hakim looked slightly uneasy. He put his arm around the Mukhtar's shoulder as if pleading with him to forget the officer's last words.

"This is a dangerous war," continued Murshed effendi. "It can creep up on you, take you by surprise and then all is lost. Therefore – as the Hakim will tell you – prevention is better than cure. The new strategy we have just received from headquarters can be summed up in a few words: today our best means of defence is attack."

The Hakim, Abu Faour and the Mukhtar looked at each other. I could imagine the question marks in their eyes matching those in my own. We were holding our breath and listening attentively.

"What does a farmer do when he notices the water level has dropped?" said Murshed. "Does he wait or does he run to the spring to check the problem before his water is lost? You know the answer. We cannot leave it to chance. Our brothers are defending the front line with great courage. We need people to back them, relieve them from their duties, boost their morale. We must catch the enemy off-balance, shake their confidence, divide them, convince them there are waves of fighters behind those guns at the front."

The Hakim went pale.

"Your sons have volunteered for active service. Have no fear – they'll be under my personal command. They'll come back to you in no time, experienced and better trained to protect this lovely village of yours. Meanwhile, a few chosen ones will stay to guard and report. Victory is ours!"

Now the applause was confused and sporadic. People started talking to each other, frowning and gesticulating. Murshed effendi jumped off the bonnet and walked towards the Hakim.

"What are you saying?" the Hakim shouted.

"Hakim, they have only just begun their training. This first stage isn't enough. They're still too green to be left alone. Believe me, I know what's best for them."

"You have no right to judge what's best for our sons. We agreed to let you use the castle and train them on the clear understanding they would be guarding their village. Marching them off to the front was never mentioned. I may be old but I can still hear your words."

"Those who volunteered know what they're doing. Ask them."

The Hakim took off his jellabia, gave it to Abu Faour, brushed the officer aside and climbed onto the bonnet of the jeep. The silence was deafening.

"People of Wahdeh, you all know why we agreed to open the castle, why we agreed to the boys joining up, why we jeopardised our crops and orchards. There's no need to repeat those reasons. Today was to be the day for welcoming our lads back and beginning a new era under their protection. We have given them what we owed them: trust and confidence. Are we now going to let them go? And where to? And why? So far we've stuck together, like the great oak, many branches, one strong trunk. Like that oak, our forefathers faced all storms. Are we going to be blown over by this wicked wind today? I must warn you, do not be fooled by uniforms and shiny guns and deceitful speeches. Let us stay on board this ship together. Let no pirate take it over from us."

Pandemonium broke out. Mothers came forward to take their sons home. Fathers argued. The recruits milled around, unsure of what to do.

Mariam pulled my hair. "What's happening?" Quickly I led her away. "Keep her with you," I said to Yousra, running out to the square.

A sudden burst of machine-gun fire ripped the air. Everyone froze. It was Bou-Youn trying to restore order. Instantly, Murshed and Abu Janjoul took out their revolvers and started shooting into the sky, driving the recruits back into line. I imagined Mariam hearing the shots, wanting to come out. My feet jerked backwards, then forward again. I had to trust that Yousra and Sitti would know what to do. Nimer shoved the women away from their sons. Abu Janjoul joined him, recklessly ramming the butt of his gun at the mothers. Rameh pushed himself between them, trying to shield the women. Um Faour slammed her slipper across Bou-Youn's face. Behind her bars,

Hilweh screamed and clapped, dropping the rest of her shredded flag. The dogs barked furiously. Scuffles broke out around the jeep, drawing in the tarbooshless Mukhtar, the Hakim, Murshed and Abu Faour. The Mukhtar spat in Bou-Youn's eyes.

I plunged head on into the wall of backs and shoulders and pushed my way through. I reached the jeep with a torn shirt. My uncle was flat on his back on the bonnet, his arms flung back and clinging to the windshield, banging his heels while Murshed pulled at his legs. "You're not taking our lads away! Over my dead body!" the Hakim cried. When Murshed saw me coming he grabbed my uncle round the waist and dragged him off the jeep so roughly that the Hakim fell to the ground. "Take him home!" Murshed shouted.

"This is his home! Where's yours?" I snarled while helping my uncle up. I looped my arm around him and dragged him out of the brawl.

The Hakim was damp with sweat. His breathing was disrupted by fierce spasms of coughing. We had to stop several times, leaning on walls or trees while he gasped for air. Every time he tried to say something he choked.

When I finally got him home, Amti Wardieh rushed to prepare a tub of hot water. We sat the Hakim on the sofa, took off his shoes and socks, and gave him a glass of lemonade. Then we sank his freezing feet in the steaming water. He was shivering. His teeth rattled. His face looked like a ravaged bulldog's. Amti rubbed his shoulders. "Easy now, easy *habibi*, easy my love."

"Despair is not when you fail," the Hakim had once said, "but when you realise you're down for good."

I could only hope, for Wahdeh's sake and mine, that the Hakim wasn't down for good.

Thirteen

Amti Wardieh found Faour's diary under his mattress at the Castle and gave it to me. The Hakim and I wondered why Faour was addressing the diary to Hilweh. Considering that almost everything was known to everybody in Wahdeh, this revelation showed shy, quiet Faour in a new light. We'd known him to be a bookworm and a poet, but we never guessed he thought so much about poor Hilweh. "Well," Amti shook her head, "she's there, isn't she? Above the square all day long. He's been seeing her since he was a child. He probably feels compassion towards her. He's always been different, this Faour."

The diary read:

Dear Hilweh,
This is day one at the training post. I'm still not sure I want to be here. I guess I did it just to escape the shop and my father and gloomy Wahdeh at this time of year. But also curiosity. Ever since I was a kid I've wondered what the inside of the Peacock Castle was like. Now I'm inside and finally seeing what was hidden: the thick stone walls and low arched doorways, the high ceilings, so high you'd think there was no roof above, everything as barren as a ghoul's den. And it's freezing cold. It makes me feel kidnapped, alien, yet my home is a bird's flight away. So you're not alone. We are all prisoners. Only we don't always see the bars.

Day two: Lights out at ten. Lights on at six. We're all knackered. I'm writing from inside my sleeping bag - a surrogate womb. Inside it I struggle to warm my feet while moving my arm and holding the book. The ranger boots hurt. My feet are like baked potatoes but frozen. I'm wondering what kind of dreams you have. I've often fantasised about the images that bubble up in your head. You're rocking behind the bars of your window, I step out of the shop, you see me, you miaow like a kitten. I think you're saying something nice to me. Miaow, goodnight for now.

Day three: Military training is like stepping on weighing scales but instead of reading figures you read questions. Who am I? Do I belong here? Is there a real war out there? Am I on the right side of it? The longer I stand on the scales the more I realise that the answers are not within my reach. I wonder what's happening at the square. Is there anyone left in Wahdeh? Go to sleep now, Hilweh, don't wait for me. I'm nothing but a jungle of question marks at the moment, yet the answer I desire most is sleep, deep dreamless sleep.

Day four: I think I'm going through some kind of change. At this stage I'm unable to explain it. But I can feel it. A nineteen-year-old village boy, a hundred and seventy centimetres, sixty-five kilograms. Under pressure, full of fears and uncertainties. Fit to salute the flag and drink patriotism like horse piss. Believes in nothing but leaving this country. The rest is meaningless. Yet something is changing inside me, for good or bad I'm not sure. I talk to my mother during lunch break and she goes home and talks to my grandmother, then they both talk to my father. It's a hell of a bridge to cross to reach one's own father, but he seems to be listening. Check him out for me, Hilweh, will you?

Day five: An integral part of training is the handling of firearms. Quite an experience, considering my total ignorance of the subject; something alien to me is becoming an extension of my being. "The G3 should become another appendage of yours. Remember the one you were born with? This is the same. You have to treat it with love," said our trainer.
Are they trying to substitute our innate appendage of love with another? Imagine, dear Hilweh, they're asking you to consider the bars of your window an extension of your arms. Madness is everywhere, believe me.

Day six: Just got back from night guard. Can't move my fingers, let alone think. My head is like the ceiling of a big factory with hundreds of fans whirring – VRRRRRRRR VRRRRRR – and I'm desperately looking for the switch. Help me sleep, Hilweh. Rock behind your window. Rock, rock. I keep your image in my head, but my father steps out of the shop. The square is empty. He says to himself, right; now I can do my moustache. He hangs the little mirror on the outer wall, gets his little tweezers and begins his meticulous dig for the grey whiskers. It makes you go bonkers. You scream with laughter, and once you started throwing your slippers at him! I think he's now stopped this performance. Anyway, his moustache is all grey now, haven't you noticed?

Day seven: Today I learned the true story of the dreaded Bou-Youn. He belongs to a secret order in the army known as the Butcher Band. They have officers and generals in their ranks. They believe in complete annihilation, deep skin cleansing and no prisoners. They also believe that recruits should witness a real death before going into battle. So what was called an "accident" when he killed a boy in his previous post was a murder. Scary stuff. I know you can keep a secret, Hilweh: I'm not giving my neck to the Butcher Band. I'm not a silly farm boy easy to fool with empty rhetoric. They have their cattle, their cannon fodder. I'm happy to be the black sheep.

Day eight: If I had to describe what it's like being here, I'd say I am in a vast warehouse where everyone is agitated to the brink of freaking out. Nothing clear is ever said to us. Zero communication. Everyone has their own motives. Their own theories. Call it a collection of private vendettas. Or a conference of the blind – the blind leading the blind. After a farcical false alarm tonight we were swept into turmoil. Fear is rife. Murshed, the leader of this pack, said he was sending us to the battle front. (Another secret for you, Hilweh.) I'm getting bad vibes from this, and cold feet. Actually I feel as if I'm walking backwards, in a trance.

Day nine: Night guard again. For the first time, I feel like going back home. I saw the lights of Wahdeh and spotted our house and imagined them all sitting by the fire. The smell of their gathering hovered about my nostrils like a strong memory in a deep dream. A blue sadness engulfed me. Mostly I missed sitting in the corner wrapped in a blanket, reading, my feet tucked under my granny's bottom. I guess one has to yearn for a simple thing like that to discover its true value.

Day ten: That's it. I'm out of here as soon as I can. Bou-Youn will kill me at the Baptism of Fire if I stay. He hates my guts. Today we were doing camouflage and survival. He forced me to drink dirty stagnant water. I threw up. He made fun of me. "A feeble spirit dies like that," he said, "vomiting." Had I had a live shot in my new appendage I would have killed the bastard.

Day eleven: I'm scheming, on the alert for a loophole. My father has finally agreed, my granny gave her blessing; as for Mama, she'll cover for me. It hurts to say this, but I should have listened to Dad. He objected to my enrolment, so automatically I disobeyed him. Already I can see his "told-you-so" nod, but that's nothing compared to what Bou-Youn might do to me. I must go now. I may never see you again, Hilweh, but I'll try, just to hear your miaow for the last time.

Three days later Faour escaped during the lunch break. My aunt remembered seeing him the same day, moving like a sleepwalker. He hadn't even greeted her. "He must have been shit scared – didn't write anything the last couple of days," my uncle said. He was still holding the book in his hands, pondering. He looked shocked, indecisive.

"Penny for your thoughts, Uncle?"

The Hakim shook his head slowly, gloom filling his face. "Just think with me, Adam, how many like Faour are leaving the country every day? How many more good minds can we afford to lose?"

Fourteen

Some weeks after his escape, I received this letter from Faour:

Dear Adam,

I'm sure you know by now that I'm in Caracas. My father was dead scared about my safety; he made me swear not to tell anyone about my escape until I was out of the country. Hope you understand.

Where shall I start?

I was surprised to find every member of my aunt's family waiting for me at the airport. Sandra, my cousin, later told me that my aunt had refused to have my name written on a sign board, "like a stranger's", she'd said. "My blood will know him in a crowd of a million." Evidently blood is a good sleuth. If you ask me, I think family likeness does a better job. Oval face, black hooded eyes under beetle-brows, projecting lips, a low forehead turning my bristly black hair into a squirrel's hump – how many such mistakes did God make? My genes came from my mother's side. My aunt was the image of my mother, so she couldn't get it wrong. I saw her. She saw me. The genetic magnet worked: "*Ya habibi*, bury me, bury me!" She sniffed and kissed me repeatedly like a starving bird. She was inhaling the scent of Wahdeh, the soil, the pine trees, the sacred dust of Lebanon, she said, and sobbed over my shoulder. Then my two cousins, Paulo and Pedro, and their father, Uncle Najeeb, took turns welcoming me with strong but less ceremonial hugs. Last but not least, Sandra.

How to describe Sandra? Most important, my dear Adam, the genetic likeness from our mothers' side has been discontinued by the graceful interference of Uncle Najeeb. His offspring bear none of their mother's features. Instead, a mixture of refined Latinos and slender Pharaohs, especially Sandra. An unnerving contrast to the shy conservative girls of Wahdeh. Sandra is well and truly worldly. Her

Egyptian eyes have a predatory gleam, her rich mouth is sensuous, her halo of auburn curls crowns her head like an Aphrodite who bathes in milk and honey. She is very slick and very sexy. She stepped into my arms like a ball of fire. Then and there, I became the ashes she could blow away any time she chose.

We drove home in two brand-new snow-white Mercedes. I was seated in the back with Sandra. She treated me like an old chum. She slid close to me, feigning the tourist guide: "Are you thinking Wow! Caracas! Fantastic! All those lights sparkling like a million Christmas trees? Well, forget it. Because come daytime this is another picture altogether. What you are seeing is the outskirts. Shanty towns – the *ranchos*. Cardboard, tin, plastic, car wheels, you name it." Sandra put her arm around me. Her curls caressed my face, her tanned cleavage interrupted my breathing. She continued in a semi-whisper as if we were talking between two pillows: "Here live the poorest of the poor, my dear Fifo – can I call you Fifo? Remember our visit to Wahdeh? We called you Fifo then, didn't we?" I nodded, trying to rewind my memory all those years back, and managed a smile. She went on, now stroking the squirrel's hump on my skull, "Those who make it out of the *ranchos* are very lucky. Not many do, though." Her voice softened.

It impresses me that she empathises with the downtrodden. Sensitive as well as beautiful! I am smitten to the core, not only by Sandra and the warm welcome, but by the vastness, the manicured greenery and the complex web of roads. I've never seen anything like it except on TV. Being suddenly here, after the bumpy rite of passage through war-torn Beirut, is like landing in heaven after hell. Far away are the bombs and the bulging eyes of Bou-Youn and the disdainful demeanour of Murshed effendi and the gouged-out buildings of the coast and the infested streets and the doom and gloom on people's faces. Far away are the barking radio stations that drip blood and human shreds around the clock. The music has a happy beat. People dance in the streets. In cafés and bars and everywhere, even sitting in their cars, they dance. Salsa moves them, day and night, they look like race horses hurtling towards the finishing line. Only my aunt switches on stations with news, no one else wants to hear.

The big bash was waiting for me at my new home: Quinta los Cedros, a colonial villa in the heart of La Floresta where the up-and-coming Caraquenos are leafily sheltered. We reached the house of cedars around eleven-thirty that night. The vast luminous back yard bustled with more than two hundred people, musicians, a large table set beside a lighted swimming pool, waiters in white shirts carrying trays of drinks. All for me. All organised to announce my arrival from Lebanon, safe and sound and happy to become an item with sweet Sandra. But of this I had no clue that night. Was my head still there on my shoulders? Shake hands. Shake. Shake. Kiss. Kiss the ladies. Have a drink, have another. Eat. Try this. Have a drink. Come this way. Meet our friends. Sandra guiding me arm in arm, hand in hand, answering my unasked questions, never leaving me for a moment. She refilled my drink, rum and soda and a squeeze of lemon – "Cuba Libre," she said, "my favourite, you can make it as light or as strong as you like." She filled me in about the invitees. "These people come from all corners of the world. Italians, Portuguese, Spaniards, Dutch and Lebos of course, a mezze of Venezuelan society. Commerce, trading, contraband, money-laundering, politics, all intertwined, scratch my back and I'll scratch yours. You think these people are oh so respectable? Forget it. Beneath the surface it's pure decadence. So don't be fooled by the glitter but don't be turned off by the reality. Enjoy. Go with the flow. With Paulo and Pedro you are in good hands. Saluté!"

Rum is a sneaky bastard. It moved me unawares from jet-lag to sobriety to merriment to elation to complete oblivion by the end of the evening. Fifo was dead to the world. He slept until early evening the next day when the smell of coffee woke him. "*Buenos dias, gringo.*" Sandra brought me breakfast in bed, my first ever.

Are you dizzy now with my romance? Okay, meet the family.

Paulo and Pedro are construction contractors. Their business is growing along with the oil boom. With the culture of theft and deceit nationwide, they need as many trustworthy employees as possible. Family first, of course. Sandra is studying economics and business administration, she'll become the general manager in a couple of years. And I, the cousin and potential husband, will start my training to become a foreman. Me on the ground, she on the top floor. Perfect.

The plan was laid before me casually, at dinner one evening. Neither my consent nor Sandra's was elicited. Families have heads – Uncle Najeeb's will is not negotiable. A self-made man who came to Venezuela with no money, no language, and no help except from God and the prayers of his mother back in Alexandria. He said: "You're lucky to have us. All you need to do, my dear Faour, is trust us and earn our trust. The rest is laid before you on a golden platter. We know how smart you are. Use your head. As for your heart," he smiled towards Sandra, "let us drink to both of you." I raised my glass and said I was happy and grateful and couldn't have asked for a better offer and promised to do my best and make them proud. A fresh wave of tears flooded my aunt's eyes, followed by cheers from everyone.

Next morning, Uncle Najeeb gave me pocket money. "An advance on your wages," he said. Then he slapped me on the back, put on his hat, called his driver and strolled out to his gentlemen's club. Paulo and Pedro presented me with a Vespa – "Better than a car, faster than public transport, Sandra will show you around. Next week we expect you on the building site. Meanwhile, have fun."

And what fun I'm having! My first impressions of Sandra hadn't yet included the importance of her hands. Her whole arms from the shoulders down to the tips of her fingers. The ivory texture of her skin is almost translucent, as if a beam of light radiates from inside. Her long fingers seem painted with a golden brush and her pearly nails, evenly cut to the skin like a pianist's, need no artifice to enhance their beauty. Who wouldn't put his heart in those hands? I must have felt them around my neck when she embraced me at the airport. But their full impact didn't come until we rode the Vespa together. I am the delighted captive of Sandra's arms. I love them wrapped around me while we cruise through the junctions of Caracas. I am on constant heat. Embarrassed by my lust, I make sure to have my shirt loose on top of my trousers, always. Don't laugh.

Anyway, the family believe we're already lovebirds. They rejoice. It doesn't worry them that the current chief foreman, Abu Racheed, is not impressed by me. Neither my size nor my voice fit the job, in his opinion. "Too skinny, too softly spoken," he said to Uncle Najeeb. "Don't worry," my uncle said, "we'll feed him well and get him to speak from his chest like his father. He'll do, take my word; I was just as skinny and coy as a choir boy and I managed," he added.

Abu Racheed showed me around the site of a twenty-storey complex. Shopping mall and office space. Eighty-two workers on the job. "Until your Spanish is good enough I want you just to watch and report to me. No alcohol, no drugs, no women on the site. Look out for tool thieves, especially before knocking off time." He showed me how a thief's walk is a giveaway when his pockets or underpants are stuffed with pieces of metal. "Trust nobody, make friends only outside work and be here first thing in the morning. Show responsibility, it rubs off."

While he was telling me all this, Sandra was leaning into the window of a truck near the gate talking to the driver. Wearing shredded denim shorts and causing a Richter effect on the whole site. By the stern look on Abu Racheed's face I could tell he was concerned. All I wanted was to get back on the Vespa and be wrapped in Sandra's arms and fly up to the National Park on Mount Avila where we'd buy a box of *chicharon* and a couple of cold *polarsitas* and sit in the shade of a big tree munching the pork crackers and sipping the beer. The building site can wait. Abu Racheed can walk like he's done it in his pants all day long for all I care.

Sandra has begun teaching me Spanish even before term starts at the Catholica University where I am going to attend evening classes. She's amazed at the speed of my learning. I am going with the flow as she asked, letting her guide me every step of the way. If she wants more than just holding hands and hugging good morning and good night I am ready, but I am not going to blow my chances. I am happy. More than I've ever been in my entire life. I wish you were here to see how cool I am!

But now my eyes are shutting. I'll write again soon. I sent a separate letter to my family. Leave this one between us, and give my love to Yousra and Mariam.

Faour

Fifteen

Faour's letter lifted my spirits like a powerful punch of oxygen.

Love! Yes! Congratulations!

And yet...something about his letter disturbed me. Perhaps it was his description of Caracas, reminding me too much of another side of Beirut that I had hated: the slick, glossy smugness of the rich, their preoccupation with displaying wealth in ways that struck me as gross and far removed from the one thing that mattered – the land itself. Even Faour's tone seemed at odds with the fresh young lad I remembered. There was something brittle, jumpy, a nervous energy that struck a false chord with me. Is this what happened when people left the land and tried to strike roots in an alien culture? I was curious to hear more from Faour. There's an old saying that teachers learn more from their students than their students learn from them.

I decided to say nothing of all this in my reply to him. Nor could I match his happy lines.

I began with a quick weather report. It was mid-February and still no sign of snow. "Good and bad," said Sitti. "Less damage to the terraces but the soil needs its white disinfectant." At the moment we were having a strange spell of crisp sunny days followed by short heavy showers. The evenings were mostly dry and clear. The daily electricity cuts lasted between six and twelve hours, so Abu Faour was selling more batteries and fuel lamps than ever. He was keeping the shop open because he needed the money to buy medicine for his mother. Her hips were crippling her to the point of paralysis. The Hakim advised a special home where she would be taken care of properly, but Um Faour wouldn't hear of it. She said: "I'll care for her with the light of my eyes." What home for the elderly can beat that?

The country's television centres had been bombed. Transmission came and went at random for a while, then we were cut off for good, so we were back to the radio era. People took their radios with them everywhere. Each had his favourite station. Radio Volcano, for instance, promised nothing less than the end of the world. Its airwaves were served by speakers straight out of Armageddon. They vowed to kill everyone including babies and the unborn. On another wavelength, Radio Valium had an announcer nicknamed Dead Man Talking. He dispensed sweet sentiments in a deep, resonant voice: "Look forward! This ordeal is only a passing dark cloud. We'll all be back to normal soon – even better, for we'll have learned valuable lessons from our mistakes." And people nodded their submissive heads, believing him.

But the weirdest of all was Radio Anarchy. This one transmitted a freakish mish-mash of sound effects: children crying, explosions, ambulance sirens, parodies of songs, recordings from live battles, street commotion, soundtracks from hospital operating theatres. Once it broadcast the confusion of a young surgeon trying, during an electricity blackout, to stitch together the limbs of a casualty: "Is this a hand? Is that a scalpel? Oh my God . . . oh my God!" As time went on and the fighting escalated, the station became apocalyptic: "Oh very small country! A speck from the moon! A microbe in God's eyes! Yet how big you think you are with your petty feuds and tribal vendettas and child assassins. You fight not for defence but for self-destruction."

For many, 'addiction' was not too strong a word to describe their devotion to the airwaves. Yousra, for example, took her transistor everywhere. Sometimes she slept with it still blabbering away. It was useless trying to convince her that the radio would not deliver salvation. She said: "I just need to know what's going on. I need to get the full picture, no matter how ugly. I don't understand how you can distance yourself and live on your own planet while all this drama is taking place in our country. But that's you: if there's nothing you can do about something, you ignore it. I'm not like that."

As for the Hakim, the little black gadget had become his alternative crutch since he decided, at long last, to humour Amti Wardieh and stop drinking. Before that, deep purple messages from his liver showed on the veins of his nose. His chest whistled and he was forever scratching the back of his hands. All this was a great worry for Amti. She sat near him and waited. She waited in silence, watching over her shipwrecked captain, trying ever so softly to mend the broken compass of his spirit. Then one evening she snapped, in her own quiet way. "I'm going to speak my mind now, Raji," she said, "So promise not to get upset."

The Hakim dropped his head between his shoulders and his hands between his knees. "I've been drinking too much, far too much," he mumbled.

"And what is it doing to you?"

"Killing me."

"We know that, Raji. But before it does, you should also know that you're losing it. You hallucinate. You make speeches in tongues. I follow you about the house all day putting out your forgotten cigarettes. Yesterday you forgot that we'd had supper.

I'm sorry, but I must say this before it's too late, I'm afraid of you sometimes. Yes, Raji, you scare me to death."

Now he was in his practice, huddled by the stove, baking garlic, drinking camomile tea, twiddling the dial, trying to understand, analyse, construct a shred of hope. He shook the screamer for better reception, changed the batteries and fiddled with the antenna, all day.

But I told Faour not to worry: Wahdeh was in good hands, what with our two titan guardians: Abu Janjoul, the iron pump with the permanent sty; and his Friday, Abu Takka of the rattling teeth. Our heroes wore crisp fatigues, carried shiny Kalashnikovs and sported hand grenades on their hips. They hung around the square while the shop was open, then they joined their masters at the Castle for enlightenment and strategy. "Everyone avoided them like the plague, except your father; he charged them double for everything. 'War bounty!' he proclaimed."

One evening, at the end of January, while I was sipping herbal tea with my uncle and aunt, there was a knock on the door.

"Hakim . . . I . . . Hakim . . ." Abu Takka was pointing at his teeth, trying to say something.

Abu Janjoul clamped his sidekick's jaw shut. "Listen Hakim, we need your help. You hear the way he rattles? That's dangerous when he's on guard. Can you remove his teeth?"

Abu Takka freed himself from his leader's grip and yelled: "No!"

Abu Janjoul started to push him through the door, but Amti shoved him back with the palm of her hand. "No weapons inside," she said firmly.

"Leave your guns out there and come in. I can fix the rattle without extraction," the Hakim said.

Surprisingly, the boys obliged, slipping their guns behind the old sofa on the covered veranda.

Once on the recliner, Abu Takka revealed a curved set of incisors that created a gap between his lower and upper jaws. The Hakim asked him to open wide. He examined the uneven teeth, tapping each with the butt of a scalpel. Abu Takka transmitted hollow sounds of irritation at each tap. The Hakim asked Abu Janjoul and me to hold him down. Abu Janjoul immobilised his feet. I held his arms tightly by his sides. Then the Hakim started up his foot drill. Abu Takka's eyes bulged as the filing began. To distract him and drown his groans, Amti turned the radio on. The national civil defence instructor was offering advice on what to do in the event of an artillery attack. Where to find protection inside your home, what position your body should be in, whether your mouth should be open or closed. Abu Takka's was wide open. I could see his epiglottis rattling and his tonsils popping up and down. He emitted groans like a calf being branded. His limbs jerked. His chest inflated. But the Hakim carried on, pitiless. Every now and then he'd ask Abu Takka to spit out. Amti sucked out the debris with a manual pump as old as dentistry. By the time the crooked hooks were sufficiently diminished, the four of us were drenched in sweat. Our patient needed a couple of slaps across the face to come round. Then he cannonballed out of the recliner and shot through the door.

Abu Janjoul was impressed. He took a fat roll of money from his back pocket to pay for the job.

The Hakim didn't look at the money. He came closer to the young hulk, staring intently at his face. "While you're here, why don't we rid you of that stubborn stye in your pretty eye?"

"I'll just get the cauterising tools," Amti Wardieh said, pretending to look for them.

Abu Janjoul was horrified. He left us in great haste, snatching up the guns and rushing after his sidekick.

I ended my letter to Faour by writing, "I guess that living close to cruelty rubs off on everyone, for we laughed and laughed about the 'operation' until late that night. I hope you too have enjoyed the entertainment by proxy.

Now, I want to hear more about you and Sandra. Until then, have a Cuba Libre for me and I'll have an arak for you. Cheers!"

Sixteen

At last I was notified by the bank that a long-awaited package deal was available. We'd be paid a lump sum plus our severance. It was more than I'd hoped for, and far better than Yousra's dead end with the Ministry of Education: The school in Delbeh was finally turned into barracks. No schools, no deals, no answers. We were luckier than most. Thousands of companies and institutions had vanished from the map, leaving behind them a trail of misery.

On my way back from collecting my money I stopped at my uncle's. I hadn't seen him for a few days and was wondering if his decision to kick the bottle was still holding. Also I wanted Amti Wardieh and him to know the good news. Good news was a rare commodity these days.

In Amti's garden, spring was showing some timid signs. Normally nothing peeped from the soil before April. Now, in early March and with the weather warmer than usual, cyclamen were popping out in sheltered spots. Much to my surprise, Uncle Raji was waiting for me as if we had an appointment. He was standing by the practice door, clean-shaven and smartly dressed in his grey suit and dark blue tie. We hugged. He squeezed my neck against his tobacco-scented chest.

"You're looking quite your old self today, Uncle. Are you going somewhere?"

"Come in, let's have some coffee."

"Where is Amti?"

"At the grove."

"I got the money. At last, they paid me, and closed the branch."

"Thank God a thousand times, my lad. What a lucky day. I'm happy for you. Come in."

We entered the practice room. The coffee pot was waiting on the stove. The Hakim picked it up with a not-too-steady hand and poured, spilling a bit. In the ensuing silence, the dark liquid sizzling into the hot cups sounded unnaturally loud.

"Son." His voice was signalling something big. It came from the windy cave where his demons quarrelled incessantly. "I have to do something. Will you help me?"

"I'm your right hand, Uncle. Tell me."

"I heard on the radio today about a ceasefire – one that's holding. The roads are safe."

"Which roads?"

"Leading to Beirut. I want to go to Beirut. I want to go to the militia headquarters, ask them to give us back our boys. We can't go on living like this. Wahdeh looks like an open grave waiting for the dead. Mothers don't sleep. Wives don't sleep. Fathers are stone drunk. This is no longer Wahdeh, son. I want my village back, no matter what it takes. Are you with me?"

"I'm with you. But let's finish this coffee first and make sure the roads are safe. Put the radio on, please."

"I told you I heard it just now."

I smiled, pointing at the cut on his chin, "That's why you rushed and cut yourself shaving. You know how things change every five minutes. We don't want to go all the way there and then get stranded. Besides, who do we know at HQ? We can't just walk in and make demands, can we?"

The Hakim switched on the radio, avoiding my question. I thought it better to let him think it over himself. For me to dismiss his idea outright would only fuel his stubbornness. Knowing what he'd suffered at the square – the shame of losing to strangers on his own turf, in front of his own people – it was cheering to find him dry and in fighting spirits, however foolish and desperate the mission.

Safe or unsafe, the radio failed to mention any roads. It reported sporadic shelling, attempts at exchanging prisoners, foreign mediators playing at shuttle diplomacy in helicopters, but nothing about roads. A rueful smile flitted across my uncle's face as he sipped his coffee, but suddenly he was shaken by one of his nervous coughing spells. I saved the cup from his hand and got him a drink of water. Any prolonged cough could trigger bronchitis in his vulnerable lungs. As I helped him to drink and thumped his back, Abu Faour stormed the practice, breathless. "She's in . . . the square . . . Hakim!" He was shaken, struggling to get the words out. "Your mother. She's got . . ."

The Hakim's cough crescendoed. Abu Faour, still gasping for air himself, shut up. I went to the kitchen again for the pitcher and another glass.

"She's dousing with her stick," Abu Faour finally blurted out. "Like she did before the earthquake. And she looks sick, really sick."

"Did she say anything?" I asked.

"Not that I heard. I was outside my shop and saw her going round and round in circles as if she was pulled by the stick. The dogs ran away. Even the old blind bitch that follows her everywhere."

The Hakim went pale, wheezing like a wounded grouse. "Adam, run over there. Check her out. And you," he said impatiently to Abu Faour, "go and get my wife from the grove."

When I reached the square there was no sign of Sitti. The square was deserted except for Abu Janjoul and Abu Takka sitting by the fountain having a smoke. They stirred and whispered at seeing my haste. Then they straightened up, hooking their guns over their shoulders. Not now, I thought, I can do without a chat with you two. I took a back route and hastened to Sitti's cottage.

The door was shut. I pushed it, thinking it must be stuck. But it wasn't. I put one ear to the door, covered the other with my hand and listened. Not a sound, not even the swish of her steps on the straw mat. I thought of knocking softly, letting her hear my voice, but after what Abu Faour had told us I reckoned it might be wiser not to startle her. I tiptoed around the cottage and crossed the back yard looking for clues. The herbs were in need of a watering. It wasn't like Sitti to let her basil droop and her oregano wilt. I went to the windowsill and lifted myself up.

There she was, lying down on her narrow mattress near the stove, her hands crossed over her chest, her eyes closed, murmuring. Praying? Should I wait for her to finish or just go back and report to the Hakim? But then how would I learn why she'd been dowsing in the square?

"Sitti?" I called, in a quiet but audible voice. "Sitti?" No response. I called again, a little louder. Nothing.

I left the window and leaned against the wall, held by indecision. If there was danger threatening us why didn't she say something? Why retreat and close the door and lie down as if she was overwhelmed or defeated? "Sitti," I began, talking to her in my normal voice, hoping she'd listen and react, "I just came back from the bank. It's all over. They paid our severance and shut the doors. Before I heard about your dowsing I was feeling good. Now I'm confused. I don't know what to do. Please, Sitti, we are all worried sick. Just give me your voice, say something."

Silence.

There are boundaries to every intimacy, never mind that it was Sitti who had pulled me out of my mother's womb. If she'd chosen to be alone, it must be for a good reason, even if she was making me feel deserted and putting the fear of God in my heart.

I walked back towards our house fighting the faceless ghosts of worry. At the end of the narrow street the two yobs had come to meet me. "Hey Adam," Abu Janjoul called. "What's with your gran?"

"What do you mean?"

"She's been going around in circles. Tapping her stick and blabbering funny words."

"Yeah," Abu Takka added. "Something about Satan and his devils. Now, she couldn't possibly mean us, could she?"

"Ask her."

"She never speaks to us," said Abu Takka. "She walks past us as if we don't exist."

Abu Janjoul brushed the subject aside. "Never mind that. What I want to know is why she sent the dogs away from the square? Where did they go?"

"The dogs?"

Abu Takka grinned, displaying his newly filed teeth. "We're about to put them down."

"What are you talking about?" I snapped.

"There's an outbreak of rabies. We have orders to shoot all the stray dogs," said Abu Janjoul.

"These are not stray dogs. They belong to the village. They guard the hens from the foxes and the calves from the hyenas and they keep the boars away from the crops. Who's going to do all that? You?"

"Orders," said Abu Takka defiantly.

Disgust rose within me. The thought of these two clowns letting off rounds at the village dogs burned my chest. Then the penny dropped. Sitti must have sensed the danger and gone out to warn the dogs. I cleared my throat to erase the edge from my voice. At least it wasn't another earthquake.

"Look," I said. "I'm sure you guys are doing your best, but shouldn't you get legal authorisation from the Mukhtar? Then you'll be covered if anything goes wrong."

"We have our orders . . ." Abu Takka started.

Abu Janjoul shut him up. "All right, let's go."

The minute we started walking towards the Mukhtar's house I regretted my ploy. How could I have forgotten? These days the Mukhtar was anything but a figure of authority. Depressed by the recent departure of his wife who'd had enough of his binges, worried about his son at the front, frustrated by having become "a shadow in the desert," a no one in the middle of nowhere, he'd taken to the bottle even more assiduously.

His state when we arrived was even worse than I'd feared. The room stank of rot. The Mukhtar was wrapped in a filthy blanket, beside him an overflowing ashtray and a misty glass of arak. His face wrinkled up at the sight of us. He belched loudly. It was an ominous start to the interview. The two guards spoke at the same time, tripping over their words as they tried to explain how it was their duty to machine-gun the village dogs. The Mukhtar struggled to concentrate and sit up straight. It pained me to see him like a drugged giraffe battling with both his limbs and his blanket. I raised my voice above the talk.

"Mukhtar, you are responsible here. You are legally in charge. Do you understand me?"

I must have hit a hidden nerve. All of a sudden the Mukhtar shouted, "So! I'm responsible for the stray dogs now? That's all that's left for me, son of Awad?"

"Mukhtar, please. You know Rameh isn't here now. He's gone . . ."

The Mukhtar went ballistic. "Oh yes! Gone! Everyone's gone. Except you, Mister Big-Shot College Boy! You are sooo good when it comes to shooting plates and bottles, but pulling the trigger for your country? Oh no, you're nowhere to be seen!" He was shaking with anger.

"Please, Mukhtar." I leant towards him. "This is not about me. It's about the whole village. Sober up, for God's sake."

"Go to your uncle." The Mukhtar's spittle sprayed me. "See if he's sober enough to deal with this shit."

The beach bums were jubilant. They walked out in triumph, leaving me to a furious old man who was desperately craving to blow off some steam. But I wasn't departing with his curse on my back. Drunk or not, he was still a pillar of my birthplace. I had to get through to him. I sat on the sofa in front of him, breathed evenly for a while and then spoke.

"Mukhtar, I haven't come here to upset you," I said gently. "But those guys just want an excuse to go around firing their guns. If there was rabies around, you would have been notified, wouldn't you?"

"No . . . ti . . . fied?" The Mukhtar's eyes rose to the heavens. "All that schooling and still you are a stupid wimp! Who, pray tell, is there to notify about anything these days? Get out of here!" he barked, blowing fumes in my face.

I left, reeling under his insults. I didn't believe for one minute that there was rabies or that those goons were acting under orders. But was there anything I could do to stop the massacre?

I could hear Zahi and his mates calling each other to the square and their mothers screaming for them to come back; the word was out that the guards were going to shoot the dogs. I raced home, taking short cuts, knocking over baskets, treading in cow dung. I ran into the kitchen. Yousra and Mariam jumped in fright. Mariam leapt into my arms. I held her tight, silencing her while I talked to Yousra. "Listen," I said, "take Mariam to Sitti's. She's not well. You have to take your key. Then stay inside. There's going to be shooting."

These jumbled fragments quelled her questions, or maybe it was the way I looked or the quaver in my voice. She took Mariam from my arms and left the kitchen at once.

There was no one left to turn to but the Hakim. I hurried to his practice hoping he'd talk to the Abus, try to discourage them from killing the dogs. He was sitting on the edge of his chair like a traveller about to disembark after a long journey. When I told him what had happened with the Mukhtar he didn't seem to care. He looked me coldly in the eye and asked: "What about your grandmother?"

"Sitti's door was closed. She's probably resting. I didn't want to disturb her. I told Yousra and Mariam to check on her."

The Hakim gave a long sigh, stood up, grabbed his leather bag and shuffled out of his house. I was rooted to the floor, bewildered. What on earth was happening? Was there no one I could relate to any more? And today of all days, after a rift of fifty years, the Hakim sees the light and decides to visit his mother?

By the time I gained the square again I was more worried than angry. The urgent thing now was to keep the children out of the range of fire. Near the fountain, the execution gallery was ready for action. The two killers had slipped the safety catches of their guns and were holding them high. Zahi and his mates were hovering around them like wasps. I walked straight to Abu Janjoul, feeling the Hakim's bone marrow in my limbs. His power was mine.

"Can we make two things clear before you start?" I said firmly. "First, keep those kids away. Second, shoot clear of houses and livestock."

Without flinching, Abu Janjoul turned and addressed the youngsters: "You kids stay back five metres. Stay with Adam." Then he looked at me. "I need one of them for a small task. Nothing dangerous."

I thought I'd go along with him as long as he co-operated. And it occurred to me that it would be a good chance for Zahi to reinstate his leadership after Faour's 'shameful' escape. "Take Zahi," I said.

"You, Zahi!" he called. "Come here." Zahi stared at me. I nodded. He marched proudly up to us like a little soldier. Abu Janjoul gave him a plastic bag filled with fresh bones. "Go on ahead of us. When you see a dog, call it and give it a bone, then get out of the way."

This special mission was no doubt a great opportunity to show off, but walking in front of a firing squad is nevertheless a scary experience. Zahi turned his head back slowly like a deer in an unfamiliar park. He feigned a smile, perhaps hoping for encouragement. But his friends were too preoccupied with their own anticipation to indulge him. I gave him the thumbs up. He took heart and walked on.

A long nasal laugh came from behind the barred window where Hilweh was watching. She was leaning, chin on arms, looking slightly bemused, just like an ordinary young woman at her window on a sunny day, watching a childish game. The boys tittered nervously. For the first time since giving the Winchester to Rameh I wished I hadn't. The feeling startled me; what could a hunting rifle do against machine guns? Nonetheless, an obscure need to clutch something lethal surged through me like a long-dormant flame. I suppose this is what a caveman would feel when attacked.

Zahi had found the blind bitch snoozing under a leafy shrub. Sitti's favourite had been a good hunting dog before losing her sight from some unknown disease, but now she was too old to run around with the other dogs. Zahi looked back and pointed. Abu Janjoul waved for him to throw the bone. The blind bitch sniffed it warily. Since when had people brought treats to her hideout? She shuffled reluctantly out into the open and took the bait. Abu Janjoul ordered the kids to stay clear. I held them back in a huddle. Zahi joined us. Some of the boys were shivering. Sure, they'd seen blood before; they'd hung around the butcher's shop when a cow or a sheep was being slaughtered. But this, this was *killing*, like in war. The idea transfixed them.

Then came the first machine-gun fire to be heard in Wahdeh since the day at the square, only this time there was a target.

The strident cries of the killers and the whimper of the blind bitch smoked out the other dogs. They howled furiously from the lower terraces by the water reservoir, revealing their whereabouts. Parents swarmed onto the scene from every corner, screaming at their children to come home. The boys slithered out of my control, running to see the first victim in her pool of blood. They stood in front of her, looking at each other. Is that it? Is that all? People started arguing with me as if *I* had organised this massacre. I screamed at them to get their children and go home.

Abu Janjoul and Abu Takka jogged towards the reservoir. Zahi started to follow. I grabbed him by the collar.

"Let go! I have the bones," he yelled.

"They don't need the bones any more. They've found the dogs."

Zahi threw the bag down and ran off. I'd restored his medals to him, how could I snatch them back now? His pack rolled after him. I pursued them with the parents behind me. I shouted to Abu Janjoul: "Look out for the kids!" None of us had witnessed killing by gunfire inside the village before. Hunting happened in the woods, it belonged to the primitive side of life. This was slaying, like in murder or war. A thick, creepy texture veiled the air. The children became quarry to their parents, running a parallel chase to the gunslingers and the dogs. Torn between rushing to check on my grandmother and staying around to keep an eye on this bloody farce, I kept my focus on the kids; they were raw vulnerability on the run.

Down by the reservoir the killers were shooting in semicircles, spraying the whole orchard. The more their bodies shook from the tremor of their weapons, the more orgasmic they looked. The dogs barked in pain, trying to escape. One with a shot-away leg attempted to prop itself up and run but Abu Takka, laughing, shot it a second time against the reservoir wall. Another hound, hit in the buttock, was gyrating, trying to lick the wound, yelping with pain. Abu Janjoul put it out of its misery with one shot in the head. Along the top of the wall an old mongrel was about to flee but Abu Janjoul leapt up onto the parapet and fired. The mongrel teetered over the edge and slipped out of sight. Abu Janjoul, ignoring the warnings of the village lads, threw himself over the side, landing in a giant gorse bush. Above him the reservoir started to seep, running red with blood. Abu Janjoul struggled with the half-dead dog. It was crazed with pain, covered with wounds and frantic to escape. By the time someone got a ladder and pulled him out, Abu Janjoul was unrecognisable: scratched all over, bloodied and wet. The humiliation brought out the worst in him. He opened fire wildly, piling round after round into dead and dying dogs, pausing only to change magazines. Abu Takka took his cue from his chief and also went berserk, at last scaring the boys into retreating.

Trying hard not to let my stomach overtake my throat, I ran back up to check on Sitti.

Seventeen

Sitti was still lying on her mattress, delirious now, muttering incomprehensible words. Yousra and Mariam were holding her hands. The Hakim had his stethoscope glued to her chest, his head lowered as if detecting a far away beat in a distant desert. He'd made it at last. I could tell that Sitti knew the prodigal son was back. Her lightless face still held a faint flicker of triumph that rose and fell with her irregular breath. I knelt beside Yousra. She looked at me and opened her palm, showing Sitti's hand resting in hers. She stroked the wrinkled skin and the protruding veins. Her sadness met mine like a burn. Sitti had taught Yousra all she needed to know about cooking and preserves and been her link with the secrets of Wahdeh and its people. I could hear her heart's lament: How many harvests had these bony fingers brought in? How many loaves of bread had they kneaded? How many babies had they eased into the world? How many weeds had they pulled out? And how many seeds had they sown?

Mariam, holding Sitti's other hand, seemed lost in her own world. I looked at her a long while but she wouldn't meet my gaze. She must have been sensing the gap awaiting her life if Sitti was dying. She must be scared.

"Hakim? How is she doing?" I asked my uncle.

He shook his head. His tears fell on her face. Mariam leaned over and wiped them. My daughter seemed older, much older.

Suddenly the door flew open, flooding the cottage with light. It was Amti Wardieh, come straight from the grove in her galoshes and her faded tweed skirt, her grey cardigan and bedouin scarf. Her eyes opened wide at seeing the Hakim crouched over his mother. She closed the door slowly and hunkered down by the wall, speechless.

The Hakim looked up in equal amazement. He'd always assumed that his mother's wrath and the subsequent estrangement had included his wife. He had no idea of the secret bond between the two women. But I'd known better for a long time, from when I was twelve. The two women had been meeting surreptitiously in Sitti's cottage ever since Amti suspected she was barren and had no one to turn to in Wahdeh but her mother-in-law. Sitti's potions hadn't worked. It was equally possible that Amti's husband was the sterile one, but the Hakim's pride wouldn't countenance having himself tested. Regardless, Amti had continued visiting to share with Sitti their common laments over the Hakim's periodic binges.

My memory erased the gap between then and now. It had been a memorable day for a twelve year old. The snow had been falling steadily for a week; it blocked the roads, overwhelming the snow ploughs. We were sent back from school. I sank in the snow to my waist several times but I was enjoying the journey. The birds were mad with hunger; I tore up my sandwiches, tossed the bits into the air and watched the war of the wings with fascinated joy. When finally I reached Sitti's cottage I was famished. I could smell the aroma of her herb-rich cooking. But I was not expected at that time of day, and when I opened the door I saw my grandmother and my aunt together by the fire. My entrance startled them. Amti went pale. Sitti held her wrist and reassured her: "Adam can keep a secret, Wardieh. Trust me." Then she gave me something to eat and along with it fed me the secret I'd faithfully kept.

Sitti's breathing was faltering, her frail frame attacked with shudders. Her mouth was half open, her eyelids drooped slowly, her hands began to lose their grip and their warmth. The Hakim's voice came out from the valley of tears. "My mother is dying," he said, and covered his face with his hands. A crushing darkness filled me.

Suddenly an explosion rocked Sitti's cottage. She opened her eyes. A trace of colour surged to her cheeks. She looked at the Hakim and said in a clear voice, "It's all right, Raji, let it be." Still staring at him, she stopped breathing.

For a long time we sat in silence, trying to absorb what had just happened. The Hakim closed his mother's eyes but held his gaze still on her face as if leafing through their years of division and before that their memories of love. The only hand that kept Sitti's in hers was Mariam's. The hand that had fed her and bathed her and combed her hair was tucked between her little palms, hiding from death in a haven of life. Amti Wardieh had sensed the moment of parting instantly. Still hunched up in the corner, her body shuddered and began emitting short whimpers. Yousra started praying, looking up at the ceiling; her tears fell down her high cheekbones and onto her neck. I'd never seen anyone die before; my father had simply slept on, and I'd been too young to grasp the significance of his death anyway. I understood all too well the significance of Sitti's death. Sitti had vanished. I wanted to vanish with her.

A second explosion shot us to our feet. I ran out, followed by the disoriented Hakim. Mariam screamed after me but her voice was soon lost in the confusion of slamming doors and clacking shutters and the screams of terrified villagers. We sprinted to the square wondering loudly what the hell was going on. Abu Faour was frantically dragging his merchandise inside. "What's happening?" I cried.

Abu Faour pushed us into the shop. He was so shaken it took us a while to understand what he was telling us.

The story, when it emerged, was grotesque. Who could have imagined that our neighbours in Nahrieh would mistake a pathetic dog-killing for a defiant show of muscle and respond with mortars! And our 'guardians', instead of raising the white flag, had in turn responded with their inadequate guns. Then the simple-minded villagers, believing we'd been attacked in earnest, had gone out with their old German and British semi-automatics and joined the foolish party. And now, worst of all, the Castle was turning its full artillery on our neighbours, thus confirming their suspicion that Wahdeh was declaring out-and-out war!

The smell of burning filled the air. A shell had scored a direct hit on the mill house. A column of brown smoke rose from it. Another hit the stable near Rameh's cottage, igniting the hay.

I looked at the Hakim and my blood froze. In the midst of all this chaos, he was utterly still, his eyes vacant and staring, only his lips moving: "My mother is dead, my mother is dead, I have to bury my mother," over and over again. I shook his shoulders, gently, trying to bring him back to the present. My touch was too effective. A fierce light flashed into his eyes. He sprang out of the shop and into the middle of the square, shouting: "Open your windows, people of Wahdeh! Don't hide like rabbits! We have a funeral to organise! Open your doors! This is all a stupid mistake! Ignorant children playing with fire! We'll fix this foolishness. I'll fix it. Didn't I save your women and your cows from dying in labour? Didn't I vaccinate your children? Didn't I take care of your teeth and your dentures? Haven't I always stood up for you? Haven't I solved all your problems before? Here I am – I haven't deserted you. Don't desert me now. We can do this together. We can stop this madness. Come out and honour my mother with a decent funeral. She too looked after your women and your children, and now she's dead in sorrow for you. Come out!"

The Hakim's cry was falling on deaf walls. Apart from Hilweh behind her window bars, and a few headstrong boys still roaming the back lanes, not one person ventured to look out, no doubt obeying the civil defence instructions and crouching in corners and corridors, covering their children with a thousand blankets.

"We have to pull him back in, he's making a fool of himself," I said to Abu Faour.

"Uncle!"

"Hakim!" Abu Faour called, scratching his throat.

"Open your doors and come out with me!" The Hakim's voice was suddenly elated, as if there was nothing to worry about, as if peace on earth was secure in his hands. Like a dervish stumbling out of a long trance, he continued calling on his absent flock: "Let us walk together across the valley, over the river and up to our neighbours, raising the white flag and bringing good will. We've shared salt and bread together. The same birds that nest in our trees are singing from their roofs. The same clouds that bring us rain are passing over their houses. We are drinking from the same springs and breathing the same fresh air. This can't be happening, this enmity must not be the legacy we give to our children."

While the Hakim was preaching to empty balconies and shuttered windows, the Castle continued responding with mortars and long-range machine guns. The shells hissed and whistled over us. I yelled for the Hakim to come back into the shop but he was deaf to the world. I started to run towards him. Abu Faour snatched at my clothes and pulled me back: "Are you crazy? You stay here, you have a family."

I struggled with him. "Let go, Abu Faour! I can't leave him there!"

"I won't let you. Go ahead, break my bones," Abu Faour growled and began calling the Hakim names befitting a runaway madman.

But my uncle was now enraptured by a dialogue with the Almighty. He was calling on divine justice, then asking whether God had a hidden agenda that transcended the teachings of the holy book. Then he decided that God wasn't alone in controlling the universe, for Satan was not far behind. "He's still out there, the bastard, and now he's here! But God, Wahdeh is your embassy in this neck of the wood. It has its sinners, me included, but it's never been a dwelling for Satan. How can You let him take it over today? How could You?"

"He's lost it," Abu Faour muttered, still keeping his iron grip on me.

Finally the Hakim's oratory fizzled out. Drained of strength he leaned against the poplar. In a desperate last attempt to bang on heaven's door he continued talking to the shadows, moaning and clutching his hands to his head. "It's all my fault. I'm the one who handed over the key to the Castle. I'm the one who let our lads go. Don't punish the whole village for my transgressions. Let Raji Awad alone pay the price."

A long hiss was coming closer. "Uncle, come back!" I screamed, jerking myself away from Abu Faour's grip at last and running towards him.

But my cry was lost in a massive explosion that split the poplar and filled the air with a cloud of dust.

Abu Faour followed me, cursing the seven heavens and their angels. Dazed by the acrid smell of the shell, blinded by the dust and the smoking tree, we pushed on until we saw him.

He was flat on his back just at the edge of the tiny stream. His blood was spurting, dribbling into the water. He'd been hit between the shoulders. His mouth was still open, his eyes still stared at the shuttered windows. I fell on my knees beside him crying, "Uncle? Uncle! Can you hear me?"

A lopsided shadow of a smile flitted across his face, as if he'd just seen a much-loved, long-lost friend walking towards him.

Eighteen

With Wahdeh in disarray, I favoured simple solemnities for Sitti and the Hakim. There were more serious tasks to face than preparing a ceremonial funeral. Barns had been burned to the ground, stock killed in the fields. Several buildings had been damaged, including the olive press and Mariam's room. The village reservoir was now leaking. A pregnant woman had lost her first baby, and many people had sustained shrapnel injuries, among them young Zahi. "He wouldn't keep away from the street," Um Faour said, looking irritably at the dressing on her son's neck.

But the Mukhtar wouldn't hear of it. Wouldn't even speak to me. He raged to Abu Faour, "Simple solemnities! For his uncle and his grandmother! What do they learn in schools these days?"

For the Mukhtar and the elders, funerals were the alchemical moments when death played a crucial role in renewing stamina. A pause for reconciliation, forgiveness, even a cheerful sadness that reminded feuding neighbours of the good times they'd had together and of the value of being kind to each other. Families who had fought over property would now see that possessions are perishable; nothing you own in this world will go with you to the grave or take you to heaven. All we can take with us is our deeds; the love we give each other is all that survives us. So it is that people come to funerals as if waking from a foolish dream, subdued, pensive and genuinely humble.

I sat and stood like a yo-yo throughout the preliminaries before the interment, shaking hands and kissing faces, randomly engulfed by crazed women who came to excavate their own pain and throw its spittle in my face. From time to time when those who had truly loved my uncle and my grandmother took me in their arms and sobbed, I sobbed with them; then my withheld tears sprang out along with my frustration. But for the most part, I suppressed my feelings beneath the traditional mask of all mourners.

Yousra read through my tormented silence. She left Amti in the hands of more experienced women and came to stand by me, holding my arm tightly. "It will pass, Adam," she whispered. "Just think that you're doing it not for the Mukhtar or tradition but for your uncle. He would have liked a big crowd."

"Yeah," I muttered. "But Sitti wouldn't."

"Let her and the Hakim sort that out now that they're together."

"They'll only start another fight."

Yousra muffled her laughter in my shoulder and went back to the women's gathering.

Two hundred plastic chairs had been hired to accommodate everyone. These were divided between the front yard, the back yard, and the living room of the Hakim's house. The men used the outside space, the women the inside. Two black stallions were to pull an ancient hearse of carved oak and cedar wood. There would be professional mourners, dignitaries and politicians, all standing heads down before the two coffins. The futility of it all infused my sadness with frustration. I saw only a farcical tradition carried on against my will but with my own hard-earned money which I'd saved for the olive press. There would be *Zajal* poets repeating the same verses they'd used at a thousand funerals, empty words of commiseration from semi-strangers, and that terrible, tuneless, deafening music played by a twelve-strong brass band in grey and blue uniforms, summoned from the coast.

People gathered from far and wide. Wahdeh hadn't seen so many cars since the last elections; they were parked as far away as the bridge near the Castle. Many noticed and mused over the irony of the funeral traffic being organised by the very beach bums who had caused this tragedy.

With black mourning ribbons around their upper arms, Abu Janjoul and his Friday escorted a pale blue Dodge to the Hakim's house. They jumped out from the back seat and opened the driver's door to none other than Sitt Kattura. What guts, I thought, hastening to greet her. She was in a dark brown suit, her hair loosely wreathed in the traditional white scarf. She seemed thinner and rather faded.

"I've come to pay my condolences, son. May God bless and have mercy on their souls. But I want you to know that those who shelled Wahdeh were not the local militia of Nahrieh. They were mercenaries. Give my deepest regrets to Wardieh; she must be overcome with grief. Come here." One more time, one last time, Sitt Kattura took my head in her hands and kissed my brow, but her tears belied her strong control. Her eyes were swimming in them as she started the old Dodge, ready to leave.

"How is the Bey?"

"The Bey left us a month ago. He asked for a low-key funeral. Family and friends only. His death wasn't even mentioned in the papers."

"I'm sorry to hear that, Sitt Kattura. Won't you come in for a cup of coffee?"

"I'm late. I'm on my way to the port, son. Our only daughter is in Paris, she's having a baby soon. It seems I'm still useful. Goodbye."

"Bon voyage."

Then she was gone. Gone too was the single good that might have come out of this tragedy and saved us from future confrontations.

Back inside, I described Sitt Kattura's visit to Amti Wardieh but couldn't get through to her. She was still deeply in shock. Words, slaps across her face, massaging her feet and shoulders, glasses of rose water – nothing could erase Amti's glazed stare. Her body was stiff, her limbs cold. Deep shudders went through her like electric currents. Yousra kept talking to her, trying to draw her out. Um Faour and the other women argued endlessly over remedies. They finally gave up, concluding that "she wants to join him".

It wasn't until the procession started and she was held up and made to walk behind it to the cemetery that she snapped into a sudden frenzy, hitting her face, pulling her hair, tearing at her clothes and wailing. Her delirium far exceeded the habitual laments of widows her age. She was blaming the Hakim for deserting her when she needed him the most. And blaming Sitti for taking him away with her as if he were still a child. She raised her head to the Almighty and screamed: "You unmerciful! You unjust! You old fool, gambling with our lives!" Um Faour whispered to her not to blaspheme. "Ask the giver and taker of life for mercy." Amti wasn't listening. She continued screaming at the empty blue sky, *"Waynak, ya Allah, waynak, where are you, God, where are you!"* nearly drowning out the *Zajal* eulogies being sung by our illustrious vernacular poets, Zaghloul and Zein, as they exalted the virtues of the two 'martyrs' and lamented the fate of a Wahdeh left without them. Of the Hakim, Zein sang:

O tears, flow like rivers
A star has fallen from our sky
The arrow of time is broken
The eternal cedar dry
You were a prince among men
You were a father to the poor
And now your sword is bent
No longer fit for war

His hoarse voice narrowed as it rose, provoking fresh wails of grief from the mourners.

Then the tender voice of Zaghloul soared above the pine trees in praise of Sitti:

The rose that gave her fragrance
Freely to friend and foe
Has left us in grief and sadness
To join her roots below
But now she is in heaven
Her spirit a radiant dove
Of heavens there are seven
All glowing with her love

As the procession approached the cemetery, the words of Zein and Zaghloul slid imperceptibly into a lament for the whole country. The sudden death of two simple villagers had become the tragedy of the motherland. There was some truth in this, when Zaghloul sang that the Hakim had been Wahdeh's mind and Sitti its spirit. With both of them gone, what would become of us? And what would become of a whole country that was losing both mind and spirit?

Nineteen

Posthumous paperwork had always been labyrinthine, more stressful than burial itself. It took much longer and there was no sympathy to soften it. During the lawlessness of the civil war, it couldn't be done at all unless you had the money and the connections. After the funeral expenses we still had seven thousand three hundred and fifty-eight liras. Yousra and I were now earning nothing. Under the circumstances it was prudent to tend each piastre carefully. But it was necessary to complete the paperwork or we could risk losing control over our own lands.

My mother phoned from Beirut to commiserate and suggested I bring the papers there at the first ceasefire.

"Do you have the right connections?" I screamed through the static.

"No problem," she screamed back.

It lifted my spirit to hear her direct-like-an-arrow voice. She didn't say where she was calling from, probably some militia's headquarters. They were the only people with access to the remaining unsevered telecom lines. I imagined her among brain-dead brutes, surrounded by sandbags and the stench of hatred, then I flicked the picture to her scolding the rowdy tinkers who used to bring olives to the olive press. "Get in line! The mules, you donkeys, in line!" If she could handle tinkers like that she'd manage even with stoned thugs armed to the teeth. She made me feel strong. In fact, her strength of will (some might call it stubbornness), which I had inherited, had led to clashes when I was young. She'd been angry at my determination to stay in Wahdeh after my father's death, done everything she could to persuade me to come with her and Hawwa to Beirut. But once she saw I was doing so well with Amti, Sitti, and Uncle, she was right. I stayed with her for four years – weekdays, going back to Wahdeh at weekends and for the holidays. By then the mother-son dynamics had changed, or perhaps she hoped that this taste of city life might lead me to drop my dream. Apart from an occasional "You don't need that hardship, Adam, you don't need it, my son," she left me alone. We lived a peaceful co-existence during those years, Mother busy with her catering business, I with my studies and my olive press research.

The morning I set off for Beirut, I had to tear myself away from Yousra and Mariam. Yousra wanted to leave Mariam with Amti and come with me, but Mariam kicked up a fuss. I said to her, "Let me check the road. If it's safe I'll take you next week. But if you keep nagging I'll never take you again."

I loathed myself for using that petty style with my daughter. But I was late and still had to stop by Amti Wardieh to take her blessing.

"Go, may God be with you. May He open all roads and doors before you and keep you from harm. May He bring you back to us safe and sound," Amti said, holding my head in her hands. "Tell your mother I'm not upset that she didn't make it to the funeral. I know that if she leaves her apartment it'll be squatted or looted. Give her my love. Off you go, son, with God's speed."

I hadn't travelled the road to Beirut for nearly a year. The contrast was devastating. The coastal strip of towns and villages had been disembowelled. Rubble and debris and garbage were piled up along the road as if a twister and an earthquake had hit at the same time. The writing on several walls read: *Abu'l Jamajem was here*. The beheader seemed to have been everywhere. Was he one or many? How many beheaders had been turned loose? Away from Wahdeh's shelter I felt hollow and vulnerable. My survival instinct kicked into action in a duel with ghosts. I negotiated the broken asphalt as if it were a minefield. I slowed down to a crawl pretending to be a local, saluting the laid-back looters who worked with comical precision – sovereigns in their own world. I feigned a bored detachment each time I approached checkpoints, producing a matching indifference from the young men fuelled by drugs and loss of direction. They were moody, unpredictable; they'd shoot without warning and without cause. So I had to make myself as invisible as possible. The closer I came to the city, the more death was in the air. Rising from one dump was a dead child's arm, all white and slim with tiny groomed fingers grabbing hopelessly at the grey sky. It cut through my shield like a spear.

I arrived at my mother's with a sick heart. The neighbours said I had the courage of a lion. They cheered me and slapped me on the back. A couple of young men took my keys and tucked the VW behind a pile of barrels and sandbags. My mother was eager to reintroduce me, beckoning her neighbours to come and shake hands. They came, commiserated with me on the death of my uncle and Sitti and welcomed me kindly.

After they left, my mother told me everything that had happened to each family in the building: Lateef's wife had been hit by mortar shrapnel seven months before. She haemorrhaged too long before reaching hospital and had been in a coma ever since. But her ex-detective husband was refusing to turn off the life support equipment. Every morning, before the skirmishes started, he would put on a suit and tie and go to visit her. He'd return at lunch time cheerful but mute about his visits.

His backgammon partner, Abu Mounir, a former fisherman who used to give away much of his catch to his neighbours, now walked on crutches, hadn't seen the sea for eighteen months. The story behind his crutches was chilling. He hadn't had the money to send his three boys abroad, so one day they'd just disappeared. Fearing the worst he'd searched the various militia camps and barracks but failed to find them. Six months later they'd dropped in out of the blue; long beards, dirty fatigues, machine guns and an attitude to match. He was furious. He ordered them to drop their weapons, take off their fatigues, have a bath, shave and get ready to leave this "cesspool of a country." He was ready to row them all the way to America in his small boat, according to my mother. But the sons mocked their father. They said they weren't here for his blessing, they only wanted to use his roof for sniping. That did it. He shoved them out of the house. Mounir, his eldest, went berserk. He knee-capped his father and left him in a pool of blood. When Abu Mounir returned from hospital he asked the tenants never to call him Abu Mounir again. He disowned all three boys and bequeathed his belongings to the poor.

Our drama in Wahdeh paled in comparison as my mother went on. But regardless of the words I was basking in the sound of her voice. I missed her. I hadn't seen her since the previous spring, when the war had erupted and our normal monthly visits to Beirut had become too dangerous. We used to stay two days with her. Yousra would take Mariam to visit relatives and to shop while my mother updated me on her life, her catering business, her brothers and their shifty commerce in the Congo, Hawwa's news from Australia, the neighbours of course. But most importantly reminiscing the golden days of the olive press. "The only contract we needed in those days," she used to say, "was a man's word. It meant his honour, his life. Now they live by that awful proverb, *Lies are the salt of men*. Shameful." Her move to Beirut had taught her a great deal about people, good and bad alike, yet it never changed her heart or her style. She still wore black and grey, still tied her hair with a white scarf firmly knotted behind one ear. When she sat down to sip her coffee, her hands and her head and her eyes talked with her. When she laughed, her face beamed with delight. For my part I would lie on the sofa and become a video camera reporting to her the chronicle of Wahdeh, house by house.

Now, instead, I was listening to her inventory of the residents' woes. She was bewailing the collapse of moral standards – wives of good breeding becoming prostitutes, incest everywhere, drugs, broken families – when sporadic shots followed by an explosion cut her short. The whole building juddered and with it my own body. My skull filled with the tremor and transmitted it all the way down to my feet. My vision became momentarily blurred from the vibrations. We hurried to open the glass windows and close the wooden shutters. Then my mother pushed me ahead of her into the hall, where we tumbled into the stream of neighbours pouring down the stairs to the shelter.

Beirut's suburban basements had been designed as cellars and storage areas. Now that survival was the priority, they made efficient shelters. They reflected the apartments above, fitted out with mattresses, fridges, freezers, gas stoves, television, backgammon tables, decks of cards and the inevitable transistors. We sat down on a folded blanket in a corner and resumed our conversation as if this was all perfectly normal.

"When we began coming down here we feared that the confinement would create friction," my mother said. "But everyone contributed freely, not only material goods but skills and hard labour. Even our landlord - he changed from a pompous miser to a model of sweetness and light." She was whispering, although it was impossible to be overheard above the hubbub of children and radios and television and the growing sound of explosions seeping through the thick walls. She nodded towards the far end of the shelter. "People who'd never before done any manual work pitched in to build that bathroom over there." Then she turned towards the men's corner. They were split into two circles - cards and backgammon, half a dozen on each side. They were leaning against the walls and pillars watching and taking turns. "Have you got the papers on you, son?"

I took the fat envelope out of my jacket and handed it to her. She clapped it under her armpit and brought out a letter from her pocket: "Your sister," she said, then walked over to the backgammon party.

Nejmeh Awad - my mother - had always been taut and thin, but the long months of war had carved deep lines under her eyes and at the corners of her mouth. Her arthritic body had lost even more agility; she was now listing slightly, walking with her palm jammed against her left hip. She waited near the two men, obviously siding with Lateef. When the game was over, he took the envelope from her, gesturing a "Don't Worry". Then he sat on it and began the next game. He sat on the maps and deeds and wills and signatures of my nearest and dearest. He sat on the myrtle tree where all my dead gathered among the olive trees. He sat on the olive trees. He sat on their shadows. He sat on my chest, for I failed to breathe at seeing his behind resting on that precious envelope.

My mother moved over to the stove to mingle with the women. The landlord's wife, Samia, greeted her with kisses on both cheeks. An attractive bottle blonde, she had a Marilyn Monroe hairdo and a red nightgown that revealed more than it concealed. Snow White velvet slippers displayed her pedicured toenails. "Poor Samia," my mother had said, explaining that Samia's first and last attempt to produce an heir had instead produced a monster with two heads, one leg, three hands, two spinal cords, two hearts, two pairs of lungs, two reproductive organs and four kidneys. Panic and outdated drugs were blamed. He had died three hours after birth.

I opened Hawwa's letter. The low voltage light was barely enough to decipher her thin embroidery-like handwriting, but even before I began I was filled with a hot wave of longing. I remembered the tips of her delicate fingers, meticulously holding the nib dipped in ink, writing her homework as seriously as any Japanese calligrapher. I remembered her climbing trees and splashing in the water down by the river. I remembered her on our father's shoulders walking down to the grove. I remembered her drawn, pale features for that whole year after his death and how her joy had been extinguished as abruptly as his life. She'd stopped seeing her friends. She'd stopped singing and playing. Instead she'd sat for hours alone by the myrtle tree, writing letters to him, letters so different from the one I was reading now:

Dear all,
Greetings from Oz. We were so saddened by the terrible news. God bless the souls of Sitti and Uncle Raji. We are lighting candles and praying for them with you.

We are so worried about you. What on earth is happening over there? Have people lost their minds? All we see on television are bombs, fires, rubble and corpses. The newsreader warns that "some people may find the pictures distressing". We stopped letting our kids watch anyway because we don't know how to answer their questions. You have no idea how this war is affecting us; we may leave our place of birth but it never leaves us. Before this war our kids were proud of their background. They boasted about their country of origin. They shared our dream of going back one day. We taught them about the Lebanon of the cedars, the Bible, Khalil Gibran, Baalbek and so on. They went to after-school classes to learn Arabic. Now they're confused. Our reputation is destroyed. People say we are barbarians.

But our distress is nothing compared to what you must be going through every day. Here we still have law and order and peace and freedom. No one gets killed because of an identity card. How can this happen? At first I didn't believe it and then one day I saw a scene on television which still haunts me: hooded armed men stop a taxi and take the IDs from the passengers. One of them opens the door, drags out a boy, maybe ten years old, pushes him aside, and throws the rest of the IDs back into the car. The driver takes off quickly. The boy kneels down, begging and crying, but they shower him with bullets. How can a man who walks on two feet and believes in a Creator do such a thing?

I want you all out ASAP. There are so many opportunities here for anyone with energy and initiative. You can all come under the family reunion programme. All you have to do is go to Cyprus, apply and call us from there. I want to know when you are leaving so I can stop worrying. Until then, a thousand kisses from us all.

Hawwa

I looked up from the letter. My mother was beside me, shaking her head. "It's too late for me to leave. I'd rather die here and be buried next to your dad, son. But your sister is right.

You should take your family and go. This war could last for ever."

I said nothing, deadened by all the dramas around me and dying for a good sleep. I lay down, my head on her lap. The sleeping space was too tight. We would have to take turns lying down, a few hours each. She covered my ear to muffle the thuds from the shelling, but deep and satisfying sleep never visited me. Each time I drifted towards it, I'd be awakened by a cry, a scream, a huge snore or a nearer than usual explosion that made all the heads jerk up in unison: had it hit us? Yet no one dared open the door. We'd look at each other blindly and, like corks when a fish is caught, our heads would sink back under the blankets.

The pain of so many people trying to survive in this cement bunker brought closer the dilemma of what to do about Wahdeh. All my life I'd believed that violence is the language of the mentally bankrupt, for it breeds not solutions but more violence. Now the very real possibility of Wahdeh being attacked in earnest scared the hell out of me. While drifting in and out of sleep, my mind rehearsed different self-defence strategies. I raise the white flag to looters and rapists, inviting them to our homes. But Hulagu's clones see no grace in my act. They storm Wahdeh and burn it to the ground. Now I'm being shot by Nimer. But I fight back the idea of fighting back although it persists like a trapped nerve that will not let me sleep.

Somewhere out there the sun and the moon were continuing their rounds. Business as usual. But down here the familiar signals of passing time were absent. The radio told us when to prepare lunch and dinner. We measured time by the hourly news broadcasts, so there was all too much time for reflection. That, and what I was seeing all around me, made me question for the first time ever the pacifism I had inherited from my father. He could lift a huge demijohn of olive oil, hugging it to his chest as if embracing an elephant. Yet he wouldn't use his formidable strength to fight, not even to show off at festivals when every able-bodied male took turns hauling stone urns and metal bars. His picture of Mahatma Ghandi still hung in the olive press: sitting full lotus in front of a shack in the forest, smiling through his eyeglasses, all thin and poor like a beggar. "But his spirit had more stars on its shoulders than all the generals of the British Empire." My father's words, his philosophy, seemed right in Wahdeh. Even after the recent tragedy I still believed we could re-establish the harmony that had served us all so well for centuries. But now? How could I forgive and forget if my Mariam was given the wrong polio vaccine and became a vegetable like little Sousou, carried around the shelter in a sling by her eldest sister, her arms flopping like broken wings, her little face staring such big question marks that I had to avert my eyes. Seeing her shook me to the core and filled me with an unbelievable surge of rage. Children of three and four were running around the shelter with festering skin rashes, eczema, trachoma, but at least they were alive and might survive this war. Sousou would vegetate like a plant just because some under-stocked pharmacist had sold her parents an outdated vaccine and the lawlessness of the war shelved her life for ever. Were I her father, would I be sitting quietly in this shelter, or would I be out there with a gun?

Twenty

After five days in Beirut, I became a full citizen of war, learning all about the different types of shells and mortars and rockets and missiles and road mines and snipers, hearing endless stories of survival and mayhem, listening to the wisdom of residents like Abu Mounir: "Men are like fish, the big ones eat the little ones. Now they're having a banquet!"

"Let them choke on each other's bones!" I laughed, shaking hands with the fisherman.

I set off home in a defiant, focused mood. I'd done what I came to do. Lateef, whose name meant 'the kind man', had sat a couple of days on my deeds before taking them out during a lull in the skirmishes. The next day he brought them back all done for the price of stamps only. He wouldn't accept a penny for himself. But it wasn't the pride of finding a good man in Gomorrah that made me feel so upbeat, it was deliverance. I felt rescued, saved. The new ceasefire was holding, enough to organise the next looting party, bury the dead, manage the wounded, restock ammunition, and for us ordinary mortals to do whatever was necessary. Many were rushing in fierce desperation to shops and hospitals. Militiamen from all the different factions lurked everywhere, tired, loosely guarding their posts. They didn't bother me much. "They can kill us at any time, makes no difference to them," said one sardonic driver while overtaking me. Something about him was familiar. His face? Voice? The way he spoke to me as if we'd just had a drink together? His dishevelled features lurked in my mind as I drove homeward: a very thin moustache, a smile revealing almost

Draculean eye teeth, cheeks a traffic-light red. Then it came to me. The ticket attendant at Cinema Miami, Beirut Centreville. A cheap, smelly old theatre with a scratchy sound system, specialising in double-bill westerns and fifty-piaster late-night shows. I could see him now, smirking behind his glassy hole: "No change, no see!" But I always had the silver coin ready, so he'd beckon me ahead of other punters still scrambling in their pockets for change. His cinema is gone – burnt to the ground – and with it all the cowboys and Indians who used to entertain insomniacs and brainweary students like me. Funny, I'd completely forgotten those nights, sinking into a squeaky seat with my bag of stale popcorn, barracking for the Indians, because they belonged to the land, like me.

I reached Wahdeh much faster than anticipated. The smell of thyme and oregano and bay rushed to greet me as I entered the side road leading to the village. I took deep breaths and waved the hat of my longing to the pine trees. I said hello to the great oak. It said, welcome back. The tension in my temples and shoulders was easing off. And the expectation of seeing my daughter and my wife was rushing them towards me faster than the rolling wheels of my VW. But as I approached the little bridge leading to the castle I stopped mid-breath. There they were, back from their swamps: Nimer and his beach bums.

"Hey hey, son of Awad, where have we been?"

"Have we won the war yet, Nimer?"

"I'm glad to see you too. Listen, sorry about your uncle."

"Yeah."

"We've come back to guard the village, as promised. You have nothing to worry about." Nimer tapped the roof of my car. "I have a surprise for you. At home," he grinned. He seemed cheerful and playful, a happy man. He'd grown a stubby goatee that helped camouflage his fat lips, and his eyes twinkled weirdly.

I'd scarcely recovered from the sight of Nimer and his gang before hitting another checkpoint, at the entrance to the square. This one was manned by our previous guardian angel, Rameh, now looking satanic in a bushy beard and oversized fatigues and armed to the teeth: grenades, dagger, revolver, and a cylinder-chambered machine gun. A few locals stood with him carrying Kalashnikovs. To my astonishment, Hilweh was there too, dressed up in a floral skirt and a white pullover, her hair combed into two neat plaits adorned with red ribbons. She was sitting near Rameh on a wooden cart, holding a bunch of wild flowers. As I stopped she stood up and gave me a flower and a beatific smile. I opened the car door. Rameh stretched his arms wide and hugged me fiercely, sobbing his sorrow over the Hakim's death. The other boys came and kissed me on the cheeks.

"Did the dog over there bite you?" Rameh asked, pointing at the Castle.

"There are no more dogs in Wahdeh, Rameh. I see you made up?" I said, arching my eyebrows at Hilweh.

"Yes. She saw me and didn't scream. I waved to her. She waved back. I don't know. What do you think?"

"Maybe she didn't recognise you, with your beard and all."

"Oh, she recognised me all right. I went up to her, I did. I took a bunch of red poppies and climbed the stairs. Her mother was feeding her. She went all white and mute with fear, her mother. But I knew in my heart that Hilweh was ready. Don't ask me how. I just saw a different, livelier look in her eyes, and I thought what the hell, you know."

"And? Did she take the flowers, Romeo?"

"She did. And since then she's kept that same grin, all day long. What do you make of that?"

"Miracles still happen. Just don't make a hasty move now. Watch out."

Rameh took me in his arms again. I thought, here is another happy man today.

More hugs and tears greeted me at home from Yousra and Mariam. Even Abu Faour came over and buried his bald head in my chest. They'd been worried sick about my safety.

As Yousra served coffee on our veranda, Abu Faour filled me in. "Apparently Rameh heard what had happened the day the dogs died. He came back like a storm out of hell. The Mukhtar was sitting in my shop. Rameh took his wrath out on him, accusing him of negligence and calling him a murderer. 'You senile old drunk,' he yelled, and kicked the Mukhtar's stool until his tarboush fell to the floor. The Mukhtar was badly shaken. He'd suffered enough scorn after failing to bring about reconciliation with the funerals. Then that same afternoon, the second day after you left, Nimer announced his own comeback, with a hail of bullets and a military jeep. Rameh took position with his boys on the municipality roof. We held our breath expecting a massacre."

Abu Faour was sweating. His bony nose dripped onto his jacket. He wiped it with his arm and stared at Yousra as if asking her to continue the story.

"What happened?" I asked, looking from one to the other.

"Nimer's wife."

"Nimer's *what?*"

"Nimer's wife. There she was, walking down the road with two little boys and waving a white handkerchief," Abu Faour said, scanning my face with flickering eyes. "She stopped the escalation."

"Yes," Yousra said, "Nimer married a widow with twin boys. A very distinguished lady. She brought her furniture from Beirut. Some furniture! Abu Faour gave them the ground floor."

"You mean . . . " I looked at Abu Faour. "Nimer is living next door with this woman? But that was Faour's apartment! You spent years preparing it for him!"

"I had no choice. Nimer walked into the shop and took the key, no please, no thank you." Abu Faour sipped his last drop of coffee and shuffled back home, leaving me stunned.

Then I remembered: *I have a surprise for you. At home.* Indeed he had.

Yousra was all praise for the new bride. She said they clicked from the first glance. "You know how you look at someone and say to yourself, yes, I can go to this stranger and befriend her? I don't know, but some faces are open and welcoming, others aren't. I mean this woman hadn't come here out of choice. She'd never heard of little Wahdeh. And yet, not a trace of snobbery. Despite her ordinary jeans and polo necks and trainers, despite the downcast eyes, Sana can't help sparkling like a queen. The gossip rippled so fast people were coming from everywhere to take a look: this refined woman conducting the transfer of her sumptuous belongings with a couple of ragged oafs who hadn't a clue what they were handling. And yet, she was so *nice*, so polite, telling them shyly how to handle each item and where to place it."

"Didn't anyone help? What was his lordship doing?"

"Nimer? You should've seen him, rushing back and forth and sweating his groin out. Subservient, self-effacing like a crushed louse. The whole scene was so weird that people didn't know how to react. They just watched in silence, awed. As for Sana, she kept a dignified distance. Approachable but classy, you know what I mean. You could tell she was well-bred, with that long neck and glossy chestnut pageboy and perfect legs and straight back. I watched her move and kept thinking, years of ballet classes have gone into that body. Discipline and grace. And you know what? I was as flabbergasted as everyone else. I couldn't move. She was like an extraterrestrial. But when they finally finished unloading and she disappeared inside the house with her sons and Nimer, I felt like crying."

"Why?"

"I couldn't bear to imagine her intimacy with Nimer. I just couldn't."

"But who is this woman?"

"She was married to a wealthy jeweller who was kidnapped by masked militiamen and put naked in a freezing bath in midwinter for a couple of weeks until he pleaded with his family to cough up the ransom. By the time they gathered the money, he was dead. But Sana didn't know that. The kidnappers told her where to deliver the ransom, then abducted her as well and raised the stakes, asking the family for more. I don't know exactly where Nimer came into all this, except that he apparently rescued her and then induced her to marry him. She told me that much. I think she doesn't want to talk much about Nimer, so let's keep what we know to ourselves. I like her. And she adores Mariam. Wait till you meet her, she's something else. Oh, I forgot – this came while you were away."

She handed me a letter from Faour.

Twenty-one

Dear Adam,

My deepest condolences. Mother wrote to me about the tragedy. Thinking of Wahdeh without the Hakim is unthinkable. I don't know how you're coping. Truly I wish I was with you. Whenever I imagine the Hakim's absence from his veranda, gazing at the cliff, the orchards, the pine forest and Wahdeh's houses, I feel that the whole village has sunk into darkness. The terrible news kind of puts my own into perspective, but here goes.

The first months here passed like a dream. I mastered the routes in and out of Caracas. I began to order my own meals in Spanish, even have a snappy conversation now and then. I caught a couple of thieves at the building site and began to count in Pedro and Paulo's eyes. Sandra took me out nearly every night after my evening classes. We ate in restaurants, at street vendors, at parties, moving between the student hangouts but never clinging to a particular group. We were cordially welcomed and warmly farewelled wherever we went. It seemed to me that Sandra was restlessly rolling from place to place, unwilling to drop anchor: a smooth way to enjoy herself while avoiding the contempt of too much familiarity. It suited me fine. I was meeting new faces all the time and practising my *español* on them all. If I made mistakes we had fun correcting them and moved on to more mistakes and corrections and fun. There were no strings attached in these drifting encounters. No real friendships. Just easy going, cool, ciao, ciao, see you soon kind of thing.

Then one day Sandra said, "Can I ask you a question, Fifo?" I said sure. She said, "Don't you want to be more independent of me, move about on your own, do what you feel like doing, you know? We're together every day, maybe you want to go out with some other people, now that you're acquainted with the city and all?" We were standing in a cafeteria near the university, Sandra's elbow resting on my shoulder, her whispers close to my ear. Blood was stranded in my veins. I couldn't grasp what looked like the dark side of the moon that had been shining on my life so far. The little girl (now in a woman's body) who came to visit us in Wahdeh was turning into a careless Latina about to throw my heart to the dogs.

Sandra must have read the dismay on my face. She tried to soften the blow. She turned to face me, clasping both arms around my neck. "I mean, like, what about when I start studying for my exams, or going on work experience trips? And anyway there are things you're keen on that I'm not."

That much at least was true. She wasn't into books and museums and art galleries and theatre like me. And there was no other music to her ears besides the beat of the drums. Movies, yes, but action movies. Still, I was enjoying the box office hits from Hollywood's factories of superguns and incredible hulks, and dancing to the interminable drums, completely numbed by alcohol and the heat of the seedy audience. Just to be with my Sandra. For until then I'd been under the impression that Sandra wasn't just humouring a family guest but attaching me to her daily life as a prelude to our betrothal. I couldn't imagine being separated from her apart from school and work. But when you've become hopelessly twisted around someone's little finger, you don't argue. You endure their twists in bleeding silence.

So it was, my dear friend, that I ventured out on my own. I aimed for the multi-purpose cultural centre – L'Ateneo de Caracas – close to the museums, theatres and parks. I spent my after-hours studying modern and classical paintings, watching plays and browsing in bookshops, alone, a ribless, sinless Adam (!) ejected from paradise. Missing Sandra made me thwart contact with strangers. I was quenching my thirst for culture, hoping to weather this new situation with time.

I was seeing Sandra less and less every day, though she hadn't changed her demeanour one bit, still hugging me and showing an interest in what I was doing and asking if I'd met any exciting people.

She said exams were approaching, she had to study with friends, hadn't forgotten about me. Come the summer, she added, we'll spend more time together. I said, "What about the family? What shall I tell my mother when she calls, she thinks we are an item. She's knitting us the same colour jumpers."

"You don't need jumpers here, the weather's always hot," Sandra said.

After three weeks of my unwanted freedom, we went out to see a thriller chosen by Sandra. She was holding my hand and squeezing it in glee at the silly stunts as always, but the emotional current that used to electrify me was not there. One message my body can read clearly is the language of hands. I guess I absorbed it from my grandmother when she used to take my hand in hers and communicate her feelings in eloquent silence. The message Sandra's hand was transmitting that evening told me something was wrong for sure.

We left the cinema after the heroic jump from the aeroplane and the final kiss in the clouds and strolled by the river.

You know me, I'm not by nature a confrontational person but there comes a time in a man's life when either he resigns himself to lifelong timidity or breaks the pattern and stands up for himself. Sandra must have read my mind. "Fifo," she said reflectively, "do you love me?" I couldn't believe it! So that's all it was? A love test? Relief washed over me. Gone was my tension, clear became the sky inside me, "Of course I love you, you know that I . . ." Sandra put her hand over my mouth, "Sure, I'm your cousin, I'm attractive and sexy and rich and all that. But suppose I wasn't. Suppose I was ugly and poor, would you still love me?"

At that moment Sandra swam straight into my soul. I was already smitten by Sandra the salsa queen, the photo straight out of a fashion magazine. Here was a new face to Sandra, a real woman who wanted a real lifelong love that would transcend the decay of the flesh and reach for the highest emotional union. My response was an outpouring of joy: "Sandra, I would love you in any shape or form. We are destined for each other. I adore you. I love the very earth you walk upon."

There was a long silence as I waited for her to echo my absolute devotion. Instead she continued in a more careful tone: "What if, say, you'd met me when I was married and in love with my husband? What then? Would you want to break up my home?"

This wasn't at all what I'd expected but, still floating in my euphoria, I answered from my heart rather than my head: "No, no, never! I wouldn't dream of destroying your happiness, your happiness means everything to me."

Sandra's face lit up, she threw her arms around me and kissed me on the lips, not deeply but enough to give me a taste of her sweetness: "Oh, Fifo, you're one in a million. It's what I hoped you would say, it means you love me for myself, it's the kind of love that lasts for ever. I think God sent you to me, Fifo."

We sat down on a bench beside the river. Sandra took my hand and pressed it fervently between both of hers. Her tone now pleading, she continued: "Fifo, please try to understand, please try to be strong and generous. Because you see, Fifo, had you come seven months earlier I would have fallen in love with you just like that. But life isn't always that neat and tidy."

She was looking straight into my eyes now, but the windows of my soul were clapping their shutters in a storm. "Fifo, I'm going to tell you a secret that has to stay between the two of us. This isn't easy but . . . well . . . the truth is, I'm in love with another man."

I was speechless, frozen. The rainbow that had stretched from the airport to the House of Cedars crumbled into darkness.

"Who?"

"His name is Ramon. He drives a truck for my brothers. He's a *Negrito* – mixed-breed, black and Indian." Sandra's hands forsook mine and rose in supplication: "And I'm hopelessly in love with him." Then she fell sobbing on my chest.

So this is where I am now, my dear Adam: back to square one. God only knows how I'm going to deal with this situation. Please say nothing to my parents until further notice. And give my love to Yousra and Mariam. I miss you all with a broken heart.

Faour

Twenty-two

I didn't have the heart to answer Faour's letter for some time, mainly because I had to tell him that his grandmother had been taken away to a home. "The house will be empty without you! My heart will remain at your feet until I die," Um Faour had cried after her mother-in-law. Little Nour wouldn't let go of her granny; she grabbed at the old woman's dress, sobbing furiously. Zahi became aggressive towards his father, calling him names and throwing stones at the Volvo as it took off to the home. But old Fatat had to go. Her health had deteriorated since Faour's departure. While the younger ones had sought refuge and comfort in her, Faour was her own pillar of support. He'd slept in the same room as her. Now she was waking up alone and crippled by the pain of her rheumatoid arthritis. Outside the nursing home the medicines she needed were unavailable and her condition had become unbearable without them. So Nimer used his 'connections' and managed to find her a decent place in the same home as his father the Mukhtar.

Every time I sat down to start a letter to Faour, my spirit darkened with the memory of Fatat's departure. It was like uprooting the old oak from the entrance to Wahdeh's land, like watching the cliff crumble and crush the pine forest beneath it. Today I was trying again, sitting before a blank page at the kitchen table. Yousra was cleaning Mariam's room. Mariam was playing next door with the twins. Over at the Hakim's house, Amti Wardieh was hanging out laundry. All the coloured garments were gone, only black mourning clothes flapped in the wind, stark against the white background of the flowering almond tree. I had waved to her, she had waved back, but neither of us called out a greeting. Nothing wrong between us, but Amti's mourning had been hard to console, made even worse a few days ago when I declined - as tactfully as I could - her request that I fill the gap his death had created for Wahdeh. She'd been withdrawn, hesitant that morning. I could tell she had words aching to be said. I'd spoken gently. "Amti, you're torturing yourself. Your pain distresses the whole village. Is there anything I can do? Anything at all?"

A mistake. "You could come over here a couple of hours a day," she'd said.
"Receive people, listen to them, give them advice. You are educated, you don't drink, you don't make dirty jokes. This house isn't just mine and the Hakim's. It's Wahdeh's house. Your uncle would have liked you to take over from him, my son."

Her naivety took me by surprise. To believe I could replace my uncle just because I was educated! Quite apart from his practical skills, his ability to solve people's marital and financial problems with his unique blend of cunning, proverbs and insights into human nature had taken a long lifetime to hone. What university teaches that? "Amti, people didn't come to the Hakim for words alone. They came because he knew how to treat a sore tooth, how to make eternal dentures, how to help a cow or a woman in labour. The words were a bonus. As for advice, he had a lifetime's experience, and those were different times. Look around you - would the young men toting machine guns today seek my advice? Would someone like Nimer listen to me? You haven't noticed how much things have changed because your grief is so great. But believe me, the time for wisdom like the Hakim's is gone."

She didn't answer. We'd finished our coffee in total silence. I'd kissed her brow and left.

Breaks in communication like that weren't confined to Amti and me. It was widespread throughout Wahdeh, leaving unanswered questions to grow into fearsome panics.

The biggest of these was Nimer. What was he up to? Did anyone know? In the past his lies had been swiftly unmasked, often recounted for entertainment. But now that he'd handed over the 'taxation checkpoint' to the beach bums, deeming it unworthy of his warlordship, rumour had it that he was involved in the arms and drug trade, hiding his stash in the caves beneath the Castle. His seedy business had attracted the attention of the neighbouring villages, which had positioned two long-range cannons towards the Castle and planted more mines on their side of the valley. Nimer was otherwise inconspicuous. He moved phantom-like in and out of Wahdeh. We knew he was around only when we saw his huge American jeep parked in front, outside our kitchen window. We avoided him, in denial over his love nest with the gentle Sana. "Beauty and the beast," said Yousra. Her empathy with Sana was becoming a solid friendship. Undoubtedly Sana was likable. She was a breath of fresh air in the sad, stuffy atmosphere that weighed on us with many young men still at the front. She saw in us a gleam of hope, and we felt protective towards her. "So, you're Adam," she'd said, after my return from Beirut, shaking hands with thin, delicate fingers. "I've heard so much about you – all, good," she hastened to add. But I hadn't yet had the chance to talk to her beyond neighbourly greetings. Her twins, Samer and Nader, were inseparable from Mariam, the three of them playing together all day. And as Yousra had said: "Sana adores Mariam."

I left the table and went into the back yard.

The weeds had run amok in my garden. Day after day I had watched their insidious progress, sometimes poised to start work on it, sometimes thinking of letting it revert to scrub. But we needed it for our vegetables and to protect our precious hens from snakes and rats. So finally I took my tools and crouched before the glory of a sunny spring day. I started with the fenced patch against the eastern wall of the olive press. I had seeds for parsley, radish, cucumber, and a few tomato seedlings.

Suddenly a chunky shadow fell over the weeds with a "God be with you" and Rameh crouched beside me, smelling of crude tobacco and breathing with a harsh wheeze. He'd relaxed the checkpoint at the square and taken to roaming the orchards, helping out wherever he was needed. Although freshly-shaven again, he looked disturbed.

"What's eating you, bailiff?"

He dug his sturdy fingers in the soil and wordlessly stuffed the weeds into a bag for his goat. Then he said matter-of-factly: "Nothing to make you happy, nothing to make you sad."

"Good for weeding time. Tell."

"You know Murshed effendi?"

"The unforgettable, the unforgivable."

"He is no more."

"How?"

"Shot. Close range. In his apartment."

"I'm sorry."

"I'm sorrier for me. Dumb me. Dumbest person around here." He laughed ruefully. "Turns out our officer's apartment was full of stolen goods. This time not just army stuff."

"Who do you think did him?"

"I don't know."

He hooked my gaze briefly, then went on weeding into his bag. "I hear you're going to Australia."

"You didn't answer my question, bailiff."

"Oh, son of Awad, you're either dumb or living on another planet. Or both. They're killing each other for a rug or a woman down there. What do you think this war is all about? Are you going to Australia or aren't you?"

"Why are you asking?"

"To get an answer."

"Emigration is a complicated business, Rameh. Just in case you're thinking of doing a flit."

Rameh went quiet, digging and breathing from his mouth. I wondered how to explain to him the complexity of emigration. All the paper work involved, the regulations, the correspondence. In our case writing back to Hawwa had taken long reflection and some edgy discussions. Yousra asked for more details about life in Sydney. "I don't want to sit at home and cook. I want to work," she wrote. She ended the letter complaining about my reluctance to leave. "He's so rooted here it will take an earthquake to uproot him." We argued. We were still arguing, but we had to reply, at least to keep that option open and to reassure Hawwa that we were well.

"If you go, take me with you, son of Awad." Rameh spoke wearily.

"Rameh! You should be the last to jump ship, you're the captain now."

"Captain, my ass! I'm a bailiff without land and a soldier without a war! Maybe I should just marry Hilweh and go somewhere else."

"Why go? She seems okay since you brought her down to the square."

"She's great. She looks at me all the time as if she's seeing a new man. The other day I took her to the woods and had her practise with the Winchester. You wouldn't believe how good she is."

"There you go!"

"You think?"

"I think that Sitti is up there pleading happiness for both of you."

"And the Hakim?"

"He tried to patch you up, didn't he?"

"I don't know, maybe he's too busy drinking celestial arak." Rameh looked up towards the blue sky and roared with a laugh that expelled the birds from the trees.

When he left me the back yard was as clean as a freshly-ploughed orchard. The hens were cackling, eager to get their beaks into that nice open soil. I ordered patience but they squawked even louder, so I let them out. I put my tools on the windowsill, smiling at the notion of Rameh fastening his seat belt on an airplane to Oz with Hilweh by his side.

Twenty-three

We were dipping down to Kafleet to do some shopping. Mariam was singing, "Look, look, look the sea," jumping in the back seat. For her the sea, big and blue and cool, was magic. Her little body had imprinted the joy of our trips to the sea. A mermaid since her first bath, she could be left in the water all day, she wouldn't complain or tire. Summer was coming soon. I could keep on trying to hide the war from Mariam but what about the Big Blue? No jolly jaunts to the sea this year. The sea had become the garbage dump of the war: oil slicks, broken machinery, bloated limbs of the war dead. The only thing it was good for was transporting thousands of emigrants to Larnaca.

Yousra was fiddling with the radio, looking for news. She hit upon a station broadcasting yet another message from our President with his tired slogans. Then the news proper. Armed men firing at an ambulance had caused a flour-laden truck to overturn and spill its load on a petrol station. Unidentified gunboats had been cruising our territorial waters at dawn.

"Slogans. Unknown gunmen. Unidentified gunboats." Yousra laughed bitterly. I kept my peace, hoping my silence would say "You want news, you got news". But regardless of how much a drug hurts, an addict always wants more. She changed the station. A nationwide shortage of rice was being announced, all traders instructed to ration one kilo per person per month.

"How can you ration in a country of looters?" Yousra shouted at the radio. Then she looked at me. "You haven't seen our larder lately. The lentils could last us a couple of weeks. The chickpeas no more than a month. Enough sugar but no broad beans. As for the rice, eight days at best."

"We'll stop at the first shop and get our ration."

At the first place I tried, the old shopkeeper I'd known for years had already run out of rice. He said that he had half a bag this morning, but his children and grandchildren took it all. Sorry. Other stores might still have some if I hurry.

Disappointment poured lead into my shoes. I drove to the next store, harried by the tooting horns. At the doorway a wave of pushy desperadoes engulfed me. I ploughed through hips and chests and waists, all the while being scolded, pushed back, sworn at. But I plunged on all the way to the counter.

"It's for my child!" a woman cried.

"We all have children!" the crowd chorused.

Behind the counter a young-man-turned-robot was handing out bags of rice and taking the money.

"ID, please."

"*What?*"

The robot didn't look up. "Orders. We have to write the amount and date of each purchase on the back of your ID."

I gave him my driver's licence. An old man shouted above the crowd: "What are we? Refugees? Gypsies? This is humiliating."

The robot handed me one kilogram of rice.

"Three kilos," I blurted.

"One kilo per month, per person. Per ID," he recited.

"We are three at home."

"No problem. Next time bring the other IDs."

Back at the car, Yousra lost her temper when she heard what had happened. "You and I can live on herbs if we must, but Mariam needs more than that."

I drove off promising to get more rice tomorrow. The road was narrowing and snaking around pine trees and residential villas. Soon I was stuck behind a wobbling four-wheeler loaded with gravel. The driver was blithely swerving as if performing a belly dance. The road visibility beyond the huge vehicle was nil. So I busied myself with the graffiti posted on the boot. *Don't speed up, Baba, we are waiting for you,* and *Don't speed, death is faster,* and *The eye of the envious will be blinded.* Stern stuff. But not a word about tail wagglers bouncing gravel off from all sides.

Finally the feeder into the coastal road gave me a chance to overtake.

"Mama, Baba, look! It's a lady!"

In the wing mirror I saw the trucky: a big-haired blonde with black sunglasses and black leather jacket. Mariam waved gleefully to her, prodding us to react.

Yousra laughed. "Anything men can do, women can do better."

"Is that so, Baba?"

"Ab . . . solutely!"

Cinderella behind the big wheel waved back and blew us a kiss through her pink bubble-gum.

At the entrance road to Kafleet we hit chaos. No holds barred when survival is at stake. But why drive into a traffic jam when the market is less than a hundred metres away? I parked the car and started to get out. But Yousra said: "They'll steal it just like this," clicking her fingers. "You stay here with Mariam. I don't want her jostled by the crowd."

Mariam was not happy. She sulked and turned her brooding back to us, deaf to Yousra's reasoning. Yousra gave up trying and disappeared into the maze of wooden and tin stalls scattered over the former football ground.

"Okay Mariam, listen, how about when Mama gets back *we* go to the market. She waits here and I buy you a present."

It took a while. Then she began to relent. "What present?" she whined.

"How about a colouring book?"

"Mm." Not hot at all.

"A mewing doll like you?"

"Mmm." Bad/angry.

"I give up, you chose."

"A tank."

"*What?*"

"Samer and Nader have tanks. I want one of my own."

"Tanks are not for girls. They're too hard to drive."

"Not harder than trucks. What about that lady just now?"

"Okay, a truck then – or maybe an ambulance? How about an ambulance?"

"A big one, with blue lights and a siren?"

"Okay."

Mariam's face began to light up. She sniffed back her tears. My God, not yet five and wants a tank, of all things. "Here comes a BMW, watch out," she whispered and ducked.

"What's a BMW Watch Out?"

"Tinted glass. Killers and spies. Samer and Nader told me. They kidnapped Aunty Sana and they killed their father."

From time to time, a lull in the traffic opened a vista onto the market. Before the war, this coastal town had had little significance. Now by virtue of its remoteness from the battlefields, closeness to the sea and profusion of vacant lots and shops, it had mushroomed into a refuge for merchants who had lost their businesses elsewhere. There were also hagglers and pushers and looters off loading stolen goods. The busiest spot was a secondhand clothes stall piled high with wares. A skinny young boy in shabby underwear was trying one pair of trousers after another. Too big! Too small! His mother kept handing him more, urging him to hurry up and cover his legs. Adding insult to injury the stallholder was giving him disdainful, withering looks. The boy was shivering with embarrassment, but his misery only made Mariam giggle. Yet at the next stall, a girl was trying desperately to fit her size fourteen body into a size ten dress. She had it stuck midway between chest and thigh. Couldn't pull it down or up. "*Ya haram,*" Mariam said, commiserating.

On the narrow bridge, a shiny red car moved slowly towards us followed at an odd distance by other cars. I thought its engine was stalling. But when it reached a wider stretch of road, the cars behind overtook it in a frenzy, some drivers blowing their horns and waving the victory sign, others gesturing in disgust. What was this all about? Meanwhile Mariam was naming the cars like an expert: "Honda Civic, Mazda, Toyota . . . hmm what's this one, Baba?" she asked as the red car drew closer. I could see the driver now. His hair was freshly styled, he looked happy and cocky, chewing at a long cigar. Mariam was now on my lap, her eyes riveted on the dawdling red Rover.

Suddenly I saw the rope hooked to the rear of the car, and the blackened, bloated, shredded body tied to it. Before Mariam could realise what it was, I forced her face down on my chest.

"What's the matter with you, Baba?" she cried.

"Please Mariam, just . . ."

She was fighting to free herself. "I didn't do anything wrong, honest," she whimpered.

I kept her glued to my chest and looked again at the body. Its fingers were missing, the head was hairless, the nose smashed, the mouth gaping. The eyes were dark holes. The arms were dislocated, hanging by a thread as they dragged behind the body.

My throat squeezed shut. My mind spun out of control. Words died inside me. Mariam's sobs were still echoing in my chest, but all I could do was shield her eyes from the trailing exhibit. I didn't let her go until the macabre vampire swerved his car towards the scenic seaside road. By then Mariam was convulsing bitterly. She pierced me with tearful question marks and an estranged gaze as if she'd never seen me before.

She was still sobbing when Yousra came back. I stepped out of the car, opened the boot, stuffed the shopping inside while whispering to Yousra what had happened. She blanched. She rushed to Mariam, took her in her arms and rocked her like a baby. Mariam complained about my inexplicable behaviour. All Yousra could say was: "It's okay now, it's okay."

We drove back in a bleak silence.

As soon as we reached home, Yousra took Mariam next door. I emptied the boot. Brought in the shopping. Washed my hands and face with cold water feeling like a man stranded on a high balcony during a blaze. I was restoring a face to that shredded cadaver – mine. I was pleading with my torturers to give me the bullet of mercy. Spare me the asphalt crucifixion. My distorted face crumbled, begging for one cheap shot, just one of a million cartridges wasted on stray cats and dogs, already-dead people, empty streets and walls.

I went to the kitchen with his/my imagined howls pulsing in my ears. I opened and shut the fridge with no notion of what I was doing. I lit the gas stove, stared sightlessly at the blue flame and turned it off. I pulled the drawers in and out and touched the cutlery, knives and forks and spoons left behind when Yousra's family emigrated. A few months after our wedding Yousra's widowed father and only brother had moved to Togo. Since they'd never approved of her eloping with "a farmer from nowhere", Yousra decided to ignore them: "If they ask after me, I'll respond. Otherwise, tough." The years went by with neither side softening. Even when we had Mariam and sent pictures. Even when the war began and the horrific news reached all the corners of the world, they didn't bother to find out if we were dead or alive. That did it for Yousra. "I'm dead to them. They're dead to me. End of story."

Togo, Venezuela, Australia – everyone was emigrating, even before the urgency of war. Why was I so clingy about this place? I went to Mariam's room and sat on her bed. The calendar on the wall promoted a computer company. The ad pictured a circle of children sitting around a huge computer screen filled with a nuclear mushroom. The caption read "World History on a Microchip". One day, soon, Mariam will look at the horrors of this war whether I hide her on top of a mountain or in a cave. Whether I take her to Australia or Togo or the North Pole. Ever since the war had started we had always managed to alleviate Mariam's anxiety. We'd been proud of our achievement. Today I could only remember Sitti's proverbs: *They are easy to deal with until you stop changing their nappies*, and, *The older they grow the more you worry*. I wondered how she would have handled this situation.

Yousra's voice startled me.

"The train is back on track. She's playing with the twins." Yousra sat on the bed beside me. "Sana told me some hair-raising stories about what you saw today. She's seen it all. She says it's a sport nowadays. Like in the Middle Ages, when they torched thieves and witches in public places. They drag a prisoner to a crowded area in broad daylight so the news will spread as far as possible. Sometimes loudspeakers call people out to their verandas to watch. Human beings have become cheaper than grass in the land of the alphabet. Well, wars produce monsters. What do you expect? All we can do is survive, I suppose."

"What did you tell Mariam?"

"I told her 'Your father was trying to protect you. He saw someone with a gun and thought he was going to shoot.' She bought it."

"She wanted me to buy her a tank, did she tell you?"

"No. But when the twins started to set up some war game she didn't want to play. She wanted the electric train. Come and see."

We went out to the back yard and watched as the little train trundled over bridges, into tunnels, around hills and valleys. Mariam was clearly enjoying the attention and the game, as if nothing had happened. Nothing at all.

Twenty-four

One very windy morning in late April, Rameh showed up at our door holding Hilweh's hand. He was shaven and neatly dressed. Hilweh was red-faced, like a late summer tomato, but her eyes were glowing with a thousand stars. To my delight, Rameh declared his desire to marry Hilweh. He'd re-entered his old bailiff's skin, looking to a new life. He had realised how insignificant Wahdeh was on the map: neither a strategic thoroughfare nor a dominant lookout post. His defiance of Nimer was now a thing of the past; he didn't want to get stuck in the warlord's mire. Time to swap Militiaman for Bridegroom.

Rameh continued an obviously rehearsed speech: "Son of Awad, now that your uncle, God bless his soul, is no longer with us, and our Mukhtar is in the nursing home, an orphan like myself has no one to give him the approval. Could you say the word?"

I was humbled. A normal village wedding takes into account the community. Issues like health, wealth, ancestry, family aspirations and inheritance are gone through with a fine-tooth comb until the elders give the word. But Rameh had skipped all the stages except the last, and chosen me to bless his union. My uncle's spirit wafted by, inspiring the words, "Be blessed. Go. Make peace with Nimer. You are the better man. I'll ask Yousra to approach Hilweh's family on your behalf."

"God bless!"

"Gobls," Hilweh echoed.

Rameh was making the event even more memorable by choosing the first Sunday in May for his wedding, the date of our customary spring feast. He also wanted the ceremony to take place at the Castle's outer court. With the Hakim's eternal leave and the Mukhtar's illness we had been too disheartened even to consider celebrating spring this year, let alone by the barracks. Rameh had once more broken a spell.

So the next day Yousra went with our silver engagement rings to visit Hilweh's family, fulfilling a crucial part of the betrothal by formally asking for the girl's hand in marriage. This had to be performed by someone trustworthy from outside both families, someone ready to take in his or her stride a yea or a nay. They could have stalled and said, "We shall consult with our relatives" or "Wait until we get the girl's approval". But Hilweh's mother ran out to the veranda ululating for all to hear, "her tongue rattling like an electric clapper," Yousra reported.

Rameh's wedding became overnight the sole orbit of interest in Wahdeh. One didn't have to eavesdrop to hear: Is she sane enough to know what she's doing? Would she be able to give him a child? Would it be a normal child? He must have lost his mind, she's crazy! And so on. Meanwhile the preparations were going ahead, enhanced by a deep sense of loyalty towards Rameh and the general compassion felt for Hilweh. Many people believed that the lifting of that curse was a sign of better times ahead.

The night before the wedding, two separate parties took place: one for the women at Hilweh's home, and one for the men at ours. It was preceded by a sincere handshake in the middle of the square between the groom and the warlord. Once more Hilweh's mother rattled her powerful tongue.

Rameh came to the party in the three-piece suit and tie Amti had picked from the Hakim's wardrobe. A time machine had pulled Rameh back from forty to twenty even before we started to drink.

"This arak is paradise," he said, raising his glass.

"That's where you're going tomorrow. Then to hell the day after!" Abu Faour said, still angry with the world but laughing.

Soon the house was shaking to the rough steps of the dabkeh. Two shepherds were blowing their double-reed flutes and Zahi, sitting up on the dining table overlooking the dance, fuelled it higher and higher with his drum.

At the first break for another refill of tabbouleh and freshly cut vine leaves, the new Nimer arrived in a crisp beige suit, yellow cowboy boots and a brown tie, trailing his watchdogs, Abu Takka and Abu Janjoul. The latter ceremoniously carried a silver box. They helped themselves to the arak. Raising his glass Nimer declaimed, with a touch of a Beiruti drawl: "A new era has begun for all of us. We should put the past behind us and begin a new chapter. One for all, and all for Wahdeh! *Kaskon*, cheers!" We cheered.

There was a long silence. What was he up to? Then he snatched the box from Abu Janjoul and presented it to the bridegroom.

With a flicker of cunning in his eyes he beckoned Rameh to open it. The bailiff obliged.

On the red velvet lining sparkled a choice 45 calibre American handgun with an ivory handle and a silver barrel.

"You want to try it out now?" Nimer asked.

Rameh, clearly wanting to shoot at the stars, reached towards the gun.

"Only one round," I interrupted. "Let's not spoil a great occasion."

So Rameh declined gracefully. Nimer did not insist. Zahi stuck his head in. "Can I try?"

"Go and beat your drum!" Rameh growled.

Meanwhile, the bride's *jalweh* was going strong. Mariam was there, clinging to Sana, both watching, for the first time, a bride being hennaed, peeled, perfumed and pampered. According to Yousra, the most moving moment was when Um Faour helped Hilweh into the white dress. "Um Faour was anxious for her dress. It was her mother's," Yousra told me. "She hadn't lent it to anyone before. But she said that though her happy years with Abu Faour were behind her, Hilweh is so innocent she could help bring back the better memories. So she squeezed her inside it one inch at a time, sweating and trembling." Hilweh had not cried like the usual bride-to-be, Yousra recounted. "She was like a child all alone at a circus. We were all clowns to her. She flew among us, electrified with joy. She kissed and hugged Mariam every five minutes. And she really took to Sana, touching her hair and her arms, admiring her green outfit with wide astonished eyes. Sana could hardly hold back her tears. I can tell you, emotions were all over the place."

On W-day, the bridal procession, led by Zahi and his friends, started from Hilweh's home. The bride had been hoisted onto a white mare adorned with a flowery collar and led by Abu Takka. Hilweh was wobbly on her mount, holding the reins in her left hand and trying to keep her balance with her right. She was followed by the women of Wahdeh. At a short distance behind, Nimer's jeep, driven by Bou-Youn, carried the bridegroom.

Beside him Abu Janjoul stood like a guard of honour, brandishing a gleaming Kalashnikov. The men behind them closed the procession singing the *hida* songs synchronised to the pace of the steep hill. First came the vows:

Come on with me
Come on come on
I'll never leave you
A day alone
I'll never leave you
Do not despair
I'll never leave you
Or be unfair

Then they named the places where the groom would like to take his beloved – prairies, valleys, rivers and the promised paradise of many children – urging her to follow:

Come on with me
Come on with me
Your love for me
Is all my life
Come on with me
You'll see no strife
Come on with me
And be my wife

I raised my voice for the last verse, Yousra looked back and blew me a kiss. For Yousra and me this first Sunday of May was always special. It was on a day like this, more than seven years ago, that she had fallen in love with Wahdeh and changed her mind about living in Beirut. Ever since, we'd ended each first Sunday in May at the olive press with a bottle of wine to commemorate the moment when Yousra had said yes. Yes, the olives *will* be pressed in this house again. Although the dream was shelved for now, the jubilation of today's procession revived my hope.

When we reached the small bridge where the ground flattened out, the women stopped, took a deep breath, wiped their faces, then waved their handkerchiefs for the first round of ululation. The older women took the lead with the most daring verses:

Eeha, welcome welcome all of you
Eeha, the spring is green the sky is blue
Eeha, their life is long, their love is true
Eeha, they'll do everything I wouldn't do
Lee lee lee

Nimer broke precedence by walking into the Castle, followed by the Abus. They disappeared inside, then reappeared on the small balcony where Murshed effendi used to stand and bark at them. Long banners of the national flag hung down the Castle walls, brightening the bleakness of the grey stone. The newest recruits had prepared the grounds with tables, chairs and a makeshift barbecue. Now they were lined up under the hawkish eyes of Bou-Youn to salute "Rameh, the best soldier this barrack has ever known".

While her husband was peacocking on the balcony, Sana rolled up her sleeves and joined the ladies preparing the tabbouleh and skewers. Wahdeh's women loathed her arrogant husband as much as they loved her. Nevertheless, they helped her pamper him with a tray of appetisers sent specially up to the balcony.

The children dived and resurfaced, bobbing on the sea of spring colours. It was heartening to see everybody in their festive attire. Apart from Amti Wardieh and a few older widows, the women had shed their sombre mourning and were floating around in flamboyant greens and yellows and reds. Even the men looked brighter than usual in their Sunday suits. Some had adorned their buttonholes with a white carnation and all were remarkably clean-shaven.

Hilweh – 'the pretty one' – had surrendered herself to helpers who wanted to recreate her younger, more radiant, image. But they had gone overboard, and the excess of powder, kohl, and rouge had done the opposite. Their attempt to augment her thin lips with crimson liner made her clownish. Circles of rouge made her rounded cheeks like those of a doll. Mercifully, the veil that fell from her flowery wedding crown softened the effect.

Nor had Rameh entirely escaped the ministrations of his own helpers. After considerable shortening of the trousers, the Hakim's suit fitted him fine but someone had waxed his shaggy moustache into the handlebars of a fearsome sheikh. And someone evidently more accustomed to a hangman's noose had knotted his tie. Rameh's face, already flushed with the grape, was beginning to turn purple at the temples. But he was happy; his smile reached all the way to his ears, his laughter nearly drowned out the loud music.

During the preparation of the meal, the physical trial commenced, using a huge crowbar, a massive stone urn, and a stone roller, each weighing well over a hundred kilos. This was the crucial moment for even the most virile bridegrooms. Some very able bodies had been shamed by their failure to shift these heavy pieces. But we all knew Rameh's strength. We'd seen him lifting a broken truck or carrying a wounded calf from the fields to the square. "Piece of cake," I whispered to Rameh as we set off to the shallow ditch at the end of the courtyard. Rameh took off his jacket and gave it to me. "Did you pass *this* test, college boy?"

"Just about. Remember?"

Despite our joking I could sense apprehension in Rameh's flustered speech and diminishing pace as we approached the moment of truth. His face was tense even after he relaxed his necktie.

The crowd formed a hushed circle around him. He filled his chest with air, and in a trial that would go down in Wahdeh's history, he tossed the urn away as if releasing a dove into the air. We all cheered but Rameh was oblivious, in a world of his own, intent on the next task. Without even a pause, he lifted the crowbar as if picking up a child and went straight on to flick the stone roller, whizzing it more than twenty metres into the roaring crowd.

So much for the trial of strength, now for the test of skill. The hubbub morphed into a rhythmic clapping as Zahi marched in carrying a flat-bottomed sieve and a glass of arak – a pageboy presenting his knight's gear. The air held its breath. Rameh held the sieve vertically with one finger inside the top of the frame and positioned the glass upright on the opposite side of the frame. He stared at it with intense concentration, willing it to do what it had rarely done for any man. Then, quick as a flash, he spun the sieve one hundred and eighty degrees and caught the glass in his teeth, downing the arak in one gulp.

The sky filled with cheers. Rameh raised his face to the heavens in thanks, his eyes misted with relief. I gave him a long tight hug. Then I helped him into his jacket and escorted him to the flower-decked platform where his bride was ecstatic with pride.

The drama of the day over (or so we thought), it was time to reward ourselves with the feast. We made our way to where a large table was groaning under the weight of a copper tub filled with tabbouleh and flanked by bowls of hummus and moutabal and grain salad and green salad and pickles. Nearby the barbecue was perfuming our festivities, while Amti headed a production line baking the thin mountain bread.

Yousra and I filled our plates and retreated to the shade of a big tree. There was no chance of catching Mariam to make it a family lunch.

As we ate we joked that the Peacock Castle had finally found its mascot in Nimer. Neither Bou-Youn nor the late Murshed effendi had fitted the bill. But the loud, vain, strutting Nimer, now smoking a fat cigar on the Castle's balcony, was the perfect peacock.

Despite the laughter all around us, spasms of melancholy surged through me. How could the same occasion contain equal amounts of joy and sadness? The scene spread out before me was both utterly familiar and yet frighteningly alien. For the first time ever the forbidden gates of the Castle were open during the spring festival, yet no one seemed to have any desire to walk in. Except, of course, Nimer and his gang. Also, there were newcomers to our celebration, the recruits who had come from outside Wahdeh. But in fact these 'gatecrashers' were joining in fully, happy themselves and happy for us. In addition, not a shot had been heard all day between the neighbouring villages. Normally (if anything in this war could be called normal), there were spontaneous ceasefires only for funerals. Most unsettling of all, this was the first time we were celebrating without the Hakim. The throne-like rock platform where Rameh and Hilweh sat had been the Hakim's place of honour, with the Mukhtar –

also missing – to his right. Although Sitti had always boycotted this festival, the stroppy independence of her act had conferred a sense of freedom on Wahdeh, a feeling that had died with her. We were no longer free, decisions were now made for us.

But . . . we were still here, still alive, which was more than could be said for thousands of others.

"Penny for them? You look miles away."

"I don't know, Yousra, somehow this day feels unreal."

"In what way?"

"Everything."

"Look over there, Mariam dashing all over the place like a little hawk. Isn't she real, and me?"

"The people are real enough, it's everything else."

"Rameh and Hilweh at last? Is that it?"

"Everything. Look, I'm really sorry, I shouldn't be brooding on a day like this, but . . ."

"Shush. It's been hard for all of us. I don't think we could have done any better. Let's just enjoy this day. It's our day too, remember?"

"I want to believe. Give me a kiss and pinch me hard."

A kiss is not just a kiss, not in public, not in Wahdeh, but Yousra's pinch put my brooding on hold.

I wasn't alone in this ambivalent mood. Um Faour approached us pensively, her eyes reddened. It couldn't have been the drink, she was a teetotaller. There must have been a fair few tears coming and going throughout the day. She sat down beside Yousra with a long sigh.

A short distance away, the musicians were beating out the dabkeh rhythms faster and faster. The keen recruits and Wahdeh's own lads vied with each other to hold hands with the girls. Some were pushing to lead the dance, while others whirled into the centre for improvised solos.

Yousra looped her arm around Um Faour's shoulders. This could have been her son's wedding, it could have been Faour's bride wearing the pretty dress. Mothers are like that. Happiness can dim their spirit when not shared with their offspring. There was no point in soothing Um Faour with words, Yousra's gestures were more eloquent: a few shared sighs, nods, and a gentle rubbing of Um Faour's back. Then we persuaded her to join us in the dabkeh, *yalla*, life is now, *ya* Um Faour, the past is past and the future is never in our hands, let's beat the dust that will be us in the end.

As we entered the dabkeh hand in hand, the ululating began all over again, this time predicting celestial joy and an eagle-like son in less than a year. Everyone was joining in now – the children and the elderly and the soldiers, the whole of Wahdeh it seemed, the circle growing and growing like a huge string of worry beads, opening from the middle. Even Nimer had descended from his balcony. No doubt spurred by jealousy of the men surrounding his Sana, he'd left the Castle and made a beeline for the centre, where he was doing the highest jumps and creating a vortex of dust with his yellow cowboy boots.

Then, just as the dance was at its frenzied peak, the music suddenly fragmented and died in a matter of seconds. The circle broke up in confusion. Through the settling dust cloud I saw several village lads running towards the little bridge, shouting. A young man with long black hair and a bushy beard, stooped under the weight of his rucksack, was walking towards us.

"Look! It's Faour!" Hilweh screamed, her first complete sentence in years.

Twenty-five

Three days after Rameh's wedding and Faour's spectacular return, we began another celebration of renewal: the spring cleaning. It had always bridged the gap not only between winter and spring but between private and public. The exposure of carpets and bedding on the flat roof tops, although banal, gave away intimate secrets. It also rang the changes. "Ah, they did buy a new cover for that ancient sofa after all." Two years ago, amid cheers, Um Faour had carried out onto the roof a brand new vacuum cleaner. Its purring legato had enhanced the familiar staccato of sticks to produce a symphony of modernity and tradition. Last year there'd been at least four more Hoovers.

Now, spring was being too moody to deliver many opportunities, so when the northerly bestowed a cool breeze and a sunny day, we grabbed it. Mariam loved to beat the dust off the hanging carpets. She called, and was soon joined by, the twins. They took turns, two beating the rugs while the other counted to a hundred.

"Remember last year?" I said to Yousra. "The beating of sticks reached all the way up to the cliff. Today Wahdeh sounds like a summer resort at siesta time."

"People are cautious. They feel watched. They don't want to be seen out in the open."

"I don't get it. Only three days ago we were having a rowdy wedding."

"Yes, and last night the shelling sounded closer to home than ever. People are scared, Adam."

Bang, bang, thirty-four, thirty-five, thirty-six. The children were having more fun than effect. Yousra was spreading the heavy blankets on the railing. Mariam was helping while describing the multitude of toys the twins had – war booty for certain. She was feeding me brand names and using hands, sticks, edges of rugs, demonstrating the mysteries of remote control. The boys were shouting over her, and the three of them jumping up and down for no sensible reason except of course to pierce my ear drums.

Finally Yousra decided "if we can't beat them let's join them," and we all began to celebrate, making dust and noise and sneezing loudly.

Soon Um Faour showed up on her roof with a stick, for we were now having long electricity cuts. Then Amti Wardieh appeared as well. Bang, bang, bang. It snowballed through the village, spreading a curtain of dust in the air but reviving that precious cycle of life.

Later that afternoon, Mariam ushered Faour into our living room, holding him by the hand. He moved slowly, as if recovering from surgery, but he looked rested. His deep black eyes were less hollowed with anguish. He'd trimmed his beard and was wearing the woollen jumper his mother had knitted for his now-aborted betrothal.

Craning her neck to scan Faour's face, Mariam asked: "Are you upset because they've taken your house?" She dreaded losing her next door neighbours if Faour claimed back his apartment.

"I've set up a lovely tent near the spring, Mariam. I don't need my apartment. Not until I marry."

"When will you marry?" Mariam was still apprehensive.

"I shall wait until you are a pretty bride and ask for your hand."

"You're too old for me," Mariam snapped and jerked her hand away.

"Then I will not marry," Faour laughed.

"Swear!"

"Promise."

"Are you satisfied now?" Yousra said, giving Mariam's bum a light tap. "Go and play with the twins."

Mariam skipped out.

Yousra put the kettle on while marvelling again at Faour's spectacular homecoming. "Your mother was so flabbergasted. Over and over crying out: 'Slap me, slap my face, hit me, I'm dreaming!' Even Bou-Youn – he'd clearly forgotten that you were a runaway fit only for a court martial. He went on and on: 'Faour! What a dark horse!' And Hilweh! You made her talk! And your mother, even forgetting about her dress and whirling Hilweh around ecstatically!" Yousra poured the coffee. "*Are* you upset because they've taken your house?"

Faour shrugged and sank into the chaise Morris. "You know I hardly used it."

"But he has no right to squat in your place. Instead of cleaning up his own father's house, that creep takes a shortcut." Yousra wasn't mincing her words. She hated Nimer.

"It's all part of the new order," I said, trying to dilute Yousra's rage. "Don't let bitterness eat your heart, Faour. Nothing can last forever, not even this ludicrous war. When it's over, Nimer will leave us like a shot."

"That's what my father says. Nimer is making shitloads of money from the black market. He'll buy himself a fancy villa and play the big shot somewhere else."

"If he's not killed first," Yousra said savagely. I wondered what was fuelling her hatred.

"Did you have a chance to talk to Nimer?" I asked.

"Yesterday morning. Just briefly as I was setting off to the valley."

"What did he say for himself?" Yousra said.

"He said: 'Don't be a stranger. I may have something for you. You know where to find me.'"

"My God!" Yousra said in disgust.

"Well, why don't you visit him? See what he wants." I kept trying to lower the temperature.

"I don't have the stomach," Faour said. "I'm not going to worry about it now anyway. I have other plans." He lifted his cup, nodding mysteriously.

"You're all secrets, aren't you?" Yousra said. "Everyone else is dying to get out of this country, and you come back all the way from Venezuela." Her unspoken question hung in the silence as we drank our coffee.

"I don't know," Faour finally said. "I got off to a bad start over there."

"But how? You're young and intelligent and you have family in Venezuela, what more could anyone hope for? Don't tell me it was only your broken heart?" Yousra was prodding.

He sighed. "Things don't always go as you plan, you know." He stirred uneasily, took a last sip of coffee, placed the cup on the tray and murmured, "*Daymeh*" – May your house always be open to guests and your coffee always served in good health. Even the standard thank you had an evasive undertone. Clearly he was not prepared to say any more about Venezuela. I took the hint. "Have you discussed restocking the shop with your father? The shelves are pretty bare. We need the shop to work properly again, your father is only going through the motions. He's stubborn, but you can convince him, I'm sure."

"It's no go, Adam. We talked it through last night. It's just that trading isn't the same anymore. It's cash and carry now and don't ask where it's coming from. The whole country is a black market now. You have to bribe the militias and suck up to warlords. We're not cut out for that kind of business."

"Maybe that's what Nimer wants to talk about," Yousra said. "He's learning the carrot and the stick. He wants to be seen as the man of good deeds. Next election you'll see his pictures up all over the place." Her temper had flared up again, but she caught it and changed the subject, "So what *are* your plans for the future?"

"I want to be a professional rug cleaner – my God, I thought we'd been invaded. The echo down in the valley sounded like a marching army, even the dust wafting through had a military smell!"

We laughed with Faour, but Yousra wasn't letting him off the hook. She cared about him and had to know he had a decent future.

"I want to write," Faour announced at last. "The only thing I learned in Venezuela is that I want to write. Would you lend me some books?"

I nodded, surprised.

"Write?" Yousra was alarmed. "Have you told your parents?"

"I did. Father wants me to be a doctor but Mother says doctors have to study for years, better to be an engineer. They both see writers as no-hopers. 'They die with no meat on their shoulders. Better even to tend the shop. At least you won't go hungry,' my father said. But Zahi hit the roof, 'The shop is mine! Faour doesn't want it.' He looked so ferociously at Dad – 'By the time I'm out of school you'll be an old man, maybe dead. The war will be finished. *I* want the shop!'" Faour mimicked his younger brother. Then he stood up ready to leave. "About the books . . ."

"Sure, come with me."

Yousra tapped him on the shoulder: "Don't be a stranger, remember?"

He followed me to Mariam's room where all our books were kept. I climbed up a stepladder, reached the highest shelf and retrieved his diary. He was dumbfounded. "Oh! So *you've* got it." He took the little book with both hands and smiled sheepishly. "Did you read it?"

"Me, Yousra, Amti and the Hakim. No one else."

"Did you think I was in love with Hilweh?"

"We did wonder."

"She's like a muse. There but not there, you know what I mean?"

"I guessed that much. Still . . ."

"Still what?"

"Well, you know, now a married woman and all, we don't want to stir the past with Rameh. He's a dangerous man."

Faour cracked up laughing. "About the books . . ."

"Sure, take as many as you like. On one condition."

"Which is?"

"I'd like to read more of your stuff. You read my books, I read yours?"

"One condition from me too: only you."

"Deal."

He perused the shelves. "Can I take this?"

"Yes."

"And this?"

"Take what you like. We've read them all."

He picked three of my favourites: Hesse's *Siddhartha*, *The Urgency of Change* by Krishnamurti, and Naimi's *Mirdad*. The quest, the questions, and the whirlwind of illusions. All philosophy, I noticed with surprise, remembering our conversation in the cave passages. I wondered what had created this new interest. Perhaps his brain was now hungry for debate, no longer satisfied writing impressions? But I kept my curiosity to myself. No doubt time would reveal what had prompted the change.

Twenty-six

That night the pounding of mortars resumed, deeper and nearer than ever. But it abated after midnight, permitting Wahdeh's roosters to fanfare the pre-dawn. Through the muslin of sleep I could hear them piercing the charcoal sky. At this hour the shepherds were setting off, guided by the stars. Babies were waking up their mothers and the elderly were beginning their murmured prayers to the Maker of darkness and light. In the barns the sleep-heavy villagers milked into metal buckets. Silently; you don't speak at the hour of the wolf. Sshsh sshsh, the white liquid foamed, rising by the minute. The southwesterly served the trees with pollen and warmth. A forlorn howl rippled across the valley. Soon the goats would be clattering out to the pastures like a river of pebbles. I turned in my bed, past and future merging. The tinkers are back, disorderly as ever, unloading their sacks of olives. "In line, you donkeys, get your mules in line!" I smell my mother's voice. Then I taste my father's whisper: "Make sure you don't spill a drop. Olive oil is sacred. Spilling it is bad luck. Like salt and bread, it shouldn't be stepped on." No one ever woke up before him, not even the roosters. His footsteps floated out of the house like sycamore wings. I knew he'd be toiling away in the olive press or out in the orchards, but I never saw him that early in the day. The strongest work image I retain is of him drenched in sweat while adjusting the hydraulic pressure. And when the shift was over and the donkey released into the back yard, my father lying on the cold floor, face down, one arm under his head, catching a half-hour snooze. It was one of his quirks; somehow, that contact with the hard cool stone triggered an instant deep sleep. Mother would wake us just before dawn, when the sky was navy blue and the square resounded to a quarrelsome chorus of barking and crowing. Breakfast: toasted pita bread with labneh, thyme in olive oil and a cup of black tea – except that Hawwa kept drinking milk as if she'd never been weaned. Then the walk to school, us kids mingling on the way to Delbeh with the older students and the grown-ups going shopping and the tinkers and the home helps on their way to more affluent homes.

Cocooned in Yousra's curves and her warmth, I didn't want dawn to end my sleep. For the first time in my life, I didn't want to greet a new day in my own birthplace. I snuggled into the hibernation of a polar bear, and dreamed:

A large flat city at night. Tall shining skyscrapers. Wide empty streets. Deserted bridges. Silence. I'm in a grey overcoat, neither cold nor warm. The collar is turned up around my neck. I'm wearing a black felt hat. Its rim partly covers my eyes. I see only the pavement, and the tips of my black patent leather shoes. I carry weightless luggage. There is no one around. Not a soul. The wind moans from time to time. Metallic birds shoot across the sky, scarcely scratching the stillness. My footsteps are soundless. I see a revolving door of the old style: dark brown wood and thick glass. I walk through the door into a hall furnished with bulky brown leather settees and lit with dim orange lights. It's a hotel. At Reception I see the arm of the receptionist laid across the surface of the desk: a black sleeve, white cuff, a gold signet ring. I think he's leaning down to fetch something. But when I reach the desk there is only the arm. It rises and gives me a key. I take it and walk towards a staircase. I climb up endless spiral stairs. The more I climb the heavier my suitcase becomes. But I'm determined to reach the door that fits my key. I grasp the key firmly and trudge doggedly up. Suddenly my now very heavy suitcase bumps against the banisters. It falls into the stairwell. It causes a deafening bang as it hits the floor.

"What?"

"Adam, wake up."

"What?"

"Can't you hear?"

Mechanically I rolled out of bed, pushed my numb limbs into khaki trousers, a denim jacket, wellies, pulled my woolly hat over my throbbing head. Sleep must have nested deep in my ears. What Yousra had heard only reached me gradually, as if the commotion outside were being shredded and blown in the wind. I opened the door to criss-crossing torches. People were milling around their rooftops in their night clothes. Perhaps one of the boys had botched a prank? The war games children played these days were causing as much anxiety as the war itself. We had hoped the scar on Zahi's neck would serve as a deterrent. Instead it was every boy's envy.

"Abu Faour, what's going on?"

"The water reservoir's been hit. We're checking our tanks. Check yours."

The reservoir had been leaking for months. Now, apparently, it had received the *coup de grace* from one of our neighbours.

Yousra handed me a torch. I climbed the ladder at the side of the house. I lifted the lid and peered into the tank. A faint shadow of the moon was trembling in the dark water. The tank was less than a third full. It wouldn't last us long. I was neither angry nor depressed. Thousands across the country were now without running water, filling their tanks laboriously from springs and broken pipes. We were simply joining the nation of water carriers. We were not dead.

Yousra was less sanguine about it. "One day we run out of rice, then electricity, then water. What's next? Gas? Wood? Oxygen to breathe?" A fist of words in the face of helplessness.

I started the car and opened the boot. Mariam appeared at the door, rubbing her eyes and yawning. "Where are you going, Baba?"

"To the spring. We're running out of water."

It took her another minute to focus. Then she pleaded: "Take me with you."

"No!" Yousra's mouth was tense. Her thick curls barely concealed the tight furrows of her brow. "There'll be a rowdy crowd down there. Go back to bed." I gave her a 'let me handle this' look, hurried Mariam into her room, helped her wash and dress at speed. Then we sprinted to the car. Yousra, scowling, hurried after us with a woollen shawl. "It'll be cold down there. Be careful." Her eyes as she handed me the shawl burnt into me the message: this is bad parenting. Yes, it was.

A few cars had already beaten us to the spring. Rameh was trying to turn a wrangle into a queue. He was shoving men and women and their containers forcefully to stop them from shoving each other. Everybody was keyed up, impatient. I thought we'd done better at cleaning the Castle that took our young men to the war. No one had argued, no one had turned a deaf ear. Now the spring – our only source of pure drinking water – was flowing generously, there was plenty for all, but the spirit of *aouneh* had gone.

Rameh saw us. "Adam! Over here!" He nudged aside a couple of youngsters who were just larking about, and ushered me near the front. "I kept your turn. After her," he said, pointing at the bending woman before me. Mariam and I brought our containers forward.

Rameh lumbered over to the incoming cars to improvise a parking lot. Through their klaxons and screeching tyres, Nimer's shining black jeep with its tinted glass surged quietly from the dusty air like a surfacing submarine. The crowd hushed. They clustered together, whispering and nodding. Did mister warlord humble himself for water? Why didn't he leave it to his cronies, better still to Abu Faour, now that he was squatting in his son's apartment? Or was he playing domestic politics, mingling with us farmers?

At the mouth of the spring, the stocky blacksmith's wife, in a crumpled nightgown and bathrobe, turned her head and spat, warding off the arrival of Satan.

It wasn't necessary. Nimer had despatched his wife to do the menial chore instead. Sana stepped out of the jeep with the twins. Mariam ran towards the boys and they disappeared into the pine trees to play. Sana fetched two twenty-litre containers and came to the spring. I reached for them.

"Thank you."

"You're welcome."

Her voice was low and slow. Her eyes were puffed. She crossed her arms and leant on the retaining wall. "Nice wedding. You know. The other day," she said. Her words were hesitant, fragmented.

"I'm glad you enjoyed it."

She nodded. "What do you think, Adam? This war . . ."

"Who knows?" I uttered the standard response to the standard question about the probable duration of the war. "Everyone has a theory. But I guess Nimer should know."

She looked away. "He's asleep."

I thought I detected a crack in her voice. I remembered Yousra's reaction whenever Nimer's name cropped up. Could it be that he was ill-treating Sana? The thought turned my spine cold. It would be shaming to us all in Wahdeh, but the darkest shame would be mine, the neighbour who knew and did nothing.

The light of day was spreading, shadows were starting to rise around us. More cars, donkeys and mules were tumbling down the dirt road. When this road was still a footpath we'd walked down it to the spring delightfully spooked by the sudden wing movements and strident shrieks of birds jolting the silence of the valley. I remember being seven or eight – the sun is bright above the cliff, Hawwa is prancing downhill before us. Mother is carrying her *jarra* on her shoulder. I struggle behind her, bearing a large pitcher. Hawwa scouts the road. When she sees someone coming our way she gives us a sign. Then Mother covers the *jarra's* mouth with her palm. When it is full of life's most precious element, the earthenware *jarra* is a symbol of fertility. But to see it empty on the way to the spring is a bad omen. Some took that superstition so seriously they'd go back home and shut their doors for the rest of the day.

"Adam!" Faour jumped down from the hilltop above the spring.

"Hey, hermit, where's your tent?" I asked.

"You can't see it from here. You need help?"

"I'm okay, thanks."

We hugged. Sana and Faour shook hands.

"We made you homeless," Sana said with an apologetic smile.

"No problem. *Mi casa es su casa*," Faour answered.

To my surprise, Sana replied in Spanish. The prodigal son and his squatter laughed and broke into a lively conversation while I filled the containers. The fact that no one around them could understand a word gave them an air of exclusivity; their faces sparkled with the glee of two children speaking Pig Latin to confound the grown-ups. I could pick out a few words here and there, some from French roots, others from Arab Andalusia, but that didn't help me share the excitement that was holding their gaze and wreathing them in smiles.

Then the containers were full. Faour offered to carry Sana's. She shook her head: "Good exercise." After saying good-bye, she walked pensively to the jeep, all animation gone. But Faour was still beaming.

"How did you know she spoke Spanish?"

"She was born in Argentina. My mother told me."

"What were you talking about?"

"Oh, nothing. This and that."

"Call Mariam for me, will you?"

Faour sprinted towards the pine trees where Mariam could be heard counting. Sana was turning the jeep slowly, awaiting her kids.

As I approached my car I heard the thin whistle of a mortar followed by salvos of heavy artillery.

There was no time to turn back before the impact of the shell hurled me to the ground. All I could see was dust, all I could smell was cordite and exhaust fumes, all I could hear were hysterical screams. Through the whirling dust, people surged and sank as if drowning in foamy waves. Bullets hailed down on us. Long-range machine guns were splitting branches, pulverising wheels and stabbing mercilessly into the trunks of the ancient pine trees.

"Mariaaam!" My mouth was full of blood and mud. Fear for her was tearing at my guts. I screamed again and again. My voice was strangling me. I choked.

Other voices were coming through:

"Over here!"

"What?"

"Inside the reservoir!"

It was twenty metres to the reservoir. Twenty-two laps and a jump and a rain of death. "No!" Yousra's voice echoed in my ears. Why hadn't I trusted her fears, why hadn't I left Mariam behind? I straightened my glasses but couldn't open my eyes anyway for the thickness of dust. I pulled as much air into my lungs as I could and propelled myself blindly towards the empty reservoir. I landed on all fours in a slime of algae and water and people.

"Baba!"

There she was, huddled in a corner with the twins. Rameh was hugging them, his eyes blazing shields. He shouted: "They're okay!" while I was finding my footing.

"Faour is shot," Mariam whimpered, turning her head, but it took me a while to distinguish Sana, leaning her back against Rameh's, with Faour resting his head on her lap. She was wrapping his arm in Mariam's shawl. At first his half-closed eyes didn't register my presence. Then his lips moved. He managed a shadow of a smile. Sana was deeply concerned. She lifted her head and lamented: "He's bleeding, he's bleeding badly!"

"Wrap it tight. As soon as they stop shooting we'll take him to hospital," said Rameh. Then, rubbing it in, he grumbled: "You should have stayed in Venezuela, stupid."

Twenty-seven
(Faour's Journal: 1)

My arm is hurting. The throbbing needles come and go, but I can still write, albeit slowly, which is rather frustrating because I want the pen to leap forward, not limp behind. I declined my mother's plea to rest at home, because it would mean leaving the spring all alone in the valley doing as it pleases. Every time I step out of my tent I discover a new plant, hear a new bird, smell a new flower. There is a fresh breath of warmth in the air, as if there were a bakery near by. So here I am, sitting on a rocky plateau with my pad and pen. Before me a majestic pine tree, the biggest for miles around, spreads an enormous umbrella of shade. Perfect surroundings. But *why* am I here? Why did I leave the dreamland of Venezuela for the hell of the civil war? Everyone wants to know. So perhaps I should start my new writing career with that and see what Adam makes of it.

In order for me to remain in Venezuela I was stuck with my aunt's family. They were my guarantors with Immigration, they gave me the job and the shelter and – in their eyes – Sandra. I had no alternative but to play Sandra's game, cover for her when she went out to meet Ramon, pretend that we were together in long outings and late nights. I was the perfect Cyrano. Call me a coward, a doormat, a wimp, if you like, for I had been calling myself much worse, names best not put down on paper. But what would you have done if you'd been in my shoes?

To top it off there was the humiliation of Sandra preferring a tattooed drunk who smelt of cheap rum and stuck a stupid ring in his ear to me. Ramon was a traitor to Paulo and Pedro who had rescued him from the *ranchos* and given him a future. In gratitude he'd seduced their sister knowing full well they would never accept him into their family; they were too proud, too prejudiced, too set in their ways, too enmeshed in Caracas society to embrace a *mulato*. There was blood at the end for Ramon, blood for Sandra and very likely for me. Pedro and Paulo would hold me responsible. Not only had I let Sandra slip out of my grasp but I had become the accomplice in this liaison. They would treat her like a slut and Ramon like a dog and me like an ungrateful shit. It would cost them the price of a dinner party to have the three of us killed and buried and forgotten.

    I tried not to think about all that while I waited in bars and cafés for Sandra to come back from her rendezvous glowing with the dew of lovemaking. But I also spent many sleepless nights in a blind rage, haunted by the desire to kill Ramon. I imagined an infinite number of scenarios, trying to plan the perfect murder that would eliminate him and bring me closer to Sandra. The destiny that had brought me halfway around the world surely had this in mind. Perhaps Ramon would meet his end in a fatal accident leaving Sandra to me.

    But wouldn't Sandra be with him? Injured? Disfigured? Burned? No! I couldn't bear to see her with raw, puckered skin. Maybe partially injured, so I take care of her until she heals and becomes indebted to me for the rest of her life? Or the accident could happen when we are all together, the three of us, and I put my life on the line to save her. "You saved my life, Fifo, my hero." Etcetera.

    By now the Cuba Libre was bouncing me up and down. I conjured up accidents involving dozens of cars, trains, motorcycles, even plane crashes. But Ramon wouldn't die.

    Then I turned it around, it's me that's hurt. The shit has finally hit the fan, the scandalous liaison has been exposed and Ramon cast out of paradise and I am in a wheelchair – just for a while. Surely Sandra would take care of me?

    But this was a dangerous scenario; Ramon might sneak in at night and they'd elope and leave me crippled for life. Even if he's killed in the same accident I can't be sure she'd nurse me and sit by my bedside until I'm well. She might hook up with someone else and I'd be back to square one, except in a wheelchair.

    I tried another accident. I cut the brakes of his truck and it rolls off a cliff and we're all stone-washed by dirt and rocks and broken metal and I save Sandra from certain death just before the truck blows up in a ball of fire with Ramon still inside. But he's not inside; he's crawled out, battered and still breathing, a malevolent look in his eyes.

Finally I took a shortcut to accomplish my mission. I couldn't trust anyone, neither destiny nor the local hit-men who might betray me and steal my money. I would have to do it myself.

It's night. I have a handgun, one neat shot in the back of his skull – better still, right through his fucking earring. Now Sandra is bereaved and lonely and dependant on me. I take care of her. I join her broken heart to mine. I lead her into my soul where I've been raising a temple to worship her. She sees the light.

Until becoming embroiled in this mess, I'd never for one second thought of killing anyone. It shook me. Through the Cuba Libre fog I could see the gap between thought and action shrinking. I was scared – of the police, of Ramon and of my own reflection in the mirror.

So I dried up. Instead of drinking I read. I had to make my pain work for me, not against me. It was all I had left. I turned to philosophy. I read books that might explain to me the difference between love, lust, infatuation, soul-mating and platonic bonding. I took notes. I tried my hand at putting some thoughts of my own on paper. It seemed to me that Love was on a planet of its own. For in the other attachments the exit is less wrenching, the hurt not terminal. With Love, your existence shifts off its axis, changes its orbit. And once you're there the end is a meteorite crashing into you. Because you see your previous existence as a void. So you cling to your Love for dear life, compelled to fulfil your loved one's every desire.

I watched Ramon and Sandra, every day, every night. Hard as I tried I couldn't escape the painful conclusion that they were truly in love. They took the kind of risks only true lovers take. They schemed like innocent children oblivious to the damage they were causing. Devoid of malice, they walked all over me with a smile on their faces.

Enlightenment finally arrived on my last night in this web of deceit. I relived in my sleep a trip the three of us had made to a native celebration by the sea. It was a long drive and the place was dangerous; it catered mainly for blacks and *mulatos* like Ramon. When we arrived at a town called Higuerote, near Barlovento, I didn't want to leave the truck. I was scared. I looked down at the beach, at the swarming darkness, and couldn't tell which was dancing, the night or the people. Sandra insisted I join the party but she said to Ramon, if your people mug him, or kill him, we're through; he didn't escape the war in Lebanon to be killed at a salsa party. Okay, he said, I'll carry him on my shoulders if I have to. Sandra hit him for that. Finally they sat me down with a bunch of drummers. They gave me a little tabla and I joined in the rhythm. Boom badaboum. I poured my soul into the deafening beat. The beat became me, I started rocking and slapping my hands on the dry skin of the drum until I drifted into a trance. Boom, Boom badaboum . . .

. . . but hey, what's going on? I'm out of my body and into Ramon's, and it's me dancing with Sandra, me, Ramon, the muscles and the machismo and even my perky earring. The waves are falling asleep, the beach is swinging with a thousand Ramons, we're drinking straight from the bottle and we're buzzing like wasps, dancing and drinking and laughing and I'm smiling down at my besotted *enamorada* and I'm saying, do we have to take Fifo with us everywhere, and she's saying, he's our alibi, remember? And I'm thinking, does he imagine he can snatch you from me by narrowing his bedroom eyes and mooning around you all the time, stupid little twerp, he hasn't a clue, women aren't won by pity but by force, boom badaboum, and now the kissing and the fondling are demanding more, and we're rushing to the truck, leaving the drummer boy alone in his boom badaboum and we're madly making love . . .

I woke up wet with semen and sweat, Sandra's *body* still pulsing in my ribs. I'd been ecstatic with pleasure during the dream but now a wave of tears rose up inside me to drown me in shame. I felt as if I'd violated Sandra. Her body was not mine.

And then it hit me like thunder. Sandra would never be in love with me. Never.

The next day, Sandra told me she was eloping with Ramon. Instead of going to work I rode the Vespa to the airport. It was the first time I saw the *ranchos* in the daytime. Some very ugly realities can look deceivingly beautiful in the dark of the night. Isn't that what had happened to me?

Twenty-eight
(Faour's journal: 2)

Had I loved Sandra as desperately as Ramon did, I would have found the courage to fight for her. The family would have forced her to marry me and we would have lived unhappily ever after, because the heart always belongs to the lost love. But what had happened had happened. Luckily no one blamed me. Sandra had left a letter behind telling the truth and clearing me of any responsibility.

My mother could only lament the chance I'd lost for a sure and prosperous future. As for my father, a growing scorn. He said he'd taken in his stride the shame when I'd escaped the last bout of training because he never wanted me to go to the Castle in the first place, and that he'd paid my airfare to Caracas willingly enough so I'd make a man of myself. "And now look at you," he screamed in disgust, "coming back empty handed, disgraced, tricked by a light-headed woman. You should have seen through her, got her drunk, made her pregnant, not treated her with puerile chivalry." My answer to that savage vision was to slam the door and leave for the valley.

Yesterday I began Krishnamurti's *Urgency of Change*. He answers questions with questions, prompting me to seek my own answers, or be swept up into a vortex of soul searching, either way leaving the book of words for the book of life: *One may hold the hand of another and yet be miles away, wrapped in one's own thoughts and problems, one may be in a group and yet painfully alone. So one asks: can there be any kind of relationship with the tree, the flower, the human being, or with the skies and the lovely sunset, when the mind in its activities is isolating itself?*

I lotused in the shade of the ancient pine tree, surrounded by thousands of its progeny. Come flood or drought, they just keep sending out new shoots while staying put, like an army of monks in perpetual worship. When I meditate I feel as if I'm vanishing inside the trees. The birds hold a conference in my ribs, the breeze disperses me like pollen across the valley. If it weren't for the sporadic exchange of mortars I could almost reach Nirvana. But with the shelling Sandra makes a forceful entry into my mind. I become trapped with her ghost, her hands, her skin, her curves, her back, straight and melodious when she walked as if made of music, the scent of her hair and that orphan kiss she once planted on my lips. She won't go away until I come out of my skin and scream: it was all a big mistake . . ake . . ake the valley echoes.

The shadow play across the valley started humming. The eastern breeze was rising. I turned to check the pegs of my little tent and a flying newspaper splatted into my face. Free delivery of today's issue:

The fierce fighting in the centre and the southeastern outskirts of Beirut took a dramatic turn last night with firearms, knives, daggers, kitchen utensils and stones used at close range. If this is not the end of civilisation, what is?

Sure, newsmen still produce newspapers to make a living, but who in their right mind reads them? Is that how this rag slammed into my face – a disgusted reader throwing it out of a faraway car window and the wind delivering it to me? On the back page were spread the most recent shots from the battlefield: a grandfather showing the camera his bleeding grandson, behind him the fire eating up his home. Next, a militiaman in a dirty cotton singlet aiming his gun at a street corner, a few steps away a dead brother-in-arms, left foot missing a shoe. Next, a grand hotel being looted – mattresses, sheets, pillows flying down from balconies into a forest of raised arms and hungry car boots. Then a succession of snaps showing the gradual incineration of Beirut Yacht Club, water joining fire against the pretty vessels.

My arm throbbed painfully. My own little pain was hurting more than the huge wound of my country. Was I selfish? Deep down I could only feel my anger. If it weren't for the children I would have spat on the whole map of Lebanon. What do I care about the shoeless 'martyr', or a looted hotel or the incinerated yacht club? The only picture that hurt me was the dead child, that helpless piece of human life so callously sacrificed by a bunch of intoxicated looters. It was a gut reaction, like the day of the shooting at the spring when I was swept towards Mariam and the twins. I only realised I'd been shot when we landed inside the reservoir. Between hearing the first shots and discovering my injury I behaved without a grain of thought, blindly propelled to achieve that one particular task: get the children out of danger. Nothing to do with chivalry or courage.

I crumpled the newspaper and threw it inside the tent. I'd start the fire with it tonight. But now I was hungry. I didn't have a watch. I was learning to read the time following the sun and the receding shade and my rumbling stomach. I pricked up my ears, listening hard through the soughing of the pine trees. My father had stopped my mother visiting me: "You don't set foot down there, woman!" Then he'd grabbed Zahi and given him the ultimate threat: "And if *you* do, I'll send you away to boarding school!" That had put the fear of God into Zahi's heart. Luckily, the embargo did not include sending me my mother's cooking, the only part of home I craved. Had my granny been here, things would have been different. But my father had taken her to a home while I was away. I loathed him for that more than anything.

The grinding purr of Adam's Beetle announced my lunch. Adam, Yousra, Sana and the three children coming to picnic on my little rocky plateau. Fiesta in the valley with Mister Hemingway, as Yousra put it a few days ago, prodding me to write something to fit the phrase. But only Adam is reading this journal. Although his comments fall short of comparison with *The Old Man and the Sea*, he is encouraging.

Mariam jumped right into my arms. She said: "All this is your mother's cooking, we only brought the oranges." She was looking boyish with her summery haircut and pink dungarees. *Oranges, O sunny, juicy oranges of my lost homeland,* we all sang while the children held hands and whirled around. Yousra opened up the pails. The smell of olive oil, onions, tomato and garlic cooked with young aubergines made me eager to dive in, but before we could eat, Sana played sister-of-mercy with her first-aid kit. Adam helped me take off my sweater. Yousra kept the children from stuffing their noses into my stitched-up wound: "Go and play your own games, you little fiends, let the man ache in peace." What ache? Sana's touch had a soothing effect on me.

Ever since she'd wrapped Mariam's shawl around my arm in the reservoir and held me tight until we were able to leave, I'd been craving her presence. She'd come over twice so far. Each time my heart would beat faster the closer she came to me.

"Boy," Sana murmured, cleaning my wound with pure alcohol, "you are so lucky. It's messy but it'll heal like a vaccination."

"How do you know," I asked.

"I helped at the hospital in Beirut. I saw many shrapnel wounds."

Gently, meticulously, like a watchmaker, she stroked the cotton wool over and over the cut while blowing cool breaths to ease the burn.

"Ouch," I grumbled, pretending.

She stroked my back, "Sorry." Her smile made me long to kiss her.

Twenty-nine
(Faour's journal: 3)

Today was a bittersweet day: taking out the stitches from one wound, opening another. It began with my second visit to Kafleet's hospital, the same place Adam and Rameh had brought me to after the shooting at the spring. Rameh had held me tight on the back seat while Adam had driven as fast as an ambulance. I'd been in such a panic then, what with all the blood and pain and fear.

The scene at the emergency hall today was the same as two weeks ago. This coastal town's hospital – our nearest – was doing brisk business: Ambulances screeched in and out like at a pit stop of a racing track. Women in shock slapped their faces and tore their hair. Armed men soiled with blood rushed through the corridors wearing the faces of those who live by blood and die in it. The ambulances kept spewing them out, sometimes in pieces, dismembered, disembowelled. One was howling, holding his entrails while his mother wobbled behind him before fainting on the floor. The colour red was so omnipresent you didn't notice it until a sudden surge of white coats.

Adam was silent beside me as we waited. He hates Kafleet. On the way here today he had recounted the body dragging episode and shown me the place where it happened. He said it was still haunting him. He said that one more scene like that might make him change his mind about staying. But he wasn't telling Yousra for she was already eager to pack. Why stay when your sister in Australia can get you out? Few people in Wahdeh have any empathy with this notion of reopening the olive press even if it would bring prosperity to the village. Sure, they remember Adam's father and the good times of the olive press, but they can't see revival as Adam sees it. In their minds, once you go to college you are no longer meant for the soil. Something must be wrong with an educated person who has a prosperous sister in

Australia and the opportunity to leave but who still hangs around dreaming of olive oil and tinkers and toil. It didn't add up. Moreover, Adam doesn't lounge around the square playing backgammon and shuffling cards. He doesn't even hunt any more, he's given away his father's rifle, the only *valuable* piece in the house, they say. Maybe he is clinging to Wahdeh's fresh air and pine climate because he had asthma when he was a child? Maybe he couldn't survive Beirut's pollution or Sydney's damp?

But the truth is much more pragmatic. Adam has it all worked out. With his savings he'll buy modern machinery, restore the dilapidated building and carry on from where his father left off. No overheads, no debts and no office hours to tie him down. He hopes that once the war is over and life back to normal his mother might be tempted to come back, even Hawwa and her family – why not? Olive oil is in demand, he argues. We'll modernise and export. Why the Spanish and Italian and Greek olive oil, but not ours?

I looked at him as we waited. His father had died before I was born, but people say Adam is the spitting image of him. Not only his thick moustache and his curly, unkempt hair and his slow tread as though the floor will crack open if he hastens his steps, but also his cogent speech and long silences. *Speech is at best an honest lie*, Naimi said in *Mirdad*. Has Adam patterned his demeanour on that? He has a gift for condensing and cutting a long story short. Yousra is no chatterbox either. They both used to help me with my maths, but while Yousra taught in the traditional way, Adam brought a handful of beans from the kitchen. He knew that abstraction blurred my reasoning. With the beans he made me *see* the movement of figures, turning my homework into fun, sometimes even finishing with a joke: Tomorrow when you eat *fassoulia* remember how numbers change and combine and become useful. Just try not to break wind in the classroom.

As a child I looked up to Adam, confided to him things I couldn't say to my father. And now I'm writing about him, even knowing that he'll soon be reading this.

It was our turn. Adam beckoned me to follow him into the surgery. He smiled again as he helped me out of my shirt. "We'll both cry like babies if you hurt him," he said to the medic, "he's our village poet." The medic chuckled: "Poets like a bit of pain, they'll hunt for it if need be." But snipping out the stitches was nothing compared to sewing them in without anaesthetic.

On the drive back I found the courage to open up about what had been gnawing at my sleep lately. It wasn't easy. It was a delicate matter and I couldn't put it as crudely as it lurked in my mind.

"Adam, can I ask you a personal question?"

Adam nodded, waiting for me to speak.

"You know when you and Yousra met – I mean when two people meet and they feel some attraction, I mean, what's the next step?"

Adam slowed his nodding. He took ten seconds to respond. "Next," he said, "they meet again and see how things evolve. There are no set rules that I know of."

"Well, if, say, you wanted to know if the other is experiencing the same feelings, what do you do?"

"Nothing in particular. It's not like driving a car where you step on the clutch and you change gear. It's a thousand things."

"I know, but how did you know for sure that you were in love with Yousra?"

Adam smiled like someone watching a movie alone in the dark. "Are you thinking of a particular person and not able to get her out of your system no matter how many times you toss in your sleep?"

"Yes."

"And you want to find out if she's losing sleep over you as well?"

"Yes."

"Now, are you going to honour me with the identity of this lucky person?"

Suddenly I wasn't as ready as I thought. Sana's name stuck to my tongue. "You know when I was injured? No, even before the shooting started. When I was chatting with Sana, remember? I felt as if I was speaking to Sandra. But the better Sandra, the ideal Sandra. Then when I jumped into the reservoir with Rameh and the children and she saw I was injured, I mean, I felt she was sharing my pain. It was something like . . ."

"Like a married woman," Adam interrupted. "Like Nimer body-dragging you through the streets of Wahdeh. Like your father getting wind of this, and then the whole village. Listen, Faour. Sandra wasn't for you even if she hadn't been with Ramon, and Sana is a mother, at least ten years your senior and trapped with a killer husband. I understand – anyone with eyes in their skull would be attracted to Sana. I, for one, love to see her around. I like to leave Mariam in her care. She's such a good person in every way that no one can know her without feeling attraction. But then what?"

"Then what? What if you slept covered by her shadow and when you woke up you felt her scent in your lungs? When she was cleaning my wound the other day I almost lost it. Almost kissed her."

"Your bouts of poetry are not helping us here, my friend. Haven't you been reading *Siddhartha*? Siddhartha learned three precious things: to think, to wait and to fast. The first two are obvious exercises of self-control. But fasting is not necessarily abstaining from food. It can also be abstaining from desire."

"Adam, I think about all this. I do. Last night I jumped out of my tent screaming. I had a nightmare. I was attacking Nimer with an axe. It was like chopping a gum tree. Instead of blood there was this milky liquid foaming all over me."

Adam sighed. Then, "I don't know what to say, but it looks like a destructive pattern with you, falling for other people's women."

"Do you really believe Sana loves Nimer like Sandra loved Ramon?"

"No, but she's still with him. His wife."

"His hostage, Adam, please."

"I know, but whatever you do, make sure to stay away from Nimer's nose."

We reached Wahdeh just after midday. Sana opened the door of Adam's house to us. I guess she thought it was one of the children at the door, so she was surprised to see me. She blushed and tried uselessly to hide a purple bruise under one eye. But when she saw how my face tightened and my eyes narrowed in concern she began to invent an accident, something stupid about a window shutter. She was a terrible liar.

I was beside myself. Another Faour surged from the rubble of Caracas: the man I wasn't when Sandra made me dance to her tune, when Ramon took me for a spineless wimp, when my father refused to believe there were balls in my groin. I took Sana in my arms: "*He* did that to you? That son of a whore!"

Luckily the children were still playing outside. Sana was so embarrassed she had buried her head in her hands, so her elbows were now resting on my chest. I wouldn't, couldn't let her go, despite the awkward embrace that was digging into my ribs. It wasn't how I had dreamt of holding her but I wasn't letting go.

Adam grabbed my good arm and propelled me firmly to the chaise Morris. "Take it easy," he said, visibly shaken.

"*Easy?*" I yelled. "No man has hit his wife in Wahdeh for as long as I can remember. Your uncle would have broken Nimer's face with an old shoe. This is happening right on your doorstep, son of Awad, what are you going to do about it?"

"What *can* I do, Faour? Put yourself in my shoes!"

"I'd shoot the bastard!"

"No!" Sana cried. "He saved my life!"

"He saved your life to enslave you and beat you up!"

"He put his own life on the line for me. How many people would do that? He sneaked me out during the night. They followed us, shot at us, but he got us through. It was dreadful. I owe him. He brought me back to my boys. I don't want him harmed."

"Okay, but why this?" Adam pointed at Sana's face.

She averted her eyes and moved closer to Yousra, as to another devotee of an occult sect. Were the two women sharing a secret? A woman's secret?

With all the authority of a priestess, Yousra spoke at last: "Stop this at once. Please don't push it any further. Sana just wants to be left in peace with her family. She can manage on her own. She doesn't need help. More importantly, she doesn't need trouble. Okay with you, Faour?"

Yousra didn't wait for my answer to what wasn't a question anyway. She walked me to the door with her hand on my shoulder: "Now call the children for lunch, will you?"

The image of Nimer roughing up Sana couldn't be washed away with a glass of arak. It hung over the dinner table and must have been mirrored in the gloom of my face. Neither the children's buzz nor the chit-chat conducted by Yousra could sedate my fury. I was sure that Nimer had caused Sana's bruise. And I resented Yousra's abrupt dismissal of the matter. I felt strongly that I had a right to know. I was staring at my food as if I could make it vanish from the plate. Sana passed me the *fattoush* bowl. I passed it on to Adam listlessly.

Then, accidentally, Sana's foot brushed against the hem of my trousers, like a tiny moth. I looked up at her. She blushed. I kicked my moccasins off and sprawled my feet under the table. She noticed me slouching in my seat and failed to hide the smile in her eyes. I thought everyone was now hearing my heart beat. My feet became receivers, waiting. When nothing happened I stopped eating again and began sulking. My whole spirit surfaced on my brow. Then her toes moved hesitantly over mine with the gentleness of an archaeologist brushing the sand off a fragile find. Was a secret love song being played under the table? Or was she merely smoothing my ruffled feathers after the earlier scene? Either way, I was happy. My heart began to sing. My anger dissipated. I started eating. Adam smiled at my transformation. He lifted his drink and talked of olives and olive oil – how we'd lost half of this year's harvest but the trees had been so generous that they'd produced more than the whole crop of the previous year. The land's mysterious power had shown clemency one more time, Adam said, sounding like a farmer from antiquity.

After lunch Sana hastened to the kitchen to help Yousra with the dishes, but her body language had changed, her ballerina sway becoming an earthy echo of the diffident message she'd delivered under the table.

My whole body was basking in a healing tonic. The arak I had sipped in slow burns was now spreading a cool euphoria through my limbs. I wanted to be alone. I thanked the women for lunch and left Adam with the children and a peanut-aided lesson in arithmetic. I sang all the way down to the valley. The crack Sandra had left in my soul was finally mending.

Thirty
(Faour's journal: 4)

At dusk I started writing to Sana. I lit my kerosene lamp and sat inside the tent trying to isolate myself from the shelling. I made several beginnings and stopped. Not because I was at a loss for words; on the contrary – there were so many that I was having a problem lining them up. Then I closed my eyes and breathed deeply. She's here, talk to her, just talk.

Dear Sana [I wrote in Spanish], *Forgive me for losing my cool but I'm glad I did. It made you send the message of your heart in the sweetest mail system ever. I want you to know that just as you're inspiring music in my words, you're also bringing life back to my life. I was lost before your golden moths honoured my feet. But please don't worry, I'll never do anything to cause you trouble. Now that we're on the same wavelength I will learn to Wait for you, Think about you and Fast my desire to be with you. It will be a great trial. Please remember that my heart beats just for you. If yours is doing the same, please do not miss any opportunity to meet me. Or shall I get injured again so that you have to tend my wounds?*

Heavy footsteps approached. A shadow loomed over my tent. "Are you alone?" said a large familiar voice.

"Yes."

"Turn the light off. You're endangering yourself." Rameh's head peered into the tent.

"Are you on patrol, bailiff?"

"It's looking bad, Faour. Worse than ever. Why don't you pack up and come with me?"

"What could happen here that wouldn't happen there, Rameh? They're shooting at random except when they're sober enough to aim at the Castle, right?"

"Yés, but if you're injured here no one will know. You'll bleed to death this time."

"He who has life shall not perish by strife."

"Use your brain before you're slain. Take your pick, Mister Philosopher. Goodnight."

"Goodnight, Rameh."

It was impossible to follow Rameh's advice and continue writing at the same time. I tried to hide the light by arching the foam mattress over my head but I almost tipped the kerosene lamp over. It was awkward and frustrating but I battled on as if pinioned inside the debris of an earthquake.

BOOMM!

The rocky platform trembled. The gush of air caused by the explosion struck the tent like a wave. I heard a harsh crack. Shocked, I crawled out of my tent.

The ancient pine tree had taken the hit. It was split right down the middle. Still standing, yes, but its mystery was gone. Under the whipping sparkle of the moon it looked humiliated. What had seemed invincible and lofty for centuries had finally fallen under the axe of war. I took in the degradation helplessly. There was nothing I could do. History was in labour and I was inside its belly.

The exchange of heavy artillery was mounting. It was becoming faster than my pulse, my ears were about to burst. Notebook in hand I hurried up the hill towards Wahdeh. Bad move. Not only was I wearing a white sweater but I had left the lamp lit in the tent, thus giving the bastards two markers. The night sky was flashing with fires. Dark red flames were rising from hill tops and the valley was streaked with rockets and bullets. Rameh's goat was cascading down the hill, her heavy dugs swinging and splashing drops of milk. Wahdeh's lights were off. On the northern hill the Castle was coughing fire. I tried to forget Rameh's words: If you're injured here no one will know. I made myself slow down to a steady walk as if going to play cards on a cool spring night. I even looked up and winked at the galaxy. A sensual Arabian crescent was out and a harem of stars bellydanced above the cliff. Whether I crawled or flew made no difference. In that blind pandemonium the only certainties were my eyes burning to see Sana, her face drawing me on. You die when your time comes, not a second earlier nor a second later. It's all been written. He who brought me to this moment when others were hiding like moles either wanted me to reach my destination or not.

The open entrance to my apartment functioned as a trench, protected by the veranda upstairs, had become a bomb shelter for my family, Adam's family and Nimer's. Everyone was huddled in the corner except Nimer. When my mother saw me, she started slapping her face with both hands as if at my funeral, perhaps mourning my dead mind. My father nodded repeatedly, no doubt for the same reason. But Mariam jumped from her mother's lap into my arms, sweet and loving as always. Even the twins, shielded in Sana's embrace, seemed happy to see me. Nader asked the forbidden question, "Did you see anybody dead on your way?" Sana's hand over his mouth, shut him up. Her eyes were reddened. She squeezed them tight in a complex message of exhaustion, exasperation with my folly, and relief. Adam, who didn't smoke, was glued to the wall puffing at a cigarette. His failure to greet me meant either that he was in another world or else stunned by my apparition. Yousra was absorbed by the transistor pressed to her ear. Zahi and Nour slept on, oblivious, covered with a table cloth.

A kerosene lantern on the floor was casting a beam on the inside of the apartment. It was the first time I had seen my door open since I had come back from Venezuela. I looked inside. It was resplendent with sumptuous furniture and ornaments, the likes of which had never before been seen in Wahdeh. An ornate dining set with eight chairs and a dresser filled the righthand side of the living area. On the left, a burgundy velvet Louis XVI style suite encircled a shiny black piano. Both walls were adorned with paintings, ten at least, all featuring lakes. The whole scene made me dizzy, it was so absurd: a nothing apartment in a nowhere village harbouring the furniture of a palace.

Sana continued to avoid eye contact with me. Her boys eventually fell asleep on her lap, frowning like peevish old men. She bent over them, abstractedly stroking their hair. The absence of her smile dimmed my spirits. Was she embarrassed because my parents were there? Or was she worried that any look between us might betray her feelings? I longed to snatch her out of this place and take her far away. I yearned for that moment when the pine tree cast its shade on my tent and my head leaned on her shoulder while she cleaned my wound. Instead I had to watch my father slouched on a narrow mattress like a beached walrus, mouth wide open, snoring.

I tried to imagine the Hakim hiding like this. No way. He would die again and again rather than hide. Even my grandmother would have dragged her bowed legs out and hit at the face of darkness with her stick. During the First World War she'd been scarcely older than I was now but already a widow, a mother of two and pregnant again. The night the Ottomans killed her husband, she had had a dream: "A knight on a white horse came to me in my sleep, Faour, and said: 'Take your children to the coast before sunrise; Wahdeh is going to be bombed.' I was nine months pregnant with your father and had two lovely little girls, three and four years old. Famine had made us too weak to travel, but I had no choice. As I was scurrying through a forest with them I heard the first bombs falling on Wahdeh. It was autumn and nothing edible was left in the soil. I was unaware that the girls were stuffing poisonous mushrooms into their mouths until I heard their groans behind me. Oh, son, don't ever ask a mother to bury her children. Somewhere, I have no idea where, I made a hole in the ground and shoved earth over them. After that I wandered, disoriented in my grief. I was on my feet for three days and three nights, unwilling to bend my body for fear of losing the child inside me. Then I saw the sea, and at that moment my waters broke. There was a fisherman hauling his net. I cried out. He came and took me on his boat to his family near by. But your father's stubborn head had already protruded and he was wailing before we reached land." From that day on she'd devoted her life to him and then to us. "They don't make women like her any more," I'd heard people say all my life.

I was thirsty. I peeled myself away from the wall and my memories, and walked over to the pitcher on the dining-room table.

"Faour, come on in." Nimer's voice creaked like a rusty gate. Framed in the kitchen doorway he sat, eating kibbeh nayeh and raw onions by the light of a candle.

I walked towards him, wishing I had a terminator that would reduce him to a traceless absence. He took a gulp from a long glass of arak. "I'm almost done, take a seat, pour yourself a drop." He swallowed and then continued, "Don't worry about your apartment, my boy. We'll leave it soon. And we'll leave all this for you. A present. I can buy the whole of Wahdeh if I want, but what for? I'm taking my family abroad. Somewhere nice, you understand?"

Nimer gulped his last swig and dropped the plate in the sink. He'd put on so much fat, his waist was one with his chest. He was wearing a track suit, looking more like a coach between games than a warlord. He was obviously feeling guilty about squatting in my house. I wanted him to feel guiltier. I wanted him to have a stroke. I wanted the arak and the raw meat to give him instant, lethal food poisoning. I wanted him to become extinct. But all I could do was stare at him with empty eyes. Meanwhile. the walls around us were quivering with the impact of falling shells. The pounding seemed to come from the earth's belly, yet Nimer was quiet, cool. Been there, done that and got Sana for a trophy. He took my scornful silence for respect and reached for a large jar on the top shelf. "Do you like souvenirs?"

I shrugged.

"Souvenirs!" he exclaimed, covering the top and bottom of the jar with both hands as if protecting a precious commodity: "These are mementos, my dear Faour, for our children and their children, preserved so future generations will know how well we fought. There are seventy-six in here. What year is this? Ha ha, same number." His voice became guttural and his eyes glazed with pride.

I was still in my own inner trench, refusing to lend him more than my physical presence. So it took me a while to realise what the jar contained. Not jam or pickles, but ears. Human ears.

Thirty-one
(Faour's journal: 5)

Hundreds of trees had been hit by the shelling, especially in the valley. Adam and I began chopping them for wood. It was practical: clearing the valley and keeping us busy. We could have done with an extra axe, and a donkey to carry the loads uphill, but we started with what we had. On our first day, Adam and I stood in wonder before the split pine tree. "Don't touch it," Adam said. "It won't die. As long as its trunk is holding it'll live."

"But it's bleeding, look!" I pointed at the sap, sparkling and dripping like tears all over the raw gash of its trunk.

"Trust me. This tree has roots all the way to the centre of the earth."

"It's split right down the middle, for God's sake!"

"We're not touching it unless it starts to decay. Stop staring at it like that. Let's go."

Despite his sensitivity to nature, Adam seemed detached about the mutilated pine. Whereas I could hear it pleading – Finish me off! Take me to the fire! – he was dismissive, insistent that it wouldn't die. I wanted to think like him, but I grieved at the memory of the majestic green umbrella when it was whole, home to the birds and squirrels and cicadas and my attempts at reaching Nirvana.

The steep slopes entailed measured journeys, treading slowly on red dirt and white rocks slippery from the morning dew. We carried the loads tied on our backs, stopping to rest for no more than a few seconds. We could do it twice a day at best, singing *Mijana* on the way down and humming *Ataba* on the way up. At the finish line, Sana and Yousra met us with a cool drink and helped us unload. I made it a habit to approach Sana as soon as we entered Adam's front yard. The scratchy sack became feather-light the minute Sana put her arms around me to loosen the knot. I closed my eyes and prayed that she would get her fingers stuck and we would stay tangled and tangoing for ever. I inhaled deeply the aroma of her jasmine perfume, breathing a quiet "thank you" that could well sound like "love you." During those precious moments the strenuous chore seemed sweet. Without Sana I would have found any excuse to chuck it in, even if it meant upsetting Adam, my only friend.

Naturally the children wanted to come with us, demanding their own tools and escalating their desire to help into tantrums. The more we ignored them the more they stamped the ground with their angry little feet against all the wicked grown-ups of the world. Mariam further fuelled the demonstration with tears. Finally Adam opted for his favourite Middle Way. He sat the children together on the ground and told them, "There are all kinds of creepy crawlies down there, spiders and snakes and lizards. They're not just ugly but poisonous too. But since you're so determined, Faour and I will take you with us one at a time. That way we can look after you. And you'll have a story to tell the others when you come back. Now choose who goes first and let us know. We'll be over there, splitting logs."

Bedlam. The twins went for each other's throats. Me! No, me! No, me! Mariam was stunned by the sudden violence of her friends. She walked backwards to her mother and watched warily. I'm not sure Adam intended this to happen, but he wasn't displeased by the outcome. He tapped my shoulder and quietly led me away.

Not much later, Samer and Nader approached, looking rather subdued. They even offered to help us. They'd obviously received some tough mama talk, so we didn't add to their misery. We just gave them a load of wood to shift from the front yard, while we carried on splitting the logs.

By lunchtime the boys still showed signs of muffled discontent, but Mariam was changed. Transformed into an aproned hostess, she laid a smart table all by herself. I imagined Sana and Yousra working on Mariam, Sana's flowing cottony voice: "Forestry is boring, leave it to the boys. Wood cutting is no fun at all. And you'd get splinters in your hands. We'd have to fish them out with tweezers and that hurts like hell. But house-keeping is a serious art, too difficult for boys." Sana employed the sweetest talk with Mariam. She probably longed for a daughter like her.

At the table, I began to sense something strange, a fizzy hush in the air. Sana and Yousra seemed oddly distant from us. They exchanged swift glances, ventriloquing things we obviously weren't meant to hear. Something disconcerting was going on. I remembered Granny and Mother behaving in this manner, like spies going undercover all of a sudden. It was usually something they were hiding from my father. But he'd always sense it. "Women," he'd declare, "are the oldest mafia on earth!" Throughout lunch, I puzzled over what the mafiosi were hiding. At one stage I feared they were discussing my flirting with Sana. Then I wasn't so sure. It was frustrating, like shooting at black objects in the dark.

That night, back in my hideout, I was reading *Siddhartha* again. It didn't help me much. I was getting impatient with the theme of Failure turned into Triumph: Go ahead, fall on your face, then look in the mirror, your bloody nose is a sign of victory! Sod that. I preferred Kamala. A woman who loves your eyes and gives you her little red mouth and teaches you the art of love. Anyway, who says that every Via Dolorosa leads to Paradise? Besides, I am living through a war, a time of chaos. I don't even know if I'll be here next winter to burn the wood I've been cutting all day. I can't think about tomorrow without fearing that it may never come. Will Wahdeh be invaded? Will Nimer take Sana away? Now, he was gone again. What if he shows up tomorrow with plane tickets to God knows where? He's keeping her and the whole village on ice about his movements. He takes off any time, day or night, sometimes for a couple of hours, then for a whole week, comes back loaded with electronic gadgets, kitchenware, sweets for Wahdeh's children. He's a will o' the wisp, and a dangerous one. My blood boils with anger and love, the lethal mix of tragedies.

Midnight. I crawled out of my tent to have a smoke. The moon was rising from behind the cliff, like a wafer dipped in blood atop a broken chalice. The starry sky was buzzing with uncertainties. The moon was still climbing, spreading a misty glow over the valley. I was a mere molecule lost in an awesome galaxy. It was scary. Never before had I experienced fear of the night. I'd slept outside every summer and spent hours contemplating heaven's trillion twinkles. Yet now the sky above wasn't lifting my spirit towards it but staring mockingly down at me.

I remembered the woman who one day had burst into the village square shouting that she was cured. She had walked on crutches most of her life. I was eight. People said she had done it with faith alone, no doctor had touched her. Faith can move mountains, she shrilled, and danced with joy until she collapsed and kissed the ground in gratitude. Men, women and children wept at the sight of her. They fell on their knees, praising the Almighty, marvelling at the power of faith.

But what is faith? Is it Your manifestation of supremacy beyond man's comprehension? Or just concentrated human determination becoming miraculous? Or is it a bridge between us and You and without it we are doomed to spin around in riddles for ever? Faith is powerful, I know, but with what shall I measure it? How do I build it up to the level of unshakable certainty?

Hear me out, God! Are You there? Are You watching over me? Or are You busy elsewhere? If this shooting star is a sign, then I have a personal request: please put Nimer's file in the ASAP tray and hoover him down into hell. Extend his present absence eternally. Snuff him off the face of this planet. After all, despite my doubts and silly insubordination, I am good and I am in love.

I was absorbed in my cosmic communication, my arms crucified against the night and my eyes swimming far away searching for answers, when I felt a feather-light touch on my shoulder . . .

. . . O merciful spirit with a thousand names! You have heard my plea!

"Sana!"

"*Habibi!*"

She threw her arms around me, her little red mouth melted on mine. The sky came down to greet us and, like sycamore wings, the stars floated around us as we rose ecstatically into the unity of His galaxy.

Thirty-two

Like Faour, I only discovered later what the women's conspiracy had been: a plan to have the boys sleep over at our house, freeing Sana to go to Faour at last. What intrigued me was the way such a delicate plot came about. Not that I agreed with Abu Faour about the universal Cosa Nostra of women, but I'd noticed signs of that special intimacy between women since I was a child, as on that snowy day when I discovered Amti's secret visits to Sitti. They seem to exchange a secret language, not always audible. 'Ventriloquing' Faour called it, and I wished he'd elaborated a bit more. I was enjoying Faour's journal and was hoping he'd keep on telling the story. But Faour's dip into the magic pond of love took the pen out of his hand.

"Not entirely," he said, as I handed him back his notebook. "I want to write poetry now: hymns of praise to the goddess of my heart."

"Great, as long as you don't go serenading all over the place."

I was both happy and fearful for Faour and Sana. A new-born love is as blind as a new-born child, and as fragile as a new moon on a stormy night. Their world was a stark contrast to life in the rest of Wahdeh: fuel shortages, massive electricity cuts, living on water hand carried from the spring. Our reservoir had not been fixed. Whatever cement we had was rationed to repair damage to houses caused by the shelling. We'd gone back a hundred years in time. "Except that a century ago," Yousra said bitterly, "the people of Wahdeh were united."

It was true. Panic and insecurity and distrust were dissipating the serenity we'd taken for granted before this war began. We longed for the times when Rameh could stand on the mill house roof calling us together to help someone. Such a call would fall on deaf ears today. People were leaving: some overseas, others drifting around the land looking for work and relative security. The other day, while Mariam was playing out with the twins, Yousra and I remembered the time she'd stumbled and fallen on her chin and her teeth had cut through her tongue. She was two years old. Wahdeh's men, women, and children gathered outside the Hakim's practice, concerned, tearful at the prospect of such a bright little girl having her speech impaired. They didn't budge until the Hakim stepped out and told them she'd be all right. This type of solidarity had now been crushed by the magnitude of events. "No one would worry about the wounded tongue of a little girl any more," Yousra said.

"I guess not."

The only reality now was self-preservation. Our community had been sliced into small units, each busy with its own fate. Our unit was waiting for word from Hawwa; the broken record of to-leave-or-not-to-leave was still scratching away, albeit quietly, through inner monologues and dreams and nightmares.

Finally Hawwa's letter arrived: our application would be processed as soon as we reached Cyprus. Our chance of getting the visas under the family reunion programme was high. "I can't think your application would be delayed for more than a month. Anyway once you're in Cyprus we can follow things up by phone. Just get there as fast as you can." She also mentioned

Mother. "Drag her onto the boat whether she likes it or not. Once she's safely here she can sue us for saving her life."

My sister had no idea what was at stake if we were to leave in haste. But we spent sleepless nights discussing possible and, at times, impossible solutions. Yousra was fed up. She wanted just to grab a few pieces of clothes and leave. She wanted our daughter to grow up in a safe environment, away from the chaos and violence. "All this may be divinely beautiful," she said after a sleepless night of rocket exchange, gesturing towards the orchards, the cliff and the sky above us, "but being here isn't paradise any more. No sign of the schools ever re-opening. Our savings running low. Our chores becoming more and more toilsome. The future has no room under our roof; we can barely cope with the present. Are you with me?"

"Of course. But say we were to leave tomorrow. We pack the light and the precious, as they say, and we hand the key to Amti Wardieh. Then we ask Rameh to mind the orchards. Fine. But what about passports? We need to be in Beirut for at least four weeks to get them. And nothing is guaranteed. Then we have to convince my mother. Beirut is not Wahdeh, you know, if you leave your property for one day you can kiss it goodbye. Let's assume Mother is convinced; we still have to sell her apartment. And selling in times of war . . . "

Yousra stormed out of the kitchen. I followed her into the bedroom. She tore her headscarf off and started yanking the brush through her hair, as if intending to flee today, her face screwed up with anger. Then she said, grinding her words, "Thousands of people are leaving the country every day. They're no better or worse off than us. In fact, many have no one on the other side to help them. They manage, they find help. What matters is getting out. We're lucky to have Hawwa in Australia."

"I know. But we don't have to rush off in a blind flight – some people aren't leaving at all. Some people still believe in this country. They could go if they chose, but they stick around, they hack it. Remember when you were offered the place in that summer school in Paris? You didn't go; you wouldn't leave your sick mother on her deathbed."

"Staying by her deathbed wasn't going to destroy me and my family. Adam, I have a bad feeling about waiting. I want out now."

"Take it easy, Yousra. We've both had a bad night. Let me finish fixing breakfast."

"Just coffee for me."

Yousra was never good at friction in the morning. It was a mistake on my part to contradict her at this hour. Fortunately her flare-ups didn't last.

I turned the gas on, filled the kettle with water, added a cardamom pod and stirred in four spoonfuls of black coffee. Within seconds the aroma began to kick my sleep-starved brain. I'd never been quick at making decisions. I'd grown up with the wisdom of counting to ten. My slow nature helped, though sometimes my pondered judgments were as regrettable as the hasty ones. However, leaving Wahdeh was my worst ever dilemma. Until now I'd been dwelling within my own world. My feet were firm on my own ground. It was a sheltered, simple life, with few surprises. It was my choice and my joy and I wouldn't change it for the world. Now, all I'd dreamt of, saved for and struggled to reach, had to be put aside, possibly for ever. I was standing in the kitchen waiting for the coffee to boil but the dynamics of war were sliding the carpet from under my feet. If I walked away now I'd leave my spirit behind. I'd become an empty shell, an addict suffering a slow cold turkey for the rest of my days. I would no longer be Adam Awad. Everything that made me what I am. Everything related to my past and to the future that had walked before me like my shadow until today. All gone. I just couldn't see myself working at the cash register of my sister's supermarket. Even if, in a few years, I could save enough to buy a piece of land, plant hundreds of olive trees and build a olive press Downunder. My imagination was so tightly linked to my past, I just couldn't fathom a life outside Wahdeh. I'd spent months since our futile crossing to Nahrieh creating scenarios for peacemakers who could *succeed* in bringing peace to our country. I suppose I needed to feel less foolish, less alone, so I went on inventing a new breed of crusaders and followed them through their lobbying, lecturing, pleading, and crying at the feet of warlords and warmongers. There were moments while I was cutting wood when in my head a limitless line of people held hands and beat a dabkeh of national unity along the entire coast. Then the naked blade of reality would fall on the log, axing my fantasy of a new salvation.

Yousra's morning mood improved with every sip of coffee. Her tenderness wafted like little breezes on a hot day. Not only in words, but in touch and gaze. "Am I too hard on you, Adam? I don't want to be. I'm sorry. I miss our harmony, the flow of everyday life, the intimacy of an evening together. I can't even remember when was the last time we made love."

"Long time," I said.

One heartfelt hug, a muffled sob and a smiling tear, and a second wind filled our lungs.

"By the way," Yousra sniffled, returning to the dailiness of life, "haven't you noticed something different lately?"

"Like?"

"Like Mariam not snuggling up with us in the morning any more. She's still sulking about the valley, you know. Why don't you take her just once?"

"Okay. Get her ready. But do we need more firewood? Pretty hefty stuff to cart all the way to Australia."

"Build a raft with it. There'll be no other transport left by the time you make up your mind."

I saw the sun's first flickering rays as we laughed.

"Baba?" Mariam's voice surprised us. She was up and ready, all kitted out in her tough gear for the valley, even carrying a light hatchet that had been hanging in the olive press for donkey's years.

"So you want to be a woodcutter now?"

"No, I just want to give you a hand. I'm not afraid of snakes."

"Why don't you check out the hens while Mama and I finish our coffee, then we'll go."

"We'll have to sneak out, to avoid Samer and Nader."

"Right. Feed the chooks and then slip through the back yard. I'll catch up with you."

The conspiracy pleased her. She ran through the living room, opened the back door and called the hens just as I did: "Chook, chook, chook..."

"So, you had it all planned," I said to Yousra.

"Last night I promised to talk to you. She slept with her clothes on."

I caught up with Mariam when she was standing on a rock overlooking Faour's tent. Her hatchet on the ground, her hands cupping her mouth, "Ooo Fa... our!" she called, a proper mountain call. She looked older than five. She looked seven, same age I was when I started helping at the olive press. I could feel back in my limbs the fretting eagerness to become a productive bee in the common hive. And what a great feeling that was. It dug deep into my primal sense of belonging to the soil of Wahdeh. Seeing Mariam in her natural habitat, on top of a rock overlooking the valley, quickened my heartbeats. All tiny and girly, yet fed by the same roots. I thought, she belongs here. She shouldn't be shipped off to a foreign land.

Faour answered back in kind. He was deep down in the valley and his voice carried a happy timbre.

Mariam was thrilled at the success of her mission. She lifted the hatchet and laid it across her shoulders, looping her arms around it. Her hair, held back with a bandana, made the fringe stick out over her eyes like the visor of a baseball cap. She walked ahead of me, positioning her feet sideways on the steep slopes, watching each step. Yet she was as agile as a rabbit. She looked so happy, but was she? Not long ago I could read her like a book. But lately I'd been detecting a fleeting sorrow flit across her face, and her eyes would dim, quite unlike her reactions to petty disappointments. Sure, she still played and looked for games. But she was also with us, a part of us. She heard what we said and she felt the tension of what we were going through. Now that the cycle of our normal life had been broken, Yousra and I disagreed a lot, we snapped at each other, our moods swung. And instead of finding refuge in each other's arms, we slept back to back more often than not. Where would all this lead? It weighed on my heart to think of Mariam bottling up her feelings like the rest of us. I wanted her to be in another zone altogether, removed from all the real and imagined fears of our present.

Then she tilted her head in a reflective way that told me Question Time was about to begin.

"Baba, why do the trees fall?"

"They get hit by rockets, you know that."
"Do they hurt?"
"Sure."
"And they die forever?"
"Well, yes. But even a dead tree is useful."
"Not like dead people."
"Dead people part with their souls. They're buried or cremated, but their souls live forever. With trees I'm not so sure."
"Where is my soul now?"
"Inside you."
"Where?"
"Everywhere. It's like fuel in a car, you don't see it, but it's there."
"I don't want to die, Baba. I want to go to Australia. Mama said people don't die in Australia."
"What else did she say?"
"She said everyone should go to Australia because it's big and it doesn't have many people."

I had no idea that Yousra was promoting Australia as the Promised Land. "Am I going too?" I teased Mariam.

"Don't be silly! Of course you are!"

Thirty-three

A big surprise greeted us when we came back from the woods. As I stepped into the living room, the scent of rose-water, medicinal strength, made my stomach leap to my throat. Her suitcase was splashed on the floor. Her scarfless head revealed more grey hair than I remembered. Her face was that of a survivor after the trial of a lifetime. Yousra was standing behind her, rubbing her shoulders. It was simply unbelievable. Nejmeh Awad was back home. "Only when I'm in a coffin, to be with your father, not a day before, shall I come back to Wahdeh." That had been her vow after my father's death. Living in the village without 'the crown of her head' had been impossible. And I wouldn't go with her to Beirut, not even in chains I wouldn't. The years rolled back in my memory like a reel of film gone off its tracks. I didn't know what to think, but I was feeling as if a huge circle of time had just closed up. Before I could utter a word, Mariam ran to her Teta.

"Bury me! My sweet, sweet darling! You've grown up sooo..." During their intense embrace, Yousra whispered to me: "The apartment was hit. Badly."

I closed my eyes, not wanting to imagine what had happened. "We need some coffee," was all I could say.

Yousra ushered Mariam to the kitchen to prepare the black remedy for all our ills. I embraced my mother and took her hands in mine and crouched by her. Never before had her presence had such a disturbing effect on me. She'd always been a rock and a shelter. Her fingers were moist and cold. I rubbed them one by one the way my father used to do for her after a long day at the olive press; warming them in the grip of my palm, then massaging slowly for the blood to flow back into their tiny vessels.

"Now tell me," I said.

"They all left the building, son, all but the snipers and me. Everyone told me I was mad. Is it mad to want to safeguard what I've worked for half my life?" She fought for breath.

"Where did everyone go?"

"East, west, north, abroad. They couldn't handle it any longer. Neither can I any more."

"Thank God you're here. So what happened next? Who did you leave your keys with – the snipers?"

My mother stared. "Son, keys were invented thousands of years after the Stone Age. That's where we are now, the Stone Age."

"How did you get here?"

"They gave me a lift to the nearest taxi. They even gave me their word of honour never to let anyone loot my home and never to snipe from my windows. And look . . ." She plunged her hand into her bra and produced a bundle of money.

"Mother!"

"What? Don't even think it. This is no blood money, it's shit money, yes, but I earned it. They actually paid me for all my catering."

I shook my head at the thought of my mother living with a bunch of killers, putting her life in danger and toiling like a captive, just to save an apartment she was going to lose anyway. It must have been heart-wrenching for her to come back here. The past had always been a forbidden territory for her. All of it. "When the sky is as silver-blue as I remember it from Wahdeh, I keep my gaze lowered until it's covered with Beirut's grey haze," she once told me.

Mariam walked in with the coffee tray. Yousra was behind her, beaming. That little gallantry brought tears to my mother's eyes. She took the tray from Mariam, then held her in her arms again and sobbed, squeezing her tightly.

Between sips of coffee, she tried to tell us what had been going on since my last visit. But her speech was fragmented, jumpy. The shock must have been devastating. I gathered that the tenants had held steady for a whole year; fought against frustration, depression, and madness. They were changing and had no clue which way the change would take them. Most marriages broke down. Then, as soon as anyone left, the snipers would take over their empty apartment.

Yousra poured us another cup. Mariam sat on the rug and laid her head on her Teta's lap. I kept warming my mother's hands in mine until she gave a sigh of relief, took a deep breath and managed to tell us what had happened that morning:

"I made coffee for the snipers, son. I was carrying the tray; walked one step, two steps; the third step threw me into the dining room. It was a rocket."

I helped her inhale more rose-water. "Thank God you're still alive, Mother. We could have lost you."

"I don't know, I really don't. Which is more merciful? Dying in a split second or of estrangement in a strange land? What on earth would I be doing in Australia at my age, son?"

Yousra must have been talking to her about Australia already, trying to persuade her.

"How about taking good care of your grandchildren, for example? Have you thought of that? Imagine the joy you would bring to our lives out there. Haven't you missed Hawwa? Don't you want to see her kids? Cheer up, Mother; you're still young and fit enough to do lots of things."

Saying this, I realised that even I, "the guardian of the last bastion" as Yousra described me, was preaching departure.

Amti Wardieh was the first to rush over, welcoming back her old friend. The two women had known happier days in Wahdeh. Childless Wardieh had been given unconditional licence to care for Hawwa and me while Mother was helping at the olive press. That had bonded them for life. It was heartbreaking how they fell on each other, sniffing and kissing and crying and shivering with emotion. Mother repeated her apology for not attending the Hakim's funeral. "I held on to something that wasn't going to last, Wardieh, forgive me, but I was feeling your heartbeats, here in mine. I cried with you and I prayed God to give you patience and peace. Wahdeh is nothing without Raji. It doesn't feel right without his open door and his thundering voice, God bless his soul." Each time they wiped each other's eyes, they shed more tears. Finally Yousra brought a chair for Amti close to Mother and helped them get hold of themselves.

Then Um Faour came in with her husband, Zahi, Faour and Nour. The little girl stood behind her mother, holding on to the hem of her dress, while Zahi took large, steady steps into the open arms of a woman he'd never seen before. Then Faour lowered his head to receive a kiss on the brow. My mother marvelled at the speed with which children grew and how the clean air of the mountains preserved the youth of their parents, a compliment quickly reciprocated by Um Faour: "You're still the same, Nejmeh, as the day you left. God only knows how much we missed you."

As soon as Yousra went back to the kitchen to make more coffee, Rameh and Hilweh arrived. "Make it five cups!" I called.

My mother was floored by the sight of Hilweh. She covered her mouth with the palms of her hands. Her eyes opened wide. "Now that is marvellous!" she cried. A threesome hug and rustic greetings from Rameh, whose emotions were seldom expressed adequately: "You're looking damn good for your age, Nejmeh. I'd thought Beirut would kill you, touch wood, hey!"

"Touch wood, hey!" Hilweh echoed.

More coffee and a crowd of reminiscing friends was all that was needed to bring my mother back to life. Everyone had a story they wanted her to recall. They argued, dusting off a misty past with contradicting memories. Each one had a different version of the same incident they wanted her to verify, giving her the last word, expressing their jubilance at her return. She was politely obliging, but I could tell that she needed much more time to reconnect her thoughts to Wahdeh's world.

Then Um Faour put the question directly to her. "Why didn't you leave before? What kept you so long?"

"Stubbornness I suppose." Now that bygones were tucked away, my mother seemed ready to tell her story. "One thing led to another. Each day was the same and yet somehow different. Even in the shelter when life was an endless walk on a tightrope and death stalked you round the clock, there were things that had to be done. People to care for, people to watch changing in totally unexpected ways. It grows on you. You become part of something over which you have no control. And one day you notice that the minds begin to play up. Take the fisherman, Abu Mounir, whose son had knee-capped him. Remember him, Adam? Well, he finally reached rock bottom in the shelter. Not only was he crippled, he was missing the sea, he was dying for endless skies and eternal waves. Instead he was seeing so many dead bodies that his eyes began to itch painfully. No rose-water, no eye drops of any kind helped. One day, it was raining rockets like the end of the world. Suddenly he took his crutches and walked out, completely deaf to our cries. Later we learned that he'd found a deserted shack by the sea, fixed it, and is now fishing, oblivious to the world around him. Good for him, I guess. Some lost it and never recovered. Bang. Gone. As if the top of their skull had been blown off. Samira, for instance. You saw what a beauty she was, didn't you, Adam, and very much together. I mean she seemed so normal, so cool, always playing the seductress, always pulling somebody's leg. One day, out of the blue, she produced a little hoe. The bombs had been gouging out the street outside our building, so Samira, with her high heels and see-through nightgown, took it upon herself to plant vegetables in those holes. 'I am dying for a salad!' she said. A couple of days later, one of the militias lured her, and she went with them. God only knows if she's alive or dead. Her husband, the landlord, never came back from his search for her. I don't know, but everyone went out of their minds in different ways. Take our retired detective, Lateef, for example, the toughest and most reliable man I've ever known. The one who helped us with the legal papers when the Hakim and Khatoum died, Adam, remember? One day he began to 'see things'. He'd put on sunglasses and cringe in a dark corner, avoiding everybody, talking to himself about aliens trying to infiltrate the police force to kill him. 'I can see them! They are coming! Hide the children!' He was shivering like a leaf in the wind. We had no choice but to take him to the mad house. Whenever he comes back to my memory I hear the sound of backgammon. Tack, tack, tack, all day. He was a winner, until his own mind betrayed him. When I first came to Beirut, he helped me set up the catering service. He sent customers my way. They treated me well. I couldn't complain. But most of them fled the war. So I ended up organising the shelter's kitchen. Now, even that wasn't so bad. I enjoyed the bickering about the menu when all we had were lentils, chickpeas, beans and rice. Cooks cook, I suppose. No matter who's eating, even snipers. But it did matter. You can't put your heart into forced labour. Your skill, yes, your heart, never. What satisfaction is there in anything done at gun point?"

You could hear a pin drop. My mother took her scarf off her shoulders and wrapped it in the usual way round her head. Her face was sweaty but her eyes had regained their sharp focus.

She'd lost her battle in Beirut. Now she was facing a new war ahead, on a new front. I could feel the phoenix of her spirit trying to flap its wings. At that moment, I wanted to walk out with her to the orchard, show her the trees, take the pitcher from the myrtle tree and see her letting the water pour down to the core of her being.

"You asked me why I stayed?" my mother smiled at Um Faour. "I thought I could protect my home and my neighbours' empty apartments from looters. I was hopeful each day that the next would be better. I am not sure I did the wrong thing. One can easily say if and if. But one ends up doing what seems feasible under the circumstances. It took a stray rocket, one among millions, to change the course of my life. Believe me, when I woke up this morning, the hope for a better day walked with me to the kitchen. I guess hope is the best legal drug ever. It keeps pushing your cart through the darkest times, like a smile carved in gold and hidden deep inside you. So I filled the kettle, lit the gas, and stood there watching the blue flame, saying my morning prayer. To my right the faraway mountain was expecting dawn. It was a particularly quiet morning. I even heard a bird and smelled the scent of spring in the air. So I thought I'd listen to the six o'clock news. Didn't I just tell you that hope is addictive? It even made an old ear like mine believe the nonsense it heard: 'This is your President! Go back to your old ways! Sleep with your doors open! The war is over!' I stopped breathing. It was unbelievable. The buzz of excitement made me sing. I put the cups on the tray and walked one step, two steps... Then I heard the familiar hiss of an incoming rocket. It could have made kebab out of me. Instead it cut across two corners and turned the bedroom into mashed potato."

Her audience laughed.

"Anyway I'm still alive, thank God. What else can I say?"

Thirty-four

Spring had handed Wahdeh over to longer days and higher skies. New birds emerged from the secret heart of the forest. First tribes of rowdy sparrows circling around the roofs and verandas, then orange-breasted robins trembling inside the leafy branches. Larks, partridges, and colonies of gulls criss-crossed the blue sky. Today, even the first screeches of cicadas, promising a hot summer ahead. With a ceasefire now holding for more than two weeks, life seemed eerily familiar. But we knew it was temporary; a ceasefire of any duration meant at best a declared pause in hostilities and a relatively safe passage between warring areas, at least for those uninvolved in the fight.

Yet even during truces the most heinous crimes were committed by those who believed vengeance was legitimate, anywhere, any time. Then there were the unexploded shells, the lone snipers, small-time warlords sorting out territorial dominance, the odd thief who would surge from the crowd, jump into your passenger seat with a gun and borrow your car forever. However, by hook or by crook, I would get our passports. I was not intimidated, but scared. I'd never feared anything I could see, be it a gun or an animal. It was the dagger in the dark, the hazy unknown, the unaimed bullet looking for a landing. The sky was never without them. I'd leave home fearful that something terrible would happen to my family while I was away. I'd drive off weighed down by their fear for me. Fear was soon running in my blood. Often, when my mind drifted into a timeout from the general madness, I'd feel a sudden jerk: wake up, it's me, your fear, remember? I was getting so used to it that it was scary not to sense it everywhere, even in my sleep. But my fear was also my shield, it kept me alert, ready to escape, or cautious enough to avoid trouble. No prescribed precautions were possible, no plans of action to escape or to deflect anything from happening. The jungle has its own laws, and the only favour you may ask of your assassin is time to say your prayers, because Fate and Destiny have your life already planned, or, as my mother put it: "It's been written on your brow before you were born. Lean on God's mercy and go, my son."

And so I went. Like a squirrel on the run, I spent the first fortnight of June commuting between Wahdeh and Beirut, trailing a heavy tail across a gutted city that had never been attractive to me in the first place. My eyes were assaulted by street graffiti, huge slogans, badly painted portraits of politicians and gloomy clerics. The absence of urban accountability was hatching mansions on hill tops: bastard architecture, no harmony, no planning. Apartment blocks, each block blocking the view of the previous one. Every patch of land or sand was an island, disconnected from the sea of islands surrounding it. Every car window was a hatch for throwing litter and garbage. Here are two hundred meters of finished road work, even my old VW feels the difference and purrs. Then bang. A ditch. And back to the potholes.

I was without help and without the necessary understanding of the new order imposed by the militias. I wished I knew what they wanted. Money? How much? Why? For what? It was all guess work. They made me wait for ever in squalid places, just to hear the dreadful, hateful, *boukra*. Tomorrow. Tomorrow is your rendezvous with miracles, and then again, tomorrow.

Once the passports were ready, the tickets would pose no problem; there were plenty of ships willing to take us. Our war was preventing the floundering maritime trade of the

Mediterranean from drowning. Hundreds of worthless vessels had been resurrected, repainted, re-engined, to help us flee our shores. Not that we needed much help, people would have cut the remaining cedar trees they so tearfully worshipped to make rafts of escape.

Finally, the only problem that remained was my mother's apartment. It was going to take at least several weeks to sell. Stories abounded of people being swindled out of their money and their property by sharks and conmen. It was a delicate task. The administration had been crap before the war. The large books that went back to Ottoman times, the grumpy civil servants who wouldn't budge without bribe, the broken doors and the smelly stairways; we were brought up to love hating them all. Now we were feeling nostalgic for them, because they meant *order* instead of the chaos of today.

Selling property and getting the paper work done properly was far more complicated than getting passports. First I had to find a buyer. Advertising was out of the question, not only because the newspapers were half their normal size and weren't publishing small ads any more, but because everything was being managed by the militias and there was no way out of dealing with them. One day, on the steps of the Land and Property Registry, I saw a mother with two small kids, crying and calling on God to avenge her. I sat beside her. "What happened, why are you crying, sister?"

"They sold my house and ran off with the money. I went back home to find strangers in it. I needed the money to leave, now where will we go? Where?"

I thought better of telling this story to my family. But that night it brewed me up a nightmare: I was in Beirut, lost, looking for my mother's address. Then I was inside the place but surrounded by hundreds of dwarfs. They asked me to have soup with them and presented me with a wooden bowl. Inside it I saw eyes floating, looking at me. Next morning, Yousra and Mother tried to explain it, each in her own way, both dismissing my dark premonitions.

"The fact that you lost your way is good," my mother maintained. "It means the place will be sold. It won't be there any more for us to worry about. And the little people are even better; they represent the minor hiccups waiting for you. As for eyes in your soup, I believe they are saying be careful, watch out, keep your eyes open."

Yousra was equally certain. "There's nothing in that dream, Adam. Your worries and fears collided with your bottled-up emotions, and your imagination found a suitable scenario to display this. Dreams aren't prophetic, we just invent their meaning."

They had already started going through our household goods; the present lull could end at any moment, delaying the trip indefinitely. I suggested staying behind to finish the sale, while Yousra, Mother and Mariam went ahead of me. The ladies were sorting out kitchenware when I voiced this option.

"Whatever," Yousra said, counting spoons, as if I'd suggested kishk instead of vegetable soup for supper.

But my mother stopped, her face drained of colour. "No way. I'll stay behind to finish the sale. You stick with your family."

"Mother, you don't drive and there's no public transport. You would be exposed to the worst kind of thugs. Who knows what might happen? How can I have peace of mind knowing you're out there dealing with this alone?"

"He's right," Yousra mumbled, still preoccupied with counting cutlery. I knew she wasn't listening. She was deep in her own world. Her answer came automatically from a long tradition of adopting my view whenever the argument involved my mother. But that's not all there was to it. Pressure had been mounting faster than she anticipated. To cope she needed to do things categorically; tidy up and pack and make lists of things to be given or kept. She needed to wrap and fold and label everything. Uprooting herself and dismantling her whole world in a few days was a rock she was pushing, while dreading it might roll over her at any time.

"Yousra!"

She looked at me, startled at my raised voice.

"I was saying to Mother that in order to save time and get out of here fast, you two could take Mariam to Cyprus while the passage is safe. You can start the applications at the embassy straight away. Meanwhile, I'll finish the sale and catch up with you. What do you think?"

"Are you saying you want to stay until the apartment is sold? What if it takes months? What if it doesn't sell at all? What if the war gets worse and you're stuck here? What then? Do we go to Australia without you? Adam, get real."

"What do you suggest we should do? Forget about the apartment? Leave it and go? Beirut isn't Wahdeh. This is our home village. Here, the risk of losing our house is next to nothing. In Beirut it's different. Once the street knows you've emigrated, your property will be taken over. We can't afford to waste twenty to thirty thousand liras. We need every piastre now, Yousra. Besides, people are now waiting three, maybe five months to get their visas. It won't take me that long to sell. I'll flog it to the first serious buyer and join you."

Yousra was not convinced. My mother feared I'd sell the apartment dirt cheap. The more I pushed my strategy, the more they resisted.

"Look at it this way," I said, "We need three things: money, safety, and those visas. All I'm doing is aiming for minimum risk."

"We all walk together. That's minimum risk." Yousra was losing patience. Her voice became biting. She seemed as far away as if we'd said goodbye on a foggy quay a long time ago.

"Son, my apartment is my responsibility. I've invested every piastre of my earnings in it. I am not going to sell it for peanuts. You go. Take your wife and your daughter. I'll catch up with you. I'll manage."

Mother was trying to sound confident, but I could tell that finally she was recognising the hassle of doing it alone. Her eyes narrowed, her mouth tensed – she was pondering my point but resisting endorsing it lest she sounded selfish. I knew how she was. She could see it was practical. It was Yousra I needed to convince. In her mind we were inseparable. Mother was a new factor that hadn't yet sunk in. And the money meant little when weighed against our safety. She was right. Mother was right. I was right. To dispel the confusion I had to make a decision, however arbitrary. I would find a buyer quickly. Someone with ready cash who wasn't a crook. Definitely a needle in a haystack. I thought of taking Rameh with me; he might still have some clout with the militias, though probably not. Then I thought of Nimer. He might give me a hand? Sickening, but hopefully the last nausea before getting seasick. I looked out of the kitchen window. The jeep was there.

I left the women without another word and stepped out the back door. Sana had taken the children on a picnic to the valley, inevitably near Faour's tent. They were high on love. Yousra and I had agreed not to interfere, but the unexpected reaction to their story was my mother's. "Let them be, son. Nimer's not man enough to keep his captive tamed. She's a beautiful piece of work. And madly in love with Faour. There is nothing anybody can do to change their hearts. Bless them."

So there I was, walking to the den of a betrayed beast. Swallowing my pride like broken glass, I knocked three times.

During the silence, I evoked the image of Nimer as a child. A chubby bundle with runny nose and constantly wounded knees. Never showed the slightest interest in girls. Seen at the square, more often than not crying, when all the other children were at school. The Mukhtar's beatings were without mercy. He didn't rear a child; he smashed a shameful image of himself. His rage at having a moron for an only son bordered on homicidal. But the paternal harshness had produced negative results. Nimer grew up in pain until he became numb to hostility. His imagination made him a pathological liar. He learned to live by fraud, no matter how pathetic.

That was the Nimer who opened the door. Not in the black school apron of his early childhood, but a stark white jellabia.

"I was sleeping, son of Awad. What's up?"

"Nimer, I want you to help me sell my mother's apartment in Beirut. I want a quick sale. No bullshit. Take your share. Consider it pure business."

"How much are you hoping for?"

"Thirty."

"It'll take two months minimum."

"Too long."

"Too high a price."

"Three bedrooms!"

"Go for twenty and hope for the best."

"A deal?"

"No guarantees, son of Awad. I'll give it my best shot."

There was no way I could tell if he was as genuine as he sounded. But I had to believe in something. Nimer and God's mercy were the only cards left on the table.

Thirty-five

Dear all, Changes in immigration laws under way. File your applications before June 25. Otherwise more delays.

The wire was dated June 19. It reached us two days later.

We sat down looking blankly at the piece of paper, Mother, Yousra and me, waiting for each other to speak. The deeds to my mother's apartment were with Nimer. There was no way of guessing when Nimer would show up. The final move couldn't be delayed any longer. My original plan was now inevitable. The family had to go before me.

My mother stood up as if nine months pregnant. "Let's pack, Yousra."

Yousra gave me a quick stroke on the shoulder. "Whatever happens to the bloody apartment, I want you with us within twenty-four hours after we get the visas, or we leave without you." Her whisper was gentle but her expression was dead serious.

I stumbled out of the house, dazed. I don't know how one feels when drowning, but I had a big need to fill up my lungs with fresh air. Mariam was skipping with the twins. My first instinct was to grab her and hold her tight. Instead I sang along with the twins: "Now she's five, she can dive, now she's six, no more tricks, now she's seven, high as heaven, now she's eight, never too late, now she's nine, like sunshine, and hop for ten, hop for eleven, hop for . . . out!" She ran to my arms. "I can go on to a hundred, Baba."

"I know. You can also go to Australia. But first walk with me."

Mariam gave me her hand, bewildered by what I'd just said. The twins screamed, it was Samer's turn. Sana came out.

"Hi," she smiled. "Are you taking her away?"

"'Fraid so."

"Well then, I have no choice." She picked up the end of the rope. Together with Nader, they began a new count for Samer.

Mariam's little palm was as tender as dough. "I heard about the wobbly tooth," I said. "Show me."

"Who told you?"

"A little bird."

"Must be Teta, she always tells."

"Why didn't *you* tell me?"

"It was a surprise."

"You were going to give me a big empty grin?"

"Yes. Look!"

"Don't push it with your tongue. It'll come out crooked."

"Shall I put it under my pillow, or is that a tall story, like Mama said?"

"You can always try; tooth fairies don't like wars, but they're still hard at work in Australia."

"Then I'll keep it till we get there."

"I have a better idea. Show me again." Mariam opened wide. I checked the loose tooth. It was holding.

"Why not try the Cypriot tooth fairies. You may get lucky."

"There are no tall stories in Cyprus?"

"Not at the moment."

"When are we going?"

"You're going the day after tomorrow with Mama and Teta. I'll follow you soon."

Mariam's face flushed. Her hand went cold. Her eyes became arrows. Then she shrieked, "You're lying! You're not coming with us! Ever!" She burst into tears and ran back to the house.

"Mariam, wait a second!"

She ran faster.

If only I could put into a story what I desperately wanted to convey to her. But the stories I knew, like those I made up, never tackled the necessity for money. Money, as she once said, grew in banks, just like olives in the orchard and water at the spring. We didn't correct her. We thought it was a cute anecdote. So how to reverse all that and explain our need for every penny, now that we were facing total upheaval? How to convince her that money did not grow in banks for everyone to help themselves? A couple of days ago we'd been talking about the boat trip to Cyprus. Mariam hadn't asked how much it would cost, she was more interested in details of the boat: how fast was it, faster than a car? And what would happen if it sank. Would they give us life jackets or rafts, and who would save us? Helicopter or submarine? She preferred the latter because she would see all the fish swimming in the belly of the sea. Her imagination was soaring and so was mine. I had turned myself into a jinni and evoked Sinbad to save us from the storm.

It had never occurred to me that war would put a curfew on Mariam's fantasies, force her to grasp the priority of matter over mind, of money over her father's company. Now, without the magic, the glow of the trip darkened in her spirit. It terrified her. And it fell on me like a bucket of ice that I was a thoughtless ass of a father. I lived with the conviction that growing up in Wahdeh was heaven for any child. I had made her believe that everything was possible with a story at hand. That was how I'd grown up: believing Sitti's stories, then growing out of them in stages of sweet and sour disillusion. Not so for Mariam. At five years of age she was abruptly facing some harsh realities.

"Mariam!" I grabbed her before she reached home and took her gently in my arms, remembering with a shudder the day I'd prevented her from seeing the body-dragging in Kafleet. No, I wasn't going to frighten her with my fears. Nor was I going to tell her a tall tale.

Her little body was stiff with anger; she turned her head away, throbbing like a naked heart. Then she blurted, "You're going to die, Baba, like everyone else staying behind!"

"Listen now, sweetheart, just pay attention to what I'm going to say, okay? Mariam, you are the most precious thing to me in the whole wide world. Would I be so stupid as to do something to hurt you? Never, right? Now, during wars, people like us try their best to save whatever they can. You know why? Because starting from scratch is very hard. It's not easy beginning a new life in a foreign country with no money. You see? I can get good money for my mother's apartment, and then take the next boat to be with you. I'm not going to die. Okay, Mariam?"

As I continued searching for words while she scrutinised me, I realised that Mariam wasn't a stranger to the situation. She'd been listening to our conversations and filling in the picture through queries of her own. The only drawback now was my sudden withdrawal from that picture. It made her feel betrayed. So, if the question of money didn't convince her, I must find another approach, something that would make her forget or at least forgive my absence from the imminent journey:

"Mariam, are you afraid of the sea?"

"No."

"What are you afraid of?"

"Nothing."

"Are you upset only because I'm not coming with you?"

"No."

"What then?"

"I don't know."

"Show me your wobbly tooth again."

"Why?"

"I just had an idea."

Mariam opened her lips slightly. I checked the next front tooth.

"Do you want to make a bet with me that I'll be in Cyprus before this one too begins to wobble?"

"No."

"What do you want?"

"I want you to bring Samer and Nader and Aunty Sana with you."

"What makes you think they want to come?"

"Samer told me the other day. He heard Aunty Sana pleading with Nimer: Let me take the children away, please."

I had fallen out of the frying pan into the fire. There was Sana a few metres away. A woman in love. She was beaming. Her eyes swam in a thousand laughs, her body swayed with intoxication, her lips shone as if freshly dipped in honey. Where was she planning to go? Was she trying to leave Nimer for the children's sake? Or was she escaping her dangerous love story with Faour before Nimer found out? Were my wife and my mother aware that Sana wanted to leave? Or was it just wishful thinking on Sana's part? Sana must be craving freedom and a new life instead of staying alone with a beastly husband. And what would Faour do with his broken heart if she left without him?

It was one hell of a downer, holding my child in my arms and thinking not how beautiful she was but how complicated life had become.

"Mariam, I can only promise to do my best. But you have to trust me."

"Bring them to Cyprus, Baba. Or I'll never trust you again."

Thirty-six

I woke up abruptly, feeling the gap where Yousra should be. All night she'd held on to me as if to the mast of a ship in distress. I'd kept rubbing her shoulders softly until we both fell asleep. But it was Mariam I was most alarmed about. Overexcitement had caused her insomnia before, and lack of sleep was the last thing she needed today. It was 3.45 a.m. The boat was leaving at ten. I went barefoot to check on her. I peered into her room. She was sprawled across the bed as usual in dreamland, but the mattress where my mother slept was empty.

There was light seeping from beneath the kitchen door. As I approached, I heard the breathless hush peculiar to women toiling closely together.

It hadn't occurred to me that in spite of all the rush and anguish, my mother would uphold tradition, let alone convince Yousra to join her in the old custom that summons hope for a safe journey. I pictured their rolled-up sleeves and their hands making the dough, the clammy mixture sticking to their skin, the repeated sprinkling of water and flour to get it right. This ritual had not taken place in our family since Hawwa left for Australia all those years ago. The Dough of Farewell would soon become bread and, once eaten, kickstart a new life for us. The suitcases would disappear from the hallway, along with the voices, the footsteps, the laughs, the cries, the smells and the shadows of the most important people in my life. My home would become a waiting quay for the next boat.

"Summer's here already," I heard my mother sigh.

"Hard time, summer."

"Winter wasn't easy."
"Summer is worse."
"The fighting is worse in summer."
"They get more vicious."
Pause.
"I worry about Sana," said Yousra.
"You wouldn't wish her situation on your worst enemy."
"I would. A bullet for Nimer, in his stupid head."
"In his useless genitals."
Pause.
"How did you know?"
"That he's impotent? His mother told me a long time ago. Who told you?"
"His wife," Yousra chuckled.

I opened the kitchen door. "I know the husband is always the last to know, but this is ludicrous!"

"Calm down, son," my mother smiled.

But Yousra was shaken. Her face paled. "Sana made me swear on my mother's grave not to tell a soul."

"And his mother did the same with me, son. She'd been desperate. She'd wanted me to speak with your grandmother, in case some old recipe could help, but your grandmother wouldn't hear of it. 'This is a curse,' she'd said, 'not a malady'. She never told a soul either. Such secrets are not made to travel."

"Does Faour know?"

"No!" Yousra cried, "It's up to Sana to tell him or not. And don't even think of telling him yourself. Faour wouldn't keep his mouth shut and then Nimer would go berserk. Please, Adam." Yousra was on the verge of tears.

I went back to my room, changed, and walked towards the orchards. This time the female secrecy infuriated me. I felt excluded. I'd regarded Nimer as a sexually rampant goon, swollen with satiated desires. My whole image of him was now shattered. So many nights I'd been jerked out of my sleep by painful images of his intimacy with the sweet Sana. How should I imagine this new Nimer?

It was still dark, but a full moon bleached my path. An unfamiliar sense of alienation shadowed my walk. I thought of Yousra's constant attacks on Nimer, of Sana's categorical refusal to harm him. I thought of my mother, condoning adultery between Sana and Faour in stark contrast to her traditional morality. And I remembered Nimer's remarks about leaving Wahdeh as soon as the war was finished. Of course. He'd go where no one knew him, all the better to pretend he was what he was not. It added up.

I saw a small fire on the rocky plateau and made a beeline for Faour's tent.

"Why are you up so early?" Faour's hostile tone stopped me in my tracks. He was behind the tent, lying down, looking at the fading stars.

"What's eating *you*?"

"I'm planning a murder."

"You want to kill the one we all want to kill?"

"He's mine. I want to deliver him back to his maker."

"I don't know how you manage your contradictions, Faour; you're in love to the brim and as much in hate."

"You said it. I have to do something before it kills me."

"Killing, my friend, is . . ."

". . . pure justice, Adam."

"So who's the judge?"

"Reason, Adam, reason. Think about it. Does he deserve Sana? No. Is he a monster? Yes. Is he destroying my life and hers? Listen my friend, when he comes back with your money, I'm going to snuff him. I'll throw him in the river. His body will end up in the sea along with hundreds of other unknown corpses. No one will know, no one will give a damn. And don't try to preach to me. You go to your own. I'll take care of mine."

"Sana won't agree."

"She won't mourn him."

"What if I spare you the trouble? I have a better idea."

"No moral lessons. I love this woman, Adam, you understand? I love her."

"Just listen, will you? How about leaving with me, the four of you, to Cyprus? I lend you the money. From there you apply for immigration."

Faour sat up, bent his knees and locked them in his arms. Then he started rocking slowly. I sat near him.

"If he catches us, we're all dead. It's too dangerous."

"Not as dangerous as killing."

"Maybe. But I wouldn't feel the same as I would if he were dead."

"If Sana agrees to my scheme?"

"Will you talk to her?"

"Of course. But there's time – you can talk to her too."

"She'll say no. Anything that puts the twins in danger is no go. It won't work."

"It's worth a try at least. Before the sword."

Faour went back to rocking.

"Give me an answer!"

"Don't push me, Adam. You are stripping me of a rare chance. I never imagined feeling good about committing a crime. I was in control before you came. I had my enemy at my feet. If I say yes to your plan, he'll walk free and I'll spend the rest of my life looking over my shoulder."

"Or dragging his cadaver."

"That's my problem."

"In a couple of hours we'll be baking the Dough of Farewell. Come over. But don't say anything about this plan just yet – we need to talk to Sana before getting Mariam's hopes up about the twins."

Faour dropped his head to his knees. He stopped rocking, but his despair had spread to me. I had come down to see him in the hope of easing my own confusion. Instead I found myself in even deeper trouble. How had I come up with that idea on the spur of the moment? Was it my promise to Mariam bypassing my brain? When I'd told my mother how Mariam had asked me to save Sana and the twins, she'd joked: "So Adam's daughter has the Noah syndrome!" But neither she nor Yousra had mentioned it again. I guess because, as Faour would put it, there was a bulky obstacle in the way.

"Are you coming to say goodbye?" I reminded him.

"In a while."

Walking home, I pondered Faour's solution. Nimer dead: a new life for two children and two lovers and a relief for the whole of Wahdeh. The fact that he was selling my mother's apartment didn't count for much alongside that vision. I had little faith that he would deliver anyway. He'd probably steal the money, or let someone squat the apartment and then ask me to buy them out and . . .

I caught my murderous musings mid-sentence. What was I doing, slithering into the law of the jungle? Me. Gandhi's disciple.

Thirty-seven

Time dragged even more after my family left. The mounting lawlessness was now spreading to the sea. Pirates emerged as if from antiquity. Unknown gun-boats attacked in the middle of the night, leaving in their wake sunken, traceless ships. Other vessels were intercepted and sent back for no reason at all. I had no idea whether my family was alive or dead. And Nimer had disappeared with the deeds and power of attorney to my mother's apartment. Waiting for him was torture. His shadow hovered over my thoughts day and night. I wanted him to come back with the money, then disappear, so that we could slip away in peace. While Nimer's absence meant freedom in love for Faour and Sana, it was sheer agony for me.

Apart from the occasional visit by Rameh, and Amti insisting on cooking and giving the house a brush every Saturday, the five of us lived in seclusion. Sana, the twins, Faour and me. No one bothered with us, and no one bothered us. Wahdeh's people had been cowed into indifference, just floating along on a raft of fruitless waiting. At times it was unbearable, especially in the mornings when all I heard was radio news and a barrage of political flak. I was missing the communal tasting of the first crops, and eating and drinking and singing, and the children playing out until after midnight. Summer was here but Wahdeh was not Wahdeh anymore. The fruits remained untouched, the unkempt orchards were turning into scrub.

I'd entrusted Amti with a few precious items and given her all my hens, so my proud rooster didn't crow under my window any more. I woke up to a mute, eerie dawn and sat on the edge of my sheetless bed. Yousra was right: sod the money; I should have left with them instead of sitting here still waiting for Nimer. Was I stupid? Or was it the fear of being down and out in an alien environment that made me cling to every piaster at any price? Or was it my slow nature? I realise things too late and keep on hoping that people will change. Why am I made like this? My father was cautious but could act on the spur of the moment. Mother was raw energy. Uncle Raji, God bless his soul, had been thunderous. So where had I got this snail-like attitude? I looked at my bare feet, comparing my toes. The left big toe was shorter than the right and slightly fatter. I tried to lift it. Dumb toe, come on, make a move. Go. It felt freshly glued to the floor. I imagined it to be the storeroom of all my ills.

Finally the dumb toe responded, took me to the bathroom and through my normal morning routine, ending up in the kitchen making coffee. The space around me was aching. I dreaded touching the walls, the water pipes, the abandoned kitchen utensils, everything felt sore, almost inflamed. A frightening strangeness was weaving a web around me. Most mornings, Sana shared my coffee, then we packed breakfast and walked with the twins to the valley to eat with Faour on the rocky plateau. But today she was cleaning her house instead. I felt marooned.

I'd become very close to Sana and come to admire much more than her beauty and sophistication. The human being behind the looks was far more interesting than I'd imagined. On those mornings when we sat and talked by the tent she'd dissected every detail of her situation with a clarity that earthed Faour's fire and doubled my sympathy. She came clean about Nimer's impotence. But she never spoke of him with anger or bitterness, even when relating his bouts of violence or his pathetic experiments with porn magazines, hormone injections, ginseng, African herbs, cocaine, and a pitiful attempt at hypnosis. "It was abracadabra performed by an imposter who put Nimer to sleep to have a go at me." Had she not fallen in love with Faour, she said, she would never have thought of leaving Nimer. "When someone saves your life you owe him sunshine ever after. They'd tortured my husband to death, and when I turned up with the money to buy him out, they blindfolded me and took me to some stinking dungeon and showed me his mutilated body. I thought I'd pass out. But the life of my boys suddenly became paramount. They were at a friend's house, and we'd been all packed up and about to flee. I couldn't let go of their faces, their features were tattooed on my eyes. I was locked up with my husband's body for four days, until I lost my voice from screaming and was about to lose my mind. They just couldn't understand: we had no more money. None. You see, my husband was a jeweller but he lost his fortune when the jewellery market was looted. The cash I had brought them in ransom was all we had left.

"On the fifth day, the door opened. A tall, bearded man with sad eyes and large lips stood there looking at me, a half-eaten sandwich in his hand. He said nothing for a long time. Then he approached, extending the sandwich to my face, as if I were a starving dog. I covered my eyes and shook my head, but he laid the sandwich on my lap and dragged my husband's body away, closing the door. That was the first time I saw Nimer. The next day, he escorted me to a bathroom: just a hole in the floor and a hose with cold water. But, God only knows how or why, he found me a fresh towel and some clean army fatigues. What I didn't know then was that Nimer watched me wash through a crack in the wall. He later told me that I was the only naked woman he'd ever seen, and that he cried at how beautiful I was.

"After that first shower, my status began to change. I was moved to a cell with a mattress on the floor and a brand new blanket, and I was given two meals a day, by Nimer. He didn't say much, sometimes not even a word of greeting. But I noticed his eyes becoming less morose as he watched me eat his cheese or falafel rolls.

"Then one day he seemed extremely disturbed. The corners of his mouth were dry and his eyes reddened, either from lack of sleep or from taking drugs, I couldn't tell. He brought me a roast beef sandwich and some salad, then closed the door and crouched near me. Strangely, I didn't think he'd rape me. His agitation was that of a child before breaking some rigid rule. He said they were going to move me out. They'd wrap me with tape and tuck me under the chassis of a truck, but they wouldn't tell him where I'd be held. Wherever that may be, he then said, looking straight into my eyes, many will rape you, many times. Then they'll shoot you and throw you in the woods. And he stood up and turned to go. Please, I begged, help me. Marry me, he answered, still averting his face. I told him about my boys. He said no problem, and left, without looking back. Death, or a life sentence with my children and a weird militiaman?

"Nimer put his life on the line the night he snatched me out and took me to my boys. I didn't tell my friend of the deal with him. I just told her I was in safe hands. At first I imagined that Nimer was avoiding physical contact because he was waiting for me to love him. It was an endearing thought, especially when he was nice to the boys and snuggled near me just seeking tenderness, like an insecure animal.

"Then everything changed, the day he brought home those ears in the glass jar. I saw the other side of him and was terrified. My fear made him edgy, and that in turn made him violent. But now I can read him like an open book. Which should make things easier for us."

It was eleven-thirty when I heard Nimer's jeep screeching around the turning by the Castle. I shouted a warning to Sana next door.

"I heard it," she called back.

Nimer arrived in a cloud of dust. He jumped out of his jeep like a hero. "Son of Awad, too many dead people are praying for you up there. You are the luckiest man alive. Come here."

I walked out to meet him in the front yard, still not believing that something positive had happened.

"You know what? I had to shoot someone in the leg to get this done for you. But you are my neighbour; he is only a fellow I'd met at the front. He tried to squeeze a commission, a fat one. He tried too hard, so what do you expect? Those people don't understand the meaning of neighbours. The nearest thing to a neighbour they know is the stuff in their underpants."

Nimer was so excited he took me in his arms and kissed me twice on the cheeks. *"Mabrouk!"* he congratulated.

My heart pounded all the way to my temples. *"Mabrouk* for what, Nimer?"

"They should have called you Thomas, not Adam. Come inside, have lunch with me."

"Did you sell the apartment?"

Nimer stopped. "You don't believe me, do you?"

"Where's the money?"

"How much did you hope for? Remind me."

"Twenty is enough."

"Are you sure? You don't need a bit more, now that you're leaving?"

"Give me twenty and keep the rest. Have you got it on you?"

Nimer's face darkened, not so much in anger as in dismay, as if I'd insulted him.

"Son of Awad, here, count this. Shame on you."

Twenty-four thousand liras in cash!

I couldn't recall a moment like this before, on the sharp edge between laughing and crying. I wanted to thank Nimer – sincerely. I wanted to apologise and make good neighbourly peace with him. But he walked away dismissively and barked: "What's for lunch, woman?" Re-marking his territory.

I went back in, feeling like someone watching himself in a movie. Incredible, yet real.

I sat counting my money, checking every note for fraud. During my years at the bank I'd learned how to spot bad money of any currency with my eyes shut. Day after day, in a windowless office, riffling through bank notes, cheques, money transfers, money orders. Nimer's money was good, every note of it. The confusing mix of joy and sorrow made me break into hysterical laughter.

I was just blowing my nose when Rameh walked in. "This really is your lucky day, son of Awad; I have a letter for you."

"You won't believe this, bailiff, but . . . "

"I know. Nimer spread the news before he reached you. He threw sweets to the kids and blabbed it to everyone at the square. He wouldn't miss a trick like that. He's learning politics, my friend."

"Well, he can have my vote – ballot paper in a bottle from Sydney!"

"Wait till you find out how much he pocketed from the sale."

"I don't want to know, Rameh. Just let me enjoy being happy for once."

Dearest Adam,
Hello from Larnaca! I'm sorry for the delay in writing, you must be so worried. Well, don't be. We're fine. Don't miracles go hand in hand with disasters? It was a miracle to set foot on dry land again. Remember the boat you saw at the port, only half afloat? Designed to

carry twenty passengers max, in safe waters only? Well, it sailed with seventy plus luggage after a few stops at smaller moorings along the coast!

By the way, your mother conceded that I was right about Mariam's clothes. She wished she'd worn trousers and comfortable shoes herself. What's the point in being well-dressed when you're being thrown around the deck by the waves? Your mother took off her high heels and sat cross-legged in a corner, her pretty *fustan* all crumpled and wet. But you know her; she finds a lesson in every failure. She said to Mariam, older people are right ninety percent of the time and today her ten percent wrong came up all at once, so she'll never be wrong again! Other than that, we didn't say much throughout the trip, we were too busy dealing with our seasickness, or, when the waves eased a bit, trying in vain to snatch a wink of sleep. Luckily the children (and there were quite a few) coped better than us. They made themselves smaller and sought shelter anywhere. Mariam found the box of lifejackets under the stairs leading to the captain's cabin and tucked herself inside it. At night the waves surfed us so high we could touch the moon that hung over us, but when we rolled down it disappeared, leaving us in total darkness. "This is a rollercoaster to hell!" one hysterical passenger cried.

Despite all this, the sea was more humane than the land. At sea, you're between the water and the sky, with your destiny and fear, your vomit, your haunting thoughts, sharing the same conditions as everyone else. We cried with joy when we saw the lights of Larnaca, but Larnaca wasn't that eager to see us. We had to wait four hours at the port before getting permission to disembark. Why? The Cypriot police decided to keep us on board in order to avoid confrontation with the passengers of another vessel "from the Other Side". But instead of feeling shamed at the way the Cypriots perceive us, some thickheads started screaming, "This is discrimination! Why make *us* wait and not *them*?" It was more sickening than the rough sea.

Anyway, we are now settled in this small guest house owned by Pani Chrisantou: a divorcée in her forties who lived in Alexandria as a child and still speaks Arabic. She is herself a refugee from Famagusta. However, her problem is not so much destitution but gambling. She collects the rent from us and squanders it at the 'green tables'. When she comes back penniless, she cries her eyes out and swears never to touch the cards again. When she wins (not that often) she's as generous as a prince with everybody.

The first few days we actually missed the sound of shelling and explosions. The silence was weird. Whenever we saw people gathering in an open place we felt like screaming: spread out, the bombs are coming!

Every day since we arrived I've taken the bus to Nicosia and I spend the morning at the Australian embassy, from 8 to 12, waiting to hear about our application. I even hear "No news is good news" in my sleep now. But I am told it will be easy for us, mainly because we are under the family reunion programme, and I am confident it will be a matter of days.

I don't want to upset you, but you hear stories here that make your hair stand on end. The immigration racketeers have been embezzling the naïve and the desperate out of their last piastre, leaving whole families with nothing more than the shirts on their backs. And you see the new money of the looters and killers zooming around in sports cars and flashy clothes, nightclubs and gambling dens, while hundreds can hardly make ends meet, and hundreds more are begging to feed their children. In short, I don't see much to be proud of, given that we are all refugees here and ought to give each other a hand. Instead, you find those who've been hurt eager to hurt others, and the better-off feigning bankruptcy.

Your mother put herself to work immediately. She persuaded Pani to lend her an old sewing machine. Then she did the rounds of the neighbouring streets, collecting clothes for mending and alterations. She also organised a 'meals on wheels' service, using local taxi drivers to deliver. She pays them in tabbouleh and hummus. As for yours truly, when I come back from Nicosia, I gather the children in a makeshift school in the front yard. I charge their parents whatever money or help they can manage.

All in all, we are keeping our heads above water, despite the prolonged phone calls to Sydney. "Hello, Australia? Give me my daughter!" your mother screams at the operator, and then she listens intently, as if Hawwa is just behind the wall. "Hello, Hawwa, speak to your mother, speak up, I can't hear you. Oh, yes, your voice is now clear, here, speak with Mariam!" On her first call she broke down in tears at hearing Hawwa's voice. She sobbed and caused those waiting their turn to cry with her. Since then, it's enough for her to ensure the connection. Then she gives us the receiver and tells us to speak her mind. "Ask her this. Tell her that."

Now Mariam. I know you're waiting. I left her to the closing paragraph on purpose. She is sunshine. You'll be surprised to see how grown up she's becoming. She swims every morning and she's picking up so much Greek that we count on her for translations when the street vendors pass by. She asks after you constantly, especially at story time when she falls out with her grandmother. "Baba knows better ones. Your stories are like school!" Mariam lost her wobbly tooth and believes you'll be here before the next one goes. She's convinced you are bringing the twins and their mother. I guess you made her think that you are Superman. But tell Sana we miss her and that she could easily get a visa to Argentina, if ever she chose to leave, because she was born there.

Write soon, now that we have a proper address. We kiss your thick moustache.

Love,
Yousra

I took my good news and the money down to Faour's tent. He was ecstatic, transfigured, an agnostic experiencing a true miracle. His past meant nothing to him any more. Today he was a migrant bird between two stations, focused on the horizon. And whether I liked it or not, I was the leader of his flock.

"The minute Nimer goes, we're out of here!" He threw his arms around me, crowing, "Buenos Aires here we come! Adios Nimer, adios the war, farewell to arms!"

"What arms, Mister Hemingway?"

"This." Faour lifted his shirt above the right hip. I recognised the hand gun: Nimer's present to Rameh on his wedding day. Faour went on, "Rameh wanted me to keep it, for self-defence. He didn't mention Nimer, but I think he knows the score."

"So you're still thinking of killing Nimer."

"Only if he stands in my way."

"Look, Faour, I'll keep my commitment to our plan, no matter what, but you in turn must promise . . ."

". . . Thou shalt not kill."

"Promise."

"But what if . . ."

"No. This is not negotiable. I am not running away from my place of birth with a trail of blood in my wake. You have to understand this, Faour."

"I understand. But if in absolute self-defence . . ."

"No! We'll be wise and cool-headed and swift as hell and we'll succeed. Now promise."

Faour's jaws quivered.

"I can't believe you're doing this to me, Adam. You're not being fair. I'm not keen on killing Nimer. That's not what it's all about. But say he's standing between you and your family and only one option is given to you or you'll never see them again? What then? This is a godless land these days, Adam, or haven't you noticed? You expect me to enter a possible duel unarmed and pray that my enemy shoots himself in the leg? What if he shoots me first? Would you rather have me dead? Meet me halfway: you make the plan, I follow. If we come face to face with Nimer, every man for himself. I won't feel betrayed if you turn your back on me then."

"I will not allow you to begin a family with murder, Faour. Just stay put behind me. We've waited long enough to be ready. Now we are."

"Okay, let's put a time limit on it. How many days should we wait for him to leave? How many days can *you* wait?"

"I have a feeling he won't stay long. He must have made some money from the sale of my mother's apartment, and most probably he's selling another. He's in business down there in Beirut, he can't risk leaving his turf for too long."

"I hope you're right. Okay, no confrontation: I am not budging from my camp until you say so. How's that?"

We shook hands. Faour opened two cans of beer he'd kept in the stream. We drank to the success of our exit and to a happy reunion with our loved ones. How amazed Yousra would be when not just I but my new little flock stepped off the boat in Larnaca – she had no idea that in her absence we'd been planning a multiple exit. And how thrilled Mariam would be that I was indeed Superman, delivering her playmates to her. My anxiety was dissipating. Now that Faour had calmed down, now that I was in control of the plan again, maybe we were on the right track. I relaxed a bit and jumped on the deck of Faour's ark.

"What will you two be doing in Argentina?"

"Catering. Like your mother. Sana's creating her own recipes, she calls her concept *La Cocina del Sur*. Olive oil, garlic, herbs and spices common to all southern cultures. We'll work together, but I'm going to continue writing as well."

I pictured the escapees of Wahdeh, serving a hotly peppered tabbouleh and calling it Exotica Mediterraneo to lure the Argentinean crème de la crème. And Faour's name rising in the world of literature. His villains would all be Nimer under different pseudonyms. And he would kill them all. Hopefully it would relieve him of his grudge.

Right now, Faour looked more like a lost shepherd than a famous novelist. His thin beard contrasted starkly with his shock of tangled hair. I dipped my fingers in it and caught a handful. "Shall we start by grooming you?"

Faour laughed.

His long hair reminded me of him in his teens, how he'd hated haircuts. Haircuts and exams. His mother used to show up at our door: "May God strike me with a thunderbolt if I have a clue why this boy sees the devil's face every time there is a test at school. He does well throughout the semester; all his marks are above average. And he's brilliant in composition and history, brilliant. Yet come the time to prepare for exams, he's out in the valley. He takes his books with him but – we know, his father spotted him and Rameh saw him many times – he doesn't touch them. He walks about like a zombie." Abu Faour had resorted to the rod. But the rod only distanced him from his son. Their communication broke down and was never fully restored. Once, I followed Faour to the valley, not far from where we were now. He was twelve or thirteen.

"Are you afraid of exams?" I'd asked.

"I don't like them. It's like being wrongly accused of something."

"What if you fail?"

"I won't. It's all stored inside my head. I walk around and remember. I don't like re-reading things. Like eating last night's meal, if you know what I mean."

Faour never failed an exam. He compensated for his weak maths with his excellent style and grasp of language.

Now the worst exam of his life was approaching.

Thirty-eight

"You sent for me, son of Awad?" Rameh's voice echoed through my empty house.

"I don't know how long we'll be gone, Rameh, and how long this war will last. I'm hoping to entrust my house to you. You're the only authority left around here."

"I'll do my best. But I won't die on your threshold."

"I'm coming back, Rameh."

"Coming back to revive the olive oil industry?"

"Of course."

"Don't look over your shoulder. This land is finished."

"I've been planning this for years. I . . ."

"You may have gone to college and all, but you're a fool to believe in olives and olive oil. All over the country people are leaving their olive groves to the goatherds. Olive oil isn't making ends meet any more. Even the best crops are sold dirt cheap to restaurants and hotels."

"Well sure, during a war no one . . ."

"Even before. I've heard it dozens of times: 'We'd plant gorse instead of olives if it would produce an income.' Look around you, how many of your generation are still tucking their lunch inside the myrtle tree and working the land? The old devils who terraced the mountains and crushed the rocks are now boasting about sending their sons and daughters to universities; they're proud of their degrees, not their ploughmanship. Lawyers, doctors, engineers . . ."

"I know, but . . ."

"No buts. Yours is the world of yesteryear, son of Awad."

"The world of tomorrow, bailiff! For years I've been gathering information; there's a growing demand for good quality olive oil. Even China's planting olives now. Why are *we* missing out? Think of the image, Rameh: the oil that breathes myrtle and thyme and sage and ancient cedars. Biblical oil from the Biblical land – people will be queuing on their knees to buy it!"

"Calm down, Adam. Listen. With the limited harvest of your orchards, or even with the full harvest of Wahdeh, you haven't a hope, not for exporting olive oil. Even if everyone stayed put and pulled together, it could only work locally, as it did before."

"To begin with, sure, we'll start small. But then we'll join with other villages, form co-ops, then companies. We've got centuries of tradition behind us, Rameh. Something like that doesn't vanish overnight. You think I'm a romantic fool, don't you. Or just fixated on some dream. Sure, that's part of it. If the olive press dies, so do my father and grandfather and countless generations of Awads, and the olive trees and the love linking us all from time immemorial. But it's bigger than that. Think of it, Rameh – the same goes for the whole country, thousands of family histories will die if we lose this continuity, this link to the soil. The land is all we have, it's the artery pumping life through our whole country. Without it we'll become just another standardised, pasteurised, corporate franchise. You must feel it too, Rameh, in your heart you remember all this, you and your father and your mule. Remember watching over the slow grinding of the olives. The huge stone, rotating at the speed of the sleepy donkey. I do it, Rameh, I clean the stone, I feed the donkey, I taste and bottle and store the new samples, and the tang of *khadeer* still lingers in my mouth, sharp like a handful of needles. I've lived it in my mind, all those years while tapping my calculator at the bank. I've closed my eyes every day with the same vision in my head, and now you come along and try to blow that vision to pieces. *You* just see a derelict olive press, stripped of its life like a dead tree, but this place, Rameh, is my raison d'être. If I die before coming back to revive it, I want to be buried in it."

I'd lost it and begun trembling, but Rameh seemed unconcerned about his trashing of my life's dream. "Whatever," he said, dismissing the issue. "Nothing-would please me more than having you back when this mad war is over. I'll watch over your house as much as possible. But remember, you're poking Nimer in the wrong rib by helping his woman escape. He won't forgive you."

"I have no choice."

"If he decides to burn your house in revenge, I'm not going to make a widow out of Hilweh, nor am I losing my child for you."

"Why did you give Faour your pistol if you're so indifferent about it all?"

"Because he was scared. But that's Faour's battle. You won't see me fighting for him either."

"Everyone for themselves, is that it?"

"Right."

"Does anyone besides you know what we're up to?"

"No one knows anything. But that's no guarantee it'll work."

"You're beginning to scare me, bailiff."

"You ought to be scared. You'll only have a few hours of darkness to get away. There's a boat sailing tomorrow, and rumour has it that Nimer's leaving tonight. I'll alert Faour. But don't make a move until I give you clearance just in case he stops at the Castle first. When he's on the road to Beirut I'll go on top of the mill house and call. Then you can get going. But fast – he might come back in a few hours. Anything else?"

"Yes. I'm giving you two spare keys. Give one to Amti Wardieh, will you? I can't bear saying goodbye to her."

In the silence that followed Rameh's exit, I went into Mariam's room. My father and my uncle and then my sister and I were born in this vaulted room. Yousra and I had left it intact, as a promise of safe return. When it had been hit on the day the dogs died we'd repaired it and vowed to preserve it for our next child and for ever. With the rest of the house almost empty, it was the only room where I felt at home. I'd been sorting out things to take on Mariam's bed. Things were scattered, or in little piles awaiting further scrutiny, hanging in the same limbo as me. Now it was time to pack in earnest. Had I put out enough socks? Are three pairs enough? No – and more underwear, too. And some more tee-shirts. Ah, and Cypriot coffee is muddy and too lightly roasted, I've heard. And cardamom may be hard to find there. I'll just pop a bag of my favourite coffee mix into a corner of the suitcase, here. Oh, and arak. Ouzo is no substitute, too sweet and murky, more syrup than liquor. I need at least one bottle, if only to celebrate on the boat. God, I'm beginning to sound like my mother. "She's taking the whole country with her!" Yousra had said. The three of us had had to stand on her suitcase to close it.

I took off my glasses and cleaned them with the bottom of my shirt. Ah! Had I packed that little yellow cloth for cleaning them properly? I did have a proper case and cloth. Somewhere. But where? What if the sea spray blurred my vision while on the deck and the wind's blowing in my face and my glasses are covered with brine, the sea looks threatening, one high wave will roll me down to the bottom of the ocean and . . .

I took a deep breath and raised my head from my suitcase. I went back to the kitchen to peer through the window in the futile hope that Nimer's jeep was gone. No. Still there, still blocking my way. I stared hard at the jeep. Breathless, I listened in case I might hear a sound. If only Sana would make an appearance, pretend she has to borrow something, so I can tell her tonight's probably the night. The silence next door is killing me. I don't want to keep imagining things. What if Sana chickens out and confesses all to Nimer?

No! I went back to Mariam's room and finished the packing. I was closing the suitcase when I heard Hilweh's voice calling Rameh. A few moments later she appeared at the door, panting, her ankles swollen and her temples pulsing like a frog's belly. Only a couple of months pregnant, yet she was looking rounded and puffed up. The goat had gone missing, she couldn't find it anywhere. "Maaa . . . go . . . go . . ." Hilweh's hands were drawing, in frantic gestures, the places where she'd looked for it.

"Ea...sy, now, Hilweh, ea...sy. The goat will come back." I spoke slowly, emphasising each word as if to a hysterical child. Her big eyes stopped blinking. She calmed down. Then she started moaning, scanning the house. Standing in the middle of the empty living room, she was running over the vacant spaces with a wounded gaze – where had everything gone? Her swollen hands clenched. Then she tilted her head and shuffled heavily to the corner, staring at where my copper lunch pail and oak stick used to hang. How could she have guessed the importance of these two things? Was she psychic?

Suddenly a surge of anguish – where *were* the pail and stick? For a few seconds my mind was blank. Hilweh hit the wall in a demand for the absent items. The wall was bare, but with Hilweh's piercing eyes pinning down its emptiness it felt crowded again. Then Hilweh shot into Mariam's room, threw open the cupboard and laughed with crazed relief. She began snatching garments out, holding them high above her head: 'Bébé . . . Bébé," dancing with Mariam's clothes. She pulled a tiny tee-shirt over her head. It looked like a bib around her neck. Next she plunged her arms into a pair of trousers and hopped up onto the bed, celebrating her new-found treasure. Not until Hilweh began jumping gleefully on the bed and the old brass frame screeched for deliverance did Rameh appear at the door. He rushed in and swept her onto his shoulder. "She's with child, you know," he said apologetically, "but she means no harm." I barely heard them leave. I was dazed. I felt seasick, though I'd never been on a boat. At that moment it came back to me: the pail and the stick were safe with Amti. My shoulders unlocked their grip on my neck and I breathed again.

I stood my luggage near the door and took off to the valley. Dusk was just opening its shutters. I was walking into the same darkening sky I'd known since the night I was born, the same galaxy that domed it, the same moon crowning the cliff and maddening the frogs into a deafening falsetto. I remembered the family story of Sitti dipping my silent body in cold and then warm water, again and again, and my mother's mouth ruptured in terror and my father's eyes drowning in prayers. And how when I finally cried my father wrapped me in warm wool and took me out and raised me high towards that same sky. Now I was desperately divorcing myself from it, walking as fast as a fugitive on my own land.

Faour's plateau was lit up by a wood fire. I could hear him reciting something. The pine tree, basking in a halo of silver moonlight, was listening to his resonant voice: "I will go to the country where the cedar is cut. I will set up my name where the names of famous men are written; and where no man's name is written I will raise a monument to the gods."

"I thought we were leaving the country where the cedar is cut."

"Adam! What are you doing here? I was just about to put out the fire and come up and join you. What's up?"

"He's still there."

"And?"

"Nothing. I just couldn't stay a minute longer in my house. I was going crazy."

I sat down. There was no beer left in the stream and I needed a drink badly enough to make me cry. Two tears turned my retinas to salt. "This is so damn beautiful," I whispered.

"Are you crying with nostalgia already?"

"I don't know."

"You want a drink? I have a bit left." Faour handed me a bottle of arak.

"You're hitting the hard stuff again?"

"Drink up my friend and let me sing you a song."

"Let me guess: Hail the Sacred Vine?"

"*Hail the wondrous root*
That feeds her tender shoot
And fills her golden fruit
With vivifying wine.
Hail the Sacred Vine!"

I drank and passed the bottle back to him. Faour's merriment eased my anxiety a little, but my mind was still roaming the distance between Wahdeh and the port, the port and the sea, the sea and Larnaca; the aching distance between my arms and Mariam; the distance that was a torture chamber crowded with Phoenician dwarfs surging out from their ships; callous fingers, sharp bones, selling and haggling and pushing and chanting the glory of their expedition. They're there; they're still there. Nothing has changed. Nothing will ever change. They were there when I waved my family goodbye, they came up to me, soliciting: money, jewellery, garments, medicine. My pitiful mercantile ancestors, the eternal beasts of mooring and farewell, each time I dared picture a happy reunion they rose up to mock me. So I drank some more with Faour as we recited more verses from Mirdad.

It was only when I stared into the fire that I noticed something like a book in the flames. I leaned over to see if it was just my imagination.

"I burned it," Faour said, laughing nervously. "The most important thing I've ever done. My own Baptism of Fire." He took a pile of books from his packed rucksack – those I'd lent him and others from Sana. He held them under my nose like evidence in a courtroom. "If I can't write something as good as these, I'd rather burn mine."

"But your poems! You don't have to publish them. Even show them to anyone. Why burn them?"

"They weren't just any old poems, Adam. I was trying to write about my love for Sana, about our miserable homeland, about my stubborn father, my poor mother, Zahi, Nour, Rameh, even Nimer. I actually had the nerve to describe their inner lives. Can you believe it? I was so full of myself, Adam. I gave myself a free hand, blithely assuming things, judging, imagining, worst of all, making prophesies!"

"Writers do all that."

"It was weak. Pathetic. Laments, hot air, that kind of thing. What do I know about people? Generally speaking, I don't even like them all that much. Yet there I was, moulding them to fit my purposes. When I was reading from Gilgamesh just now, I felt shivers running down my spine. This is a six-thousand-year-old text, and it still does that to me. Unless I do better than that, I'm wasting my time."

"I don't know why you have to measure yourself against anybody. The stuff you gave me to read I thought was brilliant. You feel you need to do better? Go ahead, who's holding you back? I don't believe you burned it just because you want to write better. I think you're scared it'll fall into someone's hands, like the diary you forgot at the Castle."

"I could have hidden it or given it to you."

"Why didn't you?"

"Because I want a fresh start. When time and space have done their work and I start again to tell our story, I want to see it as clear as crystal. Aiming high as it may sound, I want to make it a classic."

"Destruction isn't mandatory for construction."

"I worked on a building site, remember? You have to bury a lot of rubble before you can start to rise in earnest."

It pained me to see the notebook turning to ash. Faour's action felt like a betrayal. I felt entitled to know what he wrote. I looked wistfully at the powdery remains. Faour intercepted my glance. "Yeah, okay, I do regret parting with a couple of pages, and a paragraph here and there. Like describing Mariam when she skips and keeps her skirt from flying by repeatedly tucking it between her legs. Snapshots like that."

"What else did you burn, Mister Hemingway?"

"I burned a lot of stuff, my friend. A lot of stuff," he said sadly. "But it wasn't *writing*, I was exorcising my ghosts and parading my ego in a carnival of words. I'm sorry, it didn't occur to me that you'd be upset. It was one of those moments, like the last push in labour I guess, when a woman undergoes that crucial ordeal regardless of the pain involved. It was scary, but when the fire began to consume them, I felt a surge of joy. I felt free. As if I'd given something precious to a complete stranger." He picked up a stick and poked an exposed page where only a few lines in the middle could still be deciphered.

"Hah! Love and hate and life and death all in one page! All in one flash of illumination from yours truly. Adam, if only you knew how proud I was when I wrote that stuff; no self-doubt, no hesitation. I was feeling on top of the world. I thought I possessed wisdom, insight, knowledge. You know what I did? I tried to delve into why I felt different things for different people. Take my father. You remember how he treated me? Ever since I was able to understand the meaning of words he made it clear that I was his footsteps to be followed, his shadow to grow longer, and his stinking shop to become the Minimarket Supreme. He never took me on his lap or tossed me high in the air or said a tender word to me. I was the next leader of the dynasty and had to be toughened up for the job. Despite all that, I never stopped respecting him. But loving him? Did I love him? When I was in Venezuela I missed everyone in my family except him. Sometimes I would crave the smell of sweat and dough and herbs of my granny. And whenever I had a meal, my mother's hands seemed to be offering the plate to me. Every time I saw a boy running an errand it was Zahi's legs racing the wind. Any child held in loving arms pounded my chest with memories of my little sister and the long evenings we spent wrapped up together in the same blanket. And then there was Sandra. My poems revisited her time and time again, trying to understand my tangled feelings about her. I kept diving into those murky waters but my fixation on her remained, jammed inside me like a framed picture from a shipwreck stuck in the bottom of the sea. Fleeting fishes of memory pass by it from time to time, stare at it blankly, and swim away. My writing about it failed to break it, or to bury it for good. So why write if there's no salvation, no redemption? Why write at all?"

"Because there's nothing you can do better. You're asking too much, too early. You've just started. Faour, don't you realise how lucky you are? You can take your flame with you anywhere. All you need is pen and paper and enough food to keep you alive. Think how rich and self-sufficient that is. Not to need anything from anyone. You have the opportunity to realise your dream any time, anywhere, whereas a dream without the means or the talent is like carrying the world on your back and climbing."

"Yeah, but you can drop it. I can't. I carry my world inside me, with no chance of relief."

"A man's work is never finished, my friend. So what relief are you talking about?"

"When your work gives you satisfaction. So far, it's been like barking up ten wrong trees at the same time. I wrote pages and pages about Nimer. I'm glad they're gone now. You may laugh, but I kind of liked Nimer when I was a child. I used to be one of those who gathered in the square to listen to his fables. I knew from the start he was a bullshit artist, but he was a good one. He could tell an untrue story with true feeling, and with bombastic but plausible details. You could even say he was inspiring. Even at the Castle or at the mill house, his pranks were sometimes entertaining. How was I to reconcile this Nimer with the petty warlord we now know? The man who never deserved more than a kick in the butt was today causing me nightmares of murder."

"You want to solve all your problems through writing? I don't think this is what writers do, Faour. They seem to have as many troubles as everybody. Sometimes more. Your Hemingway ended up shooting himself, for example. Why don't you just write what you know and feel, the best way you can, instead of trying to reshape the world with your pen?"

"You heard me reciting from Gilgamesh. There's something like that blazing inside me, Adam."

"You are choosing the narrow path, my friend. Why don't we keep it simple? Let's go up and start our vigil and hope that Shamash is preparing a safe exit for us."

Thirty-nine

I jerked out of a doze, groggy, sweating and pulsing in my chair, puzzled at the recurrence of an old dream: I'm naked on market day at the square, I run home but I don't reach it. I run like someone escaping a ball of fire, like someone fleeing an avalanche. I look behind me. The fire and the snow are at my heels and I am still near Abu Faour's shop. The market is swarming; no matter how much I run I stay in the middle of the crowd, shamefully naked. That dream had dogged my adolescent years and kept recurring until I met Yousra. Then it vanished. We'd talked for hours about it, analysing and Freuding it to pieces. Why naked on that annual market day when other villagers came to Wahdeh to sell their produce? The insularity of a village boy suspicious of strangers? The seed of the claustrophobia I later experienced in crowded places? And what about the running and getting nowhere? Yousra suggested, "Innate tenacity fighting back against fear of naked exposure. You're timid on the outside but determined on the inside. A tough cookie, but you do everything to avoid confrontation."

My eyes were desperate to re-close, so I headed for the bathroom. Faour was fast asleep on the sofa, his head nested in the biceps of his left arm. I leaned down to cover his shoulders but the beads of sweat on his neck stopped me; he's warm enough. It was remarkable how peacefully he slept. What with all the planning and waiting we'd been through.

The neon light above the bathroom mirror filmed my features in pale, sickly gloss. I splashed my face with cold water several times. I lowered my head and let the water stun the throbbing inside it. I stared fiercely at the mirror with spidery red eyes. My walrus moustache looked enormous. For a moment I thought of shaving it off. Then I remembered when I'd done it once, how horrified Mariam had been. "Put it back!" she'd wept with bewildered bitterness.

I went to the kitchen with a towel on my shoulders. A cold gush of air from the open window made me cringe. I reached across the sink to close it and saw a shadowy light shed from a side window of Nimer's apartment. I heard a soft thud, then a voice. I stopped drying my hair and became a thousand ears. One of the boys crying. Then the other. I couldn't tell which. Then both cried and were abruptly muffled. A few seconds passed, a door slammed. There was a savage abruptness in those sounds. The ensuing silence was charged with an unsettling void. Then another slam that made me quiver. Then Nimer's barking, loud and clear :

"*Why* the suitcases under the sofa? Where the fuck you think you're going, you bloody whore? You think you can just leave me? Just like that? I made you. Me! I gave you a new lease of life. Without me you're dog shit, dog shit, dog shit, the dogs would have eaten you and crapped you and you wouldn't have seen your little bastards or the light of day, again, ever. I should have left you there to rot and die. I should have let them rape you. Look at me, look me in the eye. Why did you hide the suitcases under the sofa? *Where are you going?*"

Then silence. My heart drummed in my ears. Every muscle in my body shrank. Was Sana whispering something to calm Nimer down? Would she come up with something other than the truth? I dreaded waking Faour. I dreaded not waking him. The floor tilted beneath me. I felt cold and feverish at the same time.

"What do you mean you want to save your children? Before it was 'This is still the safest place in the country, a paradise for the kids.' So what's changed? Answer me, you bitch!" Nimer's pitch had eased down slightly but was still threatening.

Another silence. I needed to know what was happening. I imagined Sana calmly trying to subdue him, speaking in a low and composed voice that would end up deflating his wrath. I had to know more. I left the kitchen on fast tiptoes, passing Faour breathlessly. I opened the back door and went out. Through the windows beneath the jutting upstairs veranda I could see Nimer's back bent over something. Then he straightened it, lifting a suitcase. He hurled it across the room. It hit the wall and made the window rattle all the way to my stiffened limbs. "All neat and tidy! All ready to go!" Nimer chuckled sardonically.

Fuck you, Nimer, die! I heard my demons howling for my Winchester. Then I heard something else: footsteps behind me. I wheeled around to see Faour rubbing his eyes. I had to get him away, fast, before he could do anything rash. I propelled him to the far corner of the yard, where we could still see but not be heard. He was warm and unsteady with sleep. I needed to drown as much as I could of my own frustration and fear, but the suddenness of it all made me blabber: "It's not looking good. Nimer's discovered the suitcases and he's kicking up a fuss."

Faour went pale. I held him and put my arm round his neck. "Leave it – she knows what to do."

He pulled against me. "I can't see her, I can't hear her." His voice quivered with rage.

"That's good. It means she's still in control. You know Sana. She's smart. She can handle him better than we would."

"And if she doesn't?"

Faour began to shake. His eyes became traps about to go off. I had to make a move before he lost control. "Faour, I'm going to get your father."

"He's useless. Get Rameh."

"Rameh's watching from the mill house. I need at least ten minutes to reach him."

"Hurry!"

I took off towards the square. I ran faster than I'd ever run before. I ran forgetting to breathe. I ran like a whole Olympic team. My lungs kicked so hard I could hardly bear the pain flashing in my temples. I was inside my old dream, only now it was fuelling my run. I was flying and I was immobile, just like the dream. I should have asked Faour to fetch Rameh. But he wouldn't have left. He couldn't. I hoped he wouldn't go crazy, wouldn't confront Nimer with raw rage. Nimer had all the advantages, he had an automatic rifle and was inside his own house. Oh God, keep Sana in control until I get Rameh. I reached the square in less than three minutes and jumped over the stream. Just here, under the burned poplar, my uncle had been killed. Had I managed to escape Abu Faour's grip that day I would have saved him, or died with him. Why hadn't *I* gone to Nimer's now, knocked on the door and calmed things down? But how? Wasn't I the head of the snake that was smuggling his wife out of the country? Had he found out? How much did he know? *So that's how you pay me back for selling your mother's apartment, son of Awad!* It would only increase his anger. No, Rameh was best.

A thin carpet of light was unfolding down the slopes. Dawn was beginning to seep in, pale and remote like a still-born. There was no one to be seen. Wahdeh still belonged to the night. Suddenly, a volley from an automatic rifle rang out. I froze. I looked around. Where had it come from? It was too close to be from the Castle. Wherever, it was bound to wake the whole village now, so I cupped my hands and yelled towards the mill house: "Rameh!" My voice shattered the dawn.

"Awooo!" Rameh thundered across the roofs.

"Come down! Now!"

"Coming!"

I took heart. I turned and began running back.

Then three, four bursts from a handgun cut through the echoes. No mistake this time: it had come from very near my house.

All around me, windows and doors were opening. Anxious, irritable voices were asking, "Are we being attacked?" Their fear was palpable; too many villages had been taken by surprise in the early hours by small bands of militias leaving in their wake a trail of tragedies. A few men were starting their cars, driving towards the Castle, either to raise the alarm or to seek protection. Others, in their night clothes, were milling around and grabbing at me as I ran, bombarding me with questions I couldn't answer.

Three minutes to the square, a lifetime for the journey back, and all the while my feet kicking my heart and planting stop signs to every terrible thought. Nimer could just be playing his old trick, scaring Sana and perhaps Faour as well. Nothing more, nothing more. After all, Nimer knew nothing, Sana had probably come up with a plausible excuse for the suitcase by now. Behind my eyes the promised sea was mounting. Those who ran with me were chattering something about intruders having been caught red-handed. The beautiful fantasy: best case scenario. I was eager to exchange it for all the other scenarios that were storming my desperate hope.

None of them matched the scene I returned home to.

Faour's parents, together with Zahi and little Nour, were clinging to each other at the threshold of Nimer's apartment in their night clothes, shuddering, their eyes glazed. They barely noticed my arrival. Behind them neighbours were gathering, all staring at the open door in horror. A chill was rising from my feet. Those who arrived a few steps ahead of me peered through the open door and retreated, stunned, covering their faces. I pushed through the crowd and stumbled into the room.

Faour was kneeling and cradling Sana in his arms. Bullet holes covered her chest. Her white nightgown was soaked in blood. Her mouth was half-open as if about to speak, her hair in disarray. Her eyes were half-shut, showing white lines under her long eyelids. Sprawled on the sofa lay Nimer, in his track suit, two bullet holes in his neck. His eyes stared sightlessly at his Kalashnikov beside him. The gorged suitcase had scattered its contents everywhere. Thin rivulets of blood trickled across the floor, forming a demarcation line at the threshold.

The chill in my feet was spreading through my whole body as I approached Faour. He was scowling at the people behind me. "Out!" he cried, pointing his pistol at them. Then he looked up. "You should have let me kill him before!" he screamed, his eyes flooded with tears.

I kneeled beside him and hugged his head. Words were useless. Fate and destiny had turned their back on us. We'd hit rock bottom.

Faour jerked his head away, still hugging his beloved Sana, and yelled into the crowd. "Tell your children, you fucking cowards, tell your children Wahdeh once had a queen. A queen you were unworthy of having. I loved this queen. I loved the dust she stepped on. I loved the air she breathed. I loved everything she touched. And now look at her. Look what you've done to her. All of you! Cowards! Tell your bastards what a queen you've lost. I spit on your graves for a hundred years, I spit on you!" Then he broke down in a fit of violent shuddering. I tightened my arms round his shoulders. I tightened my grip on my jaw.

Outside, the crowd was growing, the cries of women mounting. I was hearing but not listening, not seeing. My eyes were stalled at the line of blood at the threshold. All those bare feet, dozens of bare feet clustered by the door. Um Faour's flipflops were incongruous. So were the big brown boots now ploughing through all the bare feet. Then the boots were in the room and Rameh's voice was booming some words it took me a long time to hear:

". . . children . . ."

Faour lifted his tearful eyes to Rameh and waved his gun towards the kitchen.

Rameh thundered into the kitchen. I heard him howl. Then he rushed past us, holding the twins in his arms. Someone's hands reached out and took them from him. They'd been tied up and beaten, but they were alive. Then Rameh turned back, moving like a raging boar. He yanked Nimer's head and spat in his face.

His gesture jolted me out of my trance. Now the doorway was blinking *Exit* all over my vision. I began revising my plan. No time left – we were fugitives now. Take off immediately. Passports and money only. Side roads to the coast. Any boatman would take us to Cyprus for a handful of dollars.

Perhaps Rameh had been revising too. He dug his hand into Nimer's pocket and threw me the key to the jeep. "The Castle's on alert – you can't use your car. The jeep's your only chance. Now move!"

He sprang to the door and pushed people aside, clearing a path. I pulled Faour to his feet. He shook me off and bent down to pick up Sana's body. There was no time to reason with him. "Give her to me, son. She's in God's hands now," Um Faour pleaded. But Faour continued walking, staring straight ahead, flicking people aside with the same handgun that had just killed Nimer.

I unlocked the jeep. Rameh snatched Sana's body from Faour and pushed him into the passenger seat. I took off in a screech of tyres and a cloud of smoke, clenching my teeth to keep calm. Fast but calm, fast but calm, I repeated like a mantra. Children were running beside the jeep, then men and women. I barely saw them, I was driving like a blind man on fire. Fast-calm, fast-calm, it wasn't working, I could hear hysterical laughter. It was coming from beside me. Faour. He had finally snapped. He was waving his gun at the people who were lining the road, jumping in his seat, shouting and laughing in a way that turned my blood cold.

And then they were behind us and the road was clear ahead. Faour was still emitting that bone-chilling laugh. I tried to screen it out, think clearly. Escaping a trail of blood changed the horizon before us. Exit had become flight, our hopeful expectations had disappeared. All we could aim for with every iota of our strength was vanishing. If only Faour would stop that awful screaming laughter that was sending tremors to my fragile concentration.

Our speed was folding away the umbrella pines, turning the olive trees into patches of haze. The contours of the land melted away. There were no hawks above the cliff this morning, no wings of salvation. The blue marble sky was cold to our escape. We were alone. Now we were out of the village, and as if in inane celebration Faour let off a volley of shots at the morning sun. We were approaching the little bridge by the Castle and his shots were being answered by a spray of machine gunfire and a loud speaker ordering us to stop.

"It's Bou-Youn! Don't listen to him, he'll kill us!" Faour shouted. I rammed the accelerator to the floor; once we reached the top of the hill and beyond the big oak we'd be out of range. I focused hard and pushed harder.

"Hell no!"

"Do it!"

"Don't shoot, Faour!"

"I have to!"

Faour aimed straight at the roadblock that had suddenly appeared. The oak tree engulfed us. Then a huge wave rose and swallowed the great oak. The boat behind my eyes capsized and drowned in the wide and endless light.

Epilogue

We're all here by the myrtle tree: my father, my uncle, Sitti. A freshly-prepared glass of arak rests on a grey rock. My uncle takes a sip. We're having our lunch. It's the olive harvest. My father has a handful of jerjar in his palm. He tenders it to me: "Here, son, fill your basket." Sitti opens the pails. Then from within the big light comes Sana with a clay pitcher and gives it to me. "You must be thirsty," she says. "Yes," I say, and look around. "Where are the boys?"
"Playing."
"Faour?"
"Writing," Sana says, and sits down with us to eat.

HISTORICAL NOTE

Our last civil war began in the 1970s and ended by stages in the early 1990s, depending on how one defines 'beginning' and 'end'. This uncertainty characterised the entire conflict. The only certainty is that we killed each other for more than fifteen years. Our fathers and forefathers had done it before us and they too always swore 'Never again,' while still unwittingly incubating the virus and keeping their powder dry for the next round. We hate each other. But we love our country to the point of believing, in the craziest way, that we have the right to destroy it *because* we've been able to rebuild it again and again.

Adam saw it chiefly as a war against his personal dream. Its history and details were not his concern. But I owe the readers of this story more explanation.

Our independence has been shaken once every ten years or so since its declaration in 1943. Outside interference always lurked behind the scene. Our differences have been used against us and thus we became a battleground for the Arab-Israeli conflict. The presence of half a million Palestinian refugees, armed and free to operate in the south of the country as well as exerting considerable power within our political fabric, turned Lebanon into a ticking time-bomb. At least half of the Lebanese population felt kinship and solidarity with the Palestinians. Christian Phalangists sought help from Israel. Tel Aviv was happy to oblige. Hundreds were sent secretly through Cyprus to receive training and indoctrination in Israel; they were convinced that a Lebanon in a sea of Muslims without a strong ally would precipitate their extinction.

Meanwhile, the Palestinian camps inside Lebanon were becoming a threat to the very existence of the Lebanese state. There were several groups, factions and fractions operating within those camps, dealing in arms and drugs and contraband and kidnapping. They received help and training from many Arab countries and from the communist block.

Pro- and anti-Palestinians differed on whether we should allow Lebanon to become a wasteland in defence of the Palestinian cause or bring the Palestinians to heel under the authority of the Lebanese government. To top it off, there was poverty among the Shiites living in the misery belt on the outskirts of Beirut; there was the political ambition of the Druze and Sunnis who'd had enough of being marginalised by Christian dominance and saw a historic opportunity to take over through their alliance with the Palestinians; and last but not least, there was the Israeli interest in seeing the Palestinians weakened.

The Syrian army usurped a deterrent Pan-Arab force formed to stop the escalation.

Eventually the Israelis invaded Lebanon and the Palestinian militias were persuaded to leave for Tunisia. International forces intervened in a bid to keep the lid on violence. They failed and left.

So, the common conception that this war was fought by Christians against an alliance of Muslims and Palestinians is not totally accurate. Christians fought their own, and Muslims and Palestinians fought amongst each other. At different times, Christians and Israelis together fought the Palestinians, Syrians fought the Palestinians on behalf of the Christians, and later the Christians fought the Syrians. At one point more than thirty different factions were involved, each making and breaking alliances with others in unpredictable ways. Massacres against unarmed civilians were perpetrated by all parties. Ideas and ideologies went to the back burner, leaving gangs of robbers and looters to rule.

In mayhem of such magnitude, fictitious Wahdeh and its people represent the disappearing microcosm of a rural life true to all Lebanese. It was my intention to place Wahdeh on the pedestal that was destroyed by the civil war. Because whatever someone's religious affiliation we did have harmony whenever we were left alone to work our land. We had common traditions and held common values, whose spirit is shown in the tragedy of Wahdeh.

J.E.H.

GLOSSARY

Abaday: tough guy or bully.
Abu: father of, followed by the name of first born child. Also a nick-name as in Abu Takka.
Ahlan wasahlan: welcome.
Aouneh: traditional communal help.
Arak: vine alcohol distilled with dried aniseed.
Ataba: songs of longing and love.
Bey: Ottoman title for civilians.
Boukra: tomorrow.
Bury me: expression of endearment.
Burghul: cracked wheat.
Charab: fruit syrup mixed with water.
Dabkeh: traditional group dance.
Effendi: Ottoman title for military personnel or police.
Fassoulia: dried white or brown beans.
Fattoush: mixed green salad with toasted pita crumbs and a sprinkle of sumac.
Gumbaz: long one-piece garment for men.
Habibi: my love.
Hakim: doctor and wise man.
Hida: slow songs of battle or love.
Jalweh: a special party for a bride-to-be and her peers and women relatives only at which they make her up and dress her and prepare her for the wedding.

Jerjar: wrinkled olives dropped by the first winds of autumn.
Jarra: large earthenware jar.
Jeddo: Grandfather.
Khadeer: crude virgin olive oil.
Kaskoun: Cheers!
Keffieh: traditional head scarf, mainly for men.
Kibbeh nayeh: raw meat pounded to a paste mixed with burghul.
Kishk: powder of cracked wheat and dried yoghourt.
Labneh: strained youghort.
Ma'sara: olive press.
Mabrouk: congratulations.
Mezze: selection of appetizers.
Mijana: cheerful songs.
Miri: Ottoman taxation.
Moutabal: roasted aubergine pounded to a paste with tahini, garlic and lemon juice.
Mukhtar: elected Notary Public.
Oumbashi: Ottoman officer.
Um: mother of ...
Sitti: Grandmother.
Tabbouleh: salad of finely chopped parsley, tomatoes, onions, and cracked wheat.
Shish barak: meat dumplings cooked in yoghourt.
Shway shway: slowly slowly.
Shukran: thank you.
Yalla: let's go, come on.

ABOUT THE AUTHOR

Born in Beirut and have been a journalist since he was sixteen, working for Al-Hayat in London and Beirut , BBC World Radio in London, Radio Monte Carlo in Paris, Harlequin Arab World (Senior Editor) in Athens.
In 1985 he immigrated to Australia with his family. He has been heavily involved in Australia's and Lebanon's arts scenes and had one novel, six collections of poetry and two of short stories published in Arabic, as well as two plays staged. Parts of his work have been translated into French, German, Spanish and Dutch. He now divides his time between Melbourne and Sereel, a small village in north Lebanon.

E-mail: jadelhage@hotmail.com

AKNOWLDGEMENT

I'd like to thank the people who've sat with me in the shade of the myrtle tree, Lydia Smith, Elizabeth Rebeiz, Melanie Ensor, Rouba El Hage, Marsha Row, Nadim Naimy, Jessica Regel, Debbie Golvan, Samar Hammam, Camil Zaroubi, Jihad Khazen, Robert Betts, Margaret Obank, Patrick Seale, Carol Willits, Dalal Smiley, and Linda Funnell, you each know the way you've helped. Without you The Myrtle Tree would never have taken root and grown. *Shukran.*

Distributed in Australia by
Smiley Communications
P.O.Box: 2130
Bayswater, VIC 3153
Tel: 03 9720 4696
E-mail: kithos@optusnet.com.au